Perfectly Imperfect

Courtney Dinkins

First Edition

Fulton Books, Inc.
Meadville, PA

Published by Fulton Books 2021

ISBN 978-1-63710-277-0 (paperback)
ISBN 978-1-63710-278-7 (digital)

Printed in the United States of America

CHAPTER 1

"Good morning, Orlando!" the DJ yells from the alarm clock speaker. "It's a beautiful humid day in July, and you already know, it's thunderstorms in the afternoon. High of one hundred, but feeling like one-oh-five. Jesus, did I read that right? Anyway, here is some Kesha to start your day with 'TiK ToK'!"

I moan as the song starts and fumble for the off button. I cannot find it and end up slamming my fist on the snooze button as hard as I can. I pull my arm back underneath the covers and try to go back to sleep. My breathing finally finds a pattern that allows my body to drift off, and my door flings wide open.

"Neveahly!" Will cries, "get the fuck up! It's graduation day!"

I roll onto my back and rip the covers off me dramatically. "I am aware of that, and whoever set my alarm will feel my wrath mightier than Thor's hammer, you cocksuckers."

Nick brushes past Will and sits on the unoccupied spot on my bed while eating a bowl of cereal. "So what's the plan after graduation, today? Are we partying or what?"

I moan. "Okay, so I guess we all don't have rooms in this apartment we cannot go to?"

Jon brushes past Will as well and sits at the foot of my bed. Will follows behind him.

"I was thinking we could go to 21?" Will suggests.

"That sounds like fun," Jon says.

I groan and try to pull the covers over my face; Nick pulls them back down. "Yeah, or Firestone. We haven't been there in a while. Chillers! That's always fun."

I sit up. "Guys, I love you, but why must we do this so goddamn early? I know I'm beautiful, but sleep is what makes this beauty happen."

Will laughs. "It's not early. It's like eleven."

I look and grab the clock and bring it to my face. "Holy shit. You do realize we need to be there in two hours, right?"

We all look at one another. Immediately, we race for the door, causing a jam. Jon makes it out first as we all scatter to the two bathrooms in the four-bedroom apartment. Will makes it to the other one, slamming the door; cackling.

I start to bang on the door. "Goddamn it, Will! I have to actually pee!" Crossing my legs trying not to pee on myself.

"You should have thought about that before you lost getting here, dude!" he yells from inside the bathroom. He turns the water on to make the feeling worse.

"I fucking hate living with guys," I mutter.

Nick laughs as he continues to eat his bowl of cereal standing up by the bathroom door. "No, you don't. You're going to miss living with all of us."

I shrug. "Will I? Am I going to miss almost falling into the toilet bowl? Or the constant hair clippings around the sink?"

Will is taking his sweet time in the bathroom, completely ignoring that there are two more people in this house who need to get ready. Jon finishes first. I make a mad dash into the bathroom with my clothes and makeup bag. I get in the shower and take a quick one, hitting all the important parts, sparing no time. I slow down with my rush job of getting ready and take time to put on my makeup, unsure if we will even make it back to the apartment for a quick wardrobe change. Hell, we might just skip the food and get extremely fucked up one last time together.

After getting out of the shower, I see Nick all dressed up, sitting on the couch playing video games with Will and Jon. I let my curls air-dry, or at least I try to let them dry, but with this Florida humidity, I highly doubt they will. I saunter back into my room to find a pair of flip-flops that match my pink Hawaiian print dress. I settle on a pair of pink ones and slide them on my feet quickly, hopping around, trying to maintain my balance. As I make my way back out to the living room, the guys continue to play the new PS3 they had just bought.

"Are y'all ready?" I ask.

No reply. I go in search of my purse as they continue to play on the gaming console.

"Have y'all seen my purse?" I ask again with attitude. *Or you guys can ignore me. That works too.*

No reply again. I roll my eyes and continue to keep searching. I decide to go into each of their rooms and look. It's a mess. Everyone's except Jon's. Which is not a surprise because he is the tidiest out of all of us. I know it drives him batshit insane when we leave dishes in the sink, which is why I'm convinced Nick and Will do it every day just to get under his skin.

I find it hanging on the back of a small light Will is using in one of the films. I grab it and stand in front of the TV.

"Uh, Nev. Could you move?" Will asks politely, looking around me at the screen.

"We have to go."

Will sighs. "I am aware of that, but we are almost done with the game, so can you move?"

I narrow my eyes and slide out of their view. I sit on the love sofa and watch the guys play. The game lasts a couple of moments longer, and Jon wins. The defeat against Will is satisfying. It is like watching your big brother lose at something, that you never can win at. I leap up from the couch and head to the front door. Will, pouting like a child, stomps his way to the door; the rest follow behind him.

Exiting the apartment, I make a mad dash to Jon's outback, hoping I can sit in the front seat and get control of the music this time. The guys take their time coming down the apartment stairs, talking and laughing. Jon whips out his keys and hits the unlock button, and I effortlessly slide into the front seat. We all settle in the hot car. We never learn, you would think by now living in Florida to wait a few minutes before getting in to allow the heat escape a bit and then get in.

Nick leans over the seat and throws a CD up front. "Here, play this."

Jon takes it and gently slides it into the CD player. "What's this?"

Nick sits back and puts his seat belt on. "You'll see."

The music starts, and within the first few seconds of the melody playing, we all recognize that it's "Bad, Bad Leroy Brown." Everyone in the car moans.

"Oh, c'mon, Nick," I beg. "Can we please listen to something else?"

"Nope. This is the last time we will all be together, and all of you can eat a dick. We are listening to my favorite song." Nick starts to sing off-key.

We start to laugh as the song continues, and the chorus comes on, and we cannot help but join in singing with him. "Bad, bad, Leroy Brown, baddest man in the whole damn town, badder than old King Kong, and meaner than a junkyard dog."

The song ends, and we laugh. The new track starts, and the song starts over.

"Are you fucking mad? Is this whole CD just 'Bad, Bad Leroy Brown'?" I turn around and ask.

Nick puts his hands behind his head and smiles. "Yup, twenty-three times, m'lady."

I turn around and rub the bridge of my nose. "I hate you. I hate you so goddamn much sometimes."

Will laughs. "I love this song," he says as he starts to fist-pump into the air.

We arrive at our college and struggle to find a parking spot. After driving around aimlessly for fifteen minutes, Jon ends up having to park in the lot over. We jump out of the car and begin the trek to the building where we are supposed to graduate. Flip-flops are not the best choice, but they are better than heels. I feel myself slipping and sliding in them, due to the lotion going back into its liquid state.

Our last names are all different; we end up breaking into our alphabetical lines. I don't really know anyone in my line, so I stick to myself. I see Jon a couple of lines ahead of me and signal for him to start texting me. Nick, being the social butterfly that he is, starts talking to anyone around him. Will and I exchange texts back and forth, joking about where others will be after graduation. *Dead? Hard-core drug problem? Blowing a director just to get a part in a movie?* I laugh at the mere thought of anyone having aspirations to actually blow a director and not get where they need to be on merit, but hey, to each their own.

I feel a poke on my shoulder and see it's one of the professors who kindly tells me to put my phone away. I roll my eyes and put it in my bra. It makes the professor a little uncomfortable, and he turns a bit red. *Sorry you're a tad bit uncomfortable, but this fashion designer at Walmart neglected to put pockets in this dress.*

We stand in line for forty-five minutes, waiting for something to happen. They begin to distribute our cap and gowns finally, and we file into the newly built auditorium. Satan, in all his evildoings and sinister ways, I somehow manage to sit next to an old fling, a hookup that happened at the beginning of the program. Nick, Will, and Jon all exchange glances as I sit there uncomfortably, trying not to make any contact with him whatsoever. *If there is a God, please let a hanging light land on this man so I do not have to deal with this. Not today, not on this day, of my graduation, where it took me forever to get a diploma.* Alas, my efforts are moot, and I feel the short stubby little finger tap me on the shoulder.

"Hey, Nev." Mark leans in for a whisper.

"No talking. I think the program is about to start," I whisper back.

I see Nick leaning over at the end of the row. I clinch my jaw and try to keep a straight face.

"I just want to say I'm sorry," he continues. "I'm sorry for everything. It was a dick thing for me to do, and I just wish I could go back and redo everything."

"Okay, coolies," I say. I take out my phone and begin to text. *Fuck that professor. What are they gonna do? Take back my degree that I paid for?*

"No, really." Mark looks around. "I really screwed up. I was so afraid of my feelings and how we got so close so fast, and I was falling for you, and then I realized I loved you."

I turn and face him. "Okay, first of all, who—" I feel the rage build, and my voice start to go from a whisper to a not so much inside voice. I look around and gain some composure. "You know what? If it gets this conversation to end, it's fine. I forgive you. Shit happens. This is a part of life."

"Really?" His eyes light up.

"Absolutely." I force myself to smile.

"Okay, good because—"

"Oh my god, Mark. That was sarcasm," I interrupt. "Not the place to have this conversation. Actually, even if we were in a different place, I still wouldn't want to have this fucking conversation with you, bro." I turn around and face the front of the stage.

Mark starts to say something, and the lights dim low. The ceremony starts, and a tall man comes out onto the stage. It's the president of our college, whom I've never seen until now. I sit there and zone out. I try not to let Mark dominate this day, like he normally does when it's not all about him, and push out the entire conversation that took place. I'm almost positive it would have turned violent if I entertained him any longer. *Ugh, the fact he is breathing the same air as me right now is aggravating. Focus, Neveahly. You finally are graduating college. Fuck that guy. He's a short little asshole who is nothing and probably won't do anything with this career. God, I hope.*

Awards are given, a skit is done, and a song is sung. I did not pay attention to any of it. I forgot to take any of my ADHD meds today, and it's starting to show. Also, I am starving. Finally, it's time to get our names called to get a piece of paper that we have fought for for the last eighteen months. Our college isn't like others; it's an accelerated program where we can graduate faster. I love it; I didn't see my family and lived with three of my best friends. It was great.

Line by line, we finally collect our degrees. Shaking hands with lab techs, professors, and the president of the college. We did the cliché thing and toss our caps into the air and scream and holler with excitement. *Hurray! I just spent eighty thousand dollars on my education, and I'm about to be in debt for the rest of my life. Fuck yeah!*

The ceremony ends, and everyone dashes out the door toward their family and friends. I push my way through the crowd, trying to make it to the exit. I wait outside for the guys. I see my fellow classmates with their families and loved ones and cannot help but thank God I didn't tell my family about my graduation. I know, it sounds messed up, but it's for the best. All of us opted not to tell our families or even want them to come down. For all of us, this isn't our first college, and I highly doubt my family would make the drive from Virginia to Florida.

I spark up a cigarette and wait. I take long drags and enjoy every bit of the sweet nicotine filling my lungs, embracing the seven minutes it's taking off my life, and let the buzz continue to flow over my body. I look at the building and think, *All the long nights and labs over and done with, the parties, the heartbreak, and now I can focus on my career and life.* I see the gentlemen walk out of the auditorium and smile.

I drop my cigarette and put it out. "Well, fellas, we fucking did it."

"We did. What the fuck did Mark want?" Jon asks.

We all begin to take off our graduation gowns.

I laugh. "He wanted to apologize for everything. Honestly, I wasn't really paying attention. All I could think about was trying not to make a scene."

Will busts out with laughter. "Really? The king of the lollipop guild wants to apologize for everything? I'm surprised you didn't knock him out."

"She was about to," Nick says. "I haven't seen Nev that angry since we ate the last of her food when we all got high."

We walk in a line together, not giving one fuck that we are walking through other people's photos. The level of unbothered we are at right now is uncanny.

"There were just so many witnesses there, and I just couldn't risk it." I take off my gown and toss it in the nearby trash.

"So you're saying you would have done it if no one was around?" Jon asks.

"I'm saying if given the opportunity, I may have done a shot-for-shot scene straight from *Reservoir Dogs*."

We cross the street and make our way back to Jon's car. The moment I open the door, I feel the heat of a thousand suns hit my face. It takes my breath away for a brief moment, and as I stand outside, Jon starts the car and blasts the air-conditioning. We wait a few more minutes, then get in. Jon shifts gears and drives us back to the apartment.

We opt to order pizza and get drunk at our place, one last time. We sit on the balcony, eating the pizza, and smoke out of the bong before we start to drink. We laugh about the good times and make fun of the crazy decisions we all have made down here in this state. I look at my best friends and smile.

"So what are you and Will going to do in DC with your bookstore?" Jon asks as he shoves pizza in his face.

I shrug. "I don't know. Hopefully not go bankrupt within the first year of having it would be fucking sweet." I light the bong and take a rip.

"How does one acquire a bookstore?" Nick asks.

"My grandfather had it, and he's dead, and I'm the only one who actually reads in the family, so he gave it to me." I pass the bong to Nick.

"That's so cool," Jon says.

"What are you going to do, Jon?" Will asks.

Jon smiles. "Travel, dudes. Travel, make movies, and see what the world has to offer me."

We all laugh.

"God, you sound so lame," Nick says as he passes the bong to Jon. "You sound like you're about to write the male version of *Eat Pray Love*."

"How is that lame? I just want to see the world and what it has to offer." Jon puts more Purple Haze in the bong.

"I like it." I smile at Jon.

Jon returns a smile. "Thank you, Nev."

Will looks at us. "Get a room, you two."

"Seriously, just fuck already," Nick chimes in.

I laugh. "What are you talking about?"

"Nothing," Jon says abruptly. He takes a rip. "Can I come see you guys in DC?"

"Duh, any time." I playfully push him.

"What are you gonna do, Nicki?" Will asks.

"Me? Stay here, surf, bang hot chicks, and smoke a lot of weed," Nick says.

"And do nothing with your degree?" I ask.

He shrugs. "I may film the chicks I bang."

"You're so fucking gross," I say in disgust.

"With consent, Neveahly!" he retorts.

We sit there, continuing to eat and smoke. We make the conscious decision, albeit the responsible decision, to go to our community tennis courts and drink and skateboard there, one last time for old times' sake.

As we walk toward the courts, we can hear the multiple parties going on from everyone who graduated today. Different music, coming from every apartment, and everyone just being on the same vibe of *we did it. We finally did it, and it only cost our eternal soul and our sanity.* Arriving at the courts, I throw the skateboard down and begin to glide on the smooth surface. Will brings his iPod and speakers, and we listen to some tunes as we drink a bottle of Jack Daniels and Jameson on the court.

We take turns riding the skateboard. Jon and I sit next to each other as we pass the bottle of Jack between the two of us. A loud bang cracks through the sound barrier, shortly followed by a light show. Fireworks, lighting up the clear night sky and dancing in front of the moon. It's a beautiful sight. I start to feel the alcohol take over my bloodstream and lie on the court and watch them go off.

Will and Nick blast some more music for the light show and dance around the illuminated courts. Will grabs Nick by the arm and drags him back to the apartment.

Jon and I decide to get up and look at the stars, away from the light show. We stumble toward the wooded area, near the picnic tables, and lay down in the well-manicured grass. The stars twinkle a little bit brighter when you know that you may not see them for a long time.

"Damn, this is it, dude," I say, watching the sky, "our last night together as a group."

Jon sighs. "Yeah"—he looks at me—"I'm gonna miss you."

I look at him and smile. "Awe, I'm gonna miss you too, bud."

I stare into his hazel eyes. We both sit up. *What in the fuck is happening right now? Is it the alcohol? Is it the bud? I never noticed how Jon's eyes are just so beautiful.*

"You know," Jon says as he scoots over closer to me, "I never thought Mark was good enough for you."

I laugh. "I mean, he is a short little asshole of a man, and his dick game was weak."

We sit close together, looking up at the night sky. A blast of fireworks dance across the sky. Blue, green, yellow. Just beautiful. I lean back on my hands and watch. I feel Jon's hand touch mine. I look down as the sky is ablaze; illuminating his hand on mine. I bite my lower lip to keep from grinning like a fool.

"Really? At graduation? Like the day we graduate and night before I leave?" I groan.

"I mean, you literally were always seeing someone, and this is the one time you aren't," Jon confesses.

"Not sure if you just called me a whore or that I can't be alone," I say slowly.

Jon laughs. "No, I'm just saying that you're extremely lovable, attractive, funny, and smart. Who wouldn't want to be with you?"

"Apparently, you for the last eighteen months!" I reply.

Jon turns to me. "Look, the minute you walked into orientation and sat down next to me, something happened. I don't know what happened, but something happened. I completely forgot why I was there. I have never met anyone as amazing as you, Nev."

I look down at the grass and back at him. "Bro, dude, ah, I'm not sure how to navigate on this."

Jon leans in to kiss me. I push him away and look at him. I bring him closer to me and kiss him again. His full lips are the one thing I've been missing for the last eighteen months. Every shitty relationship, worth it if it meant feeling these lips. I lay on the grass as he slowly leans down on me. *What the McFuck are you doing, Nev? You leave tomorrow? You gotta pump the breaks on this one.* I pull my lips away from his and sit up.

"I want to do this. I really do. Actually, I'm not gonna lie. I feel the same, but I don't want to start something, get my hopes up, and lose you," I admit.

Jon kisses me again. "You'll never lose me, Nev, but I understand."

I pull him closer to me and kiss him again. *Seriously? Are you just programmed to fuck anyone who kisses you, or are you really that horny? Stop kissing him!* I feel his hands go up my dress, and I stop it.

"I don't want to get in the way of you traveling," I say softly, "and if you want to pursue this after you're done seeing the world, then we can."

Jon kisses me again. "That sounds good to me. Just don't give up on your dream of writing, okay? Owning a bookstore is awesome, but being a writer who owns her own bookstore is even better. You can literally sell your own books."

I laugh. "I won't." I kiss him again. "Also, we breathe not a word of this to Will and Nick."

"Oh god, no," Jon agrees.

"Okay, let's head back." I to get up and start walking.

Jon grabs my hand and kisses me one last time before we get to our building.

"We will be together one day, Nev. You'll see," Jon says confidently.

I look at him. "I hope so."

We drop hands as we walk up to the apartment. We join Will and Nick, playing rock band for our last night together.

CHAPTER 2

I force my eyes open. My eyelids have been trying to peel themselves apart, but the glue from my fake eyelashes has them stuck together, forming this ultimate sticky bond. I lift my head up and see bodies scattered around the floor from the party. Beer cans cover the coffee table; stale smoke lingers and floats gently in the air as the sun illuminates through the poorly drawn curtains. I blink a couple more times to gain my focus and see the room is shoddily decorated: a couple of old movie posters and Playboy Bunny model posters—the typical apartment of a male who never really grew up. I hear my phone buzzing; I go off in search for it.

I sit up a little too fast and realize that it is a horrible idea. I take a couple of deep breaths in and out and continue to look for my phone. I keep looking, dodging the bodies that lie across the floor, barely moving, until I find my purse. I see Will's name across the screen, and immediately slide the green button over.

"Ugh, Jesus, what happened last night?" I half whisper.

"Well, good morning, sleeping beauty! Are you still at the party, or did you go home with someone?" Will cheerfully shouts through the phone.

I clear my throat from the stale beer that rests in the back of it. "It appears I am at what they call a modern-day Jones-Town. Where are you? When did you leave?"

I begin gathering my things, slowly, in fear if I move faster, the room will start spinning and projectile vomit will spew from my mouth.

"I left between the strip club and the trip to Wendy's. Wait, no, after you got the call from the football guy, I decided to bounce. You got all emotional and what the kids are calling these days 'in your feelings.' *Then* I decided to bounce."

I find my shoes resting on top of a table and slide them on.

"Cool, cool, cool. So do you know where I am? I mean, I have all my clothes on, so that's always a good start." I look around the room to see if I know anyone. No one looks familiar. *Where did I meet these people? How did Will and I even come across this gang of affiliates?*

Will laughs. "That is actually really surprising. No, I have no idea where you are, but I know where you need to be, and if you're not there in twenty minutes, we are going to have what I call a fucking Yelp disaster."

I begin to tiptoe to the front door and start to figure out how to unlock the locks. As I look at them, I feel as though I'm in an escape room, and there is some hidden code around this apartment to open this goddamn door. *It can't be that hard, Neveahly. It's three fucking locks.* I figure it out after five minutes and open the door. Slowly, I close it behind me so I don't wake up the sleeping drunks. I dig in my purse to find my headset and switch to my hands-free as I try to navigate out the apartment building.

"I am completely aware of what will happen if we are late today. Just give me a minute to figure out where I am, my dude."

I hit the elevator down button. An elderly couple is waiting beside me, getting ready to take their little dog for a walk. My hair is a mess, and I look like I've been partying all night. I smell of booze. Turning my head I flash them a half smile; they pull the tractable leash that is attached to their dog and take a step back. The awkwardness of us standing there should make me feel uncomfortable, but it doesn't. I've had my fair share of awkward waits by the elevator from a rough night of partying.

The elevator takes an eternity as I wait. I spot an exit sign off in the corner and opt to take the stairs. I wave bye to the scared elderly couple and clumsily walk to the exit door, looking like a child in her mother's heels.

"What's in it for me?" Will asks, taunting me.

I let out an annoyed sigh. "The next time we go out, I promise I will not talk about the football player or ditch you?"

I hold on to the railing as I walk down the endless flights of stairs. *How many flights of stairs are there? This is ridiculous! This is my nightmare!*

I walk out into the busy sidewalk of the city, dodging the endless rows of people getting ready to hail a cab and see Will's SUV. I let out an irritated laugh.

"Lies, but I'm out front," he says, hanging up the phone.

I open the car door and get inside. I give him a jab on the arm and immediately go into the back seat and get my workbag.

"How hard was it to say that you were outside waiting for me?" I start going through my small bag, looking for something that can withstand the summer heat in Washington D.C.

"I mean," He says as he laughs, "I wasn't going to let you go out by yourself the entire night, but I also wanted to sleep in my own bed."

I fall back on the seat and slide my shorts on. "What are you, a twelve-year-old girl who can't spend the night at a sleepover?"

"I feel like I just got a dark glimpse into your adolescent life."

I dig in my bag and look for a comb to fix my curls. "Whatever. What time did you end up really leaving last night?"

"We went back to the apartment, and you started acting weird about the football dude, and then I dipped out. I told you I was leaving, but I knew you weren't going to remember it."

I jump back into the front seat and go into his glove box and pull out my makeup bag.

"Jesus, do you have your whole life in here?"

"I do, and his name is Mike. Why do not ever call him by his name?"

Will laughs as he lights up a joint at a stop light. "I refuse, *refuse* to call him Mike when he's such a shit bag. You're so lucky I don't call him that to his face."

I shoot him a look and swipe the joint and take a drag. "He's nice," I say as I exhale the sweet-tasting smoke.

"No," Will says, grabbing the joint back. "And ask next time. Nice guys don't stand you up on your birthday at your favorite restaurant and leave you there to cry. Nice guys don't invite you to their game to have their live-in girlfriend come and be like, 'Hey! Surprise! We're still together, but can we still fuck on the side? Better yet, let's bang behind this dumpster so she won't see us.' Plus, he's not even on a good team, Nev."

"I mean, he did lay down a blanket," I say.

I shove the makeup bag back into the glove box.

"Oh, dear god."

"Dude, I'm kidding. Yeah, he didn't tell me his girlfriend was living with him or the fact that he had a girlfriend was shitty, but we worked it out. I think. I don't know what is going on at this point, but I know we are not dating. I am keeping my options open, kind of."

"It's like, you don't want to be happy," Will says.

"I do want to be happy. I want to be so happy, but I also don't want to be dragged through social media again."

Will sighs. "Which is what I don't understand why you are still with him or even entertain the idea of fucking him. He's a shit bag. Dude, his girlfriend basically assassinated your character on Twitter and Facebook and didn't even get the story right. She saw something and drew from that conclusion. Again, Shit bag did not come to your defense."

I turn up the music as we drive through DC. The city is so big and beautiful and full of life I don't even mind sitting through traffic sometimes. *Sometimes.* We pass the joint back and forth as I let my curls hang freely. We bob our head to old tunes as we approach our store. Will pulls the SUV in back, making it easier to unload all the boxes in his trunk.

I hop out of the front seat. The air is humid. A true August day in DC. I can feel my curls immediately start to frizz and my skin feel damp. I extend my arm as far as I can inside the SUV toward the cup holder to grab the set of keys to open the back door. As I make my way through the back, I turn on the lights, illuminating store. I walk toward the registers, hop behind the counter and turn on the speakers as I get ready for the day. The first album is Carole King's *Tapestry. Classic.*

A few times of going back and forth to the car, Will and I say nothing to each other. Just Carole singing her songs and me accompanying her. I get lost in the music as I sing along.

Will finally speaks up. "You can do better."

"Jesus, here we go." I groan.

I place one of the boxes on the floor.

"No, seriously, you really could. You go for these big burly guys who got nothing between their ears, and yet this is what always happens. He fucks something up, you cry about it, you write a short story, don't come out of your room unless it's to work, and you smoke pretty much our entire stash, get super drunk, and bring some dude home and start this cycle all over again." Will sighs. "I can't keep doing this."

Will starts looking through a box a woman donated with books out of print.

"How's the script coming along?" I ask, changing the subject.

I start to place books on the shelves adjacent to Will.

"How's the book coming?" Will fires back.

I laugh. "Well played."

Will comes in with the last box and places it on the floor. "I haven't been able to write in months. I've had the worst writers' block. Plus, Sharon and I have been—"

I quickly turn around. "Hold on, you're still seeing Sharon?"

Will lets out a loud sigh. "Yes, Neveahly, I'm still seeing Sharon. She's really—"

"Hello, I'm Sharon," I begin with a British accent. "I'm from England, and I've gone to the best schools, and I'm proper, and I drink tea, and I think ice coffee is gross." I laugh at my own diss. "Bro, who the fuck thinks ice coffee is gross? I mean, c'mon. She doesn't even like *South Park*."

Will starts to unpack the box in the neighboring aisle. "So she's classy. Believe it or not, Nev, some people do have morals, and not everyone likes *South Park*."

"First of all, fuck you, and second of all," I pause for a second to think, "I can't come up with a second of all, but still fuck you."

I finish putting up the comics and begin working on the Author of the Month's display in the window. He should be arriving at any moment, but luckily for us, he is running late. That's what all romance writers do when they come to our store. It drives me batshit insane, but in this case, it's working in our favor.

"She's different from the rest," Will continues.

I turn around and look at him. "How? How is she different from the rest?" I laugh. "I just want to say, not liking *South Park* doesn't make you classy. It makes you look like you don't have a sense of humor."

I hop down and walk over to him. "Look, my dude, as much as I make fun of her, I like her, I really do, but it does sound like you aren't really into her, but besides being classy, how is she different from the other chicks you've banged? Better yet, how is she remotely even lifting you up, bro?"

Will looks at me. "She just is. She encourages me to write, sometimes."

I laugh. "That's not an answer. You got to give me a reason on why she is absolutely different." I see the wheels turning in his head. "Having big tits doesn't count because that literally makes her just like the rest."

"Damn it," Will yells, "I don't know. She believes in me. I like that about her. I mean, you believe in me too, but I don't bang you."

I shudder. "Gross, you could have just left it at she believes in you."

"She makes me laugh, and she challenges me. I like that." Will leans on the counter and smiles.

"See, that's the shit I'm talking about! That's a reason to like someone. Not because they have awesome rockin' tits!"

He laughs. "She does this thing in bed—"

I hold up my hand. "And that's where I'm gonna stop you, buddy. In no way, shape, or form do I care to know what y'all do in the bedroom."

I head back to the window display to place the books by the cutout cardboard full-length body picture and see Mike is standing right there. I mean, it's hard to miss him. He's six foot five and about two hundred and I don't know how many pounds. Built like a tank.

"Ah, shit," I say loudly.

"What? Is there a line forming?" Will asks.

Will briskly walks with excitement to the front of the store. "Ah, fuck, what the fuck is he doing here?"

"Can I come in?" Mike enunciates loudly, not realizing that I can hear him perfectly from where he is.

"No, fuck you," Will enunciates back, mocking him.

"Will." I try to keep a straight face.

"What? We aren't open, and there is a line forming for this romance novelist."

Will grabs a book from the display and starts to flip through it. "God, this dude can get more poon than Nicholas Sparks himself, and I'm out here struggling to write one fucking sentence. I don't get it. He's not even that good."

I hop down from the window display. "Can you give me, like, ten minutes?"

Will looks up from the book and thinks for a brief moment. "No."

I laugh. "I'm sorry. That made it sound like I was requesting your permission. Give me ten minutes." I head out the store.

I look to the right of me and see the line forming. So many women. I can feel their vaginas throbbing all the way from where I am standing. Hey, I got to give it to this guy. Whatever he's typing on his computer to make these women touch themselves and buy this grocery store, waiting in line and see a romance novel, checkout shit is selling like hotcakes. We normally don't have this kind of item in the store, seeing how we are strictly unique books/comics, but I figured why not? Make some money.

"What are you doing here? Does your girl know you're here?" I ask mockingly.

"Don't do that," Mike says, looking me dead in the eye. "Don't stoop to her level."

"Stoop to her level? What level is that, Michael? The seventh level of hell? She is fucking insane. Who the fuck threatens someone with a sword? A sword! Also, who keeps a sword over their fucking bed, dude?"

Mike laughs. "Yeah, that shit was intense."

"That shit is not fuckin' funny. I did you a favor by coming over and offering to film your promo video. You also said that *you* were single. Had I known you were dating a crazy bitch, I wouldn't have come near you with a ten-foot pole. If you came here to say hi, hi. Now if you can see"—I point to the line forming—"I got work to do."

I start to walk back inside, and Mike grabs me by the arm gently. "No, I didn't come to say hi. I came to apologize. We broke up, and I want to make it up to you."

I roll my eyes. "Yeah? How?"

"How about we just go to Arlington tonight? Go to a nice restaurant, and we see what happens from there?" he says, pulling me closer to him.

I feel my body start to tingle. *Goddamn it.* I come back to my senses and take a step back, "I don't know. I gotta do inventory, and we have a new shipment of comic books from a warehouse that went belly up with vintage comic books we have to price out, and it's not fair to Will if I stick him with it."

"Yeah, it would be a dick move if you stuck me with it," Will says from the door.

I look back. "Don't you have some shit to do? Like, literally be anywhere else but here right now?"

"What? I'm cleaning the door window, and the windows, and—smoke bomb!" Will runs out of sight. He quickly comes back, realizing he forgot the duster, and slowly backs away, staring at Mike and me.

I roll my eyes and turn my attention back to Mike.

"C'mon, Neveahly. It's dinner in Arlington. I promise I will have you back so you can do inventory." Mike tries to entice me.

"Fine, but you gotta pick me up before booty call hours. Those are the hours before ten p.m., just in case you forgot. Pick me up at eight p.m."

"Sounds great. I'll see you then." Mike kisses my cheek gently and walks away. I open the doors for the customers, and they come rushing in. One by one, the ladies grab the books off the display and walk over to the seats and wait for the author to show up.

Will shoots a dirty glance at me. "His dick better be of a golden god for you to keep going back like this."

"Yeah, something like that."

CHAPTER 3

The author shows up three hours later than the original time. He saunters in with two women, one on each arm. I don't know why women think this is attractive because I honestly thought I was going to vomit everywhere. As he walks in, he asks for a bottle of water and acts as though we are his minions. I grab him a generic bottle of water; he flips out. I try to hold in my laughter. I apologize and go into the back and pour the generic bottle of water into a plastic cup.

"Much better," he says. What an ass.

He starts to read some very graphic parts in the book, which I guess is his signature move to get women all hot and bothered because I thought I was going to have to get a hose and spray majority of these horny housewives down. Will and I look on in amazement at what women are really into and what they think is kinky. So vanilla, so middle-class it's scary. It makes me wonder if they even heard of S&M play and if they discovered Pornhub.com yet.

The author signs some books and takes a few questions after reading and leaves. I disinfect all the chairs, just to be safe. It was a great idea to have him. We made a lot of money today, but I think we need to cool it with the romance novelists for a while. Perhaps maybe even a story time for young kids, anything but horny housewives.

Closing time finally approaches, we decide to do inventory before my date with Mike. We sit in the back room with the couple of boxes left at the back door from the warehouse, slowly pricing everything out. Box by box, we go through and look up the value online and how much we can sell it for. We start to place each one in piles by value. As I sit at the computer, the conversation quickly switches from comic books to my date.

"So I'm asking you again. Do not go on this date," Will begs.

I laugh and shake my head. "I'm going to go and see what this is about. Who knows? Maybe this could be the final push to end things with him. Maybe I just need to see how disgusting he really is."

Will shakes his head. "How? What other evidence do you need? Having a girlfriend while you guys were hooking up is not disgusting enough? Does it need to be like, baby daddy disgusting? I'm so confused right now."

I change the subject. "What are you and Sharon going to do tonight?"

He shrugs. "I have no clue. Probably smoke and cook. Watch an awesomely bad horror movie."

I narrow my eyes. "Um, I don't mind you dating other chicks, but please don't do shit we do together, okay? That's weird. That's our thing."

"Neveahly Skye Walker, are you jealous?" he asks as a huge grin creeps across his face.

I turn away from the computer to face him. "Pause, not jealous. I don't do other things with other people that we do. That's our thing. We've been doing that since college. With Nick and Jon, that's our sacred bond. To do it with someone else breaks it, and it no longer becomes ours, and you taint it with whores."

"Jesus, all right." Will goes back to picking up comics from the boxes. "I won't."

"I'm serious. If I come home, and y'all are snuggling up on the couch watching *Leprechaun in the Hood*, eating steak, and smoking, I'm breaking all your shit." I turn myself back to the computer.

"Holy shit, you need to hakuna your tatas because it's really not that serious," he says, starting to walk away.

"Try me, Will. Now how much for that action comic?" I say, pointing to the comic book in his hand.

Two hours after closing, we start to lock up for the night and head out the back. I set the alarm for the store, get into the SUV, and we make our way back to our apartment. I put on a decently nice dress. Not too fancy but nice enough that it shows that I am trying to give a shit. I told Mike to meet me downstairs for the sake of my sanity. Even though Mike cannot fully pick up on Will's sarcasm and mean jabs, it's much easier; Will won't have anything to say if he can't see him.

As I am leaving, Sharon is coming in. She offers a kind smile. I look her up and down to see she is in a pair of Will's sweatpants and a tank top. Odd, it's hotter than Satan's nut sack outside, but I get that wearing your significant other's clothes can make you feel closer to them. I stand at the door and realize I have been there for a bit longer than I wanted to. I move to the side to let Sharon in.

"Why, don't you look lovely." Sharon walks in.

"Yeah, gotta date. Have fun, you two!" I grab my purse off the coatrack and close the door behind me.

As I step outside my building, I am instantly hit with the summer heat. Even in the evening, it's unforgiving. I feel the lotion, once dry on my skin, become slimy all over again. I lean against the brick wall by the stairs and wait for Mike. I try to rub in the lotion over and over again on my arms, but I keep making it worse. I feel myself slipping and sliding in my heels as the sweat on my feet begin to form. I try to stand tall, curling my toes so I stay in place but to no avail, I keep sliding.

I feel the knots forming in my stomach, the kind of the fear of him standing me up again. Me, all alone on the sidewalk in the NOMA/Gallaudet area. In my tight black dress, in my red three-and-a-half-inch fuck-me pumps that I can barely get a grip in. *This is a bad idea. I should have listened to Will. I should just reactivate my Tinder, OkCupid, anything but give into this bullshit again.*

My mind races to the thoughts of what he could be doing. Maybe this is just a setup. Maybe his girl put him up to this, and they are laughing on the other side of the road in a car that I can't see, and the joke's on me. Oh, how big of a fool am I?

I look down at my phone to check the time. That's it. He's not coming. It's already 8:05, and he's not going to show. I pull up Facebook and start to type in his name. I click on the three dots and get to the unfriend option right when a black sports utility vehicle pulls up. The big utility vehicle stops right in front of me. I start to get nervous. *Holy shit, I'm about to get abducted.* Mike jumps out of the driver side; holding a dozen roses. *Possibly work on the execution of the pull-up next time, Michael.*

Mike, wearing a black pants and a nice top, has his long dirty blonde hair slick back into a low hanging ponytail. I put my phone back in my purse and walk toward him.

"Sorry," Mike says as he walks up to me, "traffic was horrible getting here. Holy shit, you look amazing."

"Jesus, Mike, you scared the shit out of me pulling up like that."

He laughs. "Sorry."

I grab my chest. "Wow. Okay. I just need my heart rate to go down a little bit." I walk toward him and grab the flowers. "These are nice."

"You ready?" he asks as he extends his arm for me to grab.

I look at it and grab it. "Oh, how classy. Why so fancy?"

"We're going to Arlington. It's a classy area." He grins.

"Not all of it. So where are we going to go?"

Mike opens my door and allows me to get in. He shuts it and runs to his side and jumps in the driver's seat. I thought about opening his door, but we are not there yet. We have not reached *A Bronx Tale* level in this relationship or whatever we are, and I'm not sure if we ever will.

"Well, I figured, we have dinner, go dancing, and then we could stop back at my place?" he suggests.

"Counteroffer, we get something to eat and then go back to your place and have nasty crazy sex?" I offer.

"I can get down with that," Mike says.

He signals to get back on the road, and Mike guides the vehicle toward the highway to get to Arlington. We haven't spoken in seven months or even talked about the events that led up to us not talking. As we make our way out of DC, the vibe in the SUV is awkward. I feel the rage build up and finally break the silence.

"Seven months though?" I turn to him and ask.

He laughs. "I knew this was going to come up."

"What the fuck did you think? I was going let it slide? Hey, Mike, it's coolies that your girl attacked me on social media and try to ruin my business. All is forgiven."

He sighs. "I mean, kind of?"

I laugh. "Wow."

"I couldn't talk to you even if I wanted to. Between my coach and my girl, it would have wrecked my chances of even starting in the game." He glances over at me.

"That's a new one." I laugh. "Michael, I get that you want your career to take off, but, dude, a fucking call would have been nice."

"I know, but now that our star-tight end is out for the season, I'm in!" he says with excitement. "It's like a career-ending type of injury."

"You might not want to sound excited that someone has lost their income because they are injured," I say, fully judging him.

"I'm sorry, but this is what I've been dreaming about! Ever since I was a kid."

I sigh. "Yeah, I know."

We continue to drive, and Mike continues to go on about football. I stare at the highway lights on the side of the road and start to count them. I'm lost in thought about what I'm going to drink at the restaurant and what I'm possibly in the mood for to eat when Mike asks me something.

"Sorry, what did you ask?" I snap back to reality.

"I asked if you want to eat at the steak house?" he asks again.

Mike starts to take the exit ramp off I-66 and slows down. He turns right and comes up on the restaurant.

I look at him. "I mean, we are already here, so it's kind of late to be asking that."

He shrugs. "There's a ramen restaurant down the street if you want."

I laugh. "No, it's fine."

Mike pulls around back and parks the car. He walks around to my side and opens the door. I look at him suspiciously.

"What's wrong?" he asks, concerned.

"What's with this? You being extremely nice?" I get out the car.

"I'm a nice guy, Nev."

I walk toward the restaurant. "Your definition of nice guy and my definition of nice guy are two very different definitions, sir."

He laughs as he shakes his head.

The conversation goes back to his career. We make it to the restaurant, and we are seated immediately in a nice booth. The restaurant itself is dimly lit with a soft piano playing in the background. It reminds me of a black-and-white movie I used to watch with my mom when I was younger. Our waiter comes and takes our drink order, and I go straight for my usual: a dirty Shirley, two of them, and a shot of tequila. Mike looks at me, a little bit shocked that I'm going so hard for someone who doesn't want to party tonight. Mike orders a beer and a rum and Coke.

Mike orders a huge steak, and I get the house salad. I feel his judging eyes look at me as I start to eat it. *Trust me, I'm not trying to watch my figure or am afraid to order food in front of a guy. I'm just trying to get as hammered as fast I can, in the shortest amount of time possible.* Our conversation comes to a screeching halt. Mike starts shoveling food in his mouth. Watching him eat makes my stomach turn, and I lose my appetite altogether. I order another couple of drinks while he continues to finish the huge steak.

Mike, in a twisted turn of events, settles the bill and we excuse ourselves from the table. I stand up and realize I am more buzzed than I thought and brace myself. I take a sip of water before we make our way back to the car. As we leave the expensive restaurant, Mike attempts to grab my hand, taking completely off guard, I pull away.

"What are you doing?"

"I'm just trying to be romantic. I thought that is what couples do?" he says as he looks confused.

I sigh. "We aren't dating. This is merely a trail run, Michael."

We get to the vehicle, and this time, he doesn't open my door. *I hit a nerve.* I get in, and he gets in on his side. We sit there for a brief moment, not saying anything. You can cut the tension with a butter knife; the awkward silence is diminished as Mike starts the engine.

"Do you still want to go back to my house?"

I think about my next words really carefully before I open my mouth. "We can."

A hopeful smile creeps across his face. "It's a couple of minutes away from here."

"Wait," I say, confused. "You got a new place?"

"Yeah, it's a town house. You'll love it." He looks at me and smiles.

I turn to face him. "No one is going to be there, right? I'm not going to be met with an angry girlfriend or girlfriends, will I? No swords will be drawn, and no *Kill Bill* action scenes will happen tonight? Because I've had a lot to drink, and I don't think I could defend myself all that well."

He shakes his head and laughs. "I promise, Nev."

We take off down the street. I start to feel nervous. I do not like not being in control of a situation, and especially after what happened last time. I feel the knots again forming tighter than before in my stomach. He takes his right hand off the steering wheel and grabs my hand. I don't reject it this time, and I lace my fingers with his. We ride and listen to music on the streets of Arlington. Mike's hand moves from mine onto my thigh. I smile. My cheeks get hot as I move my thighs apart.

We hit a red light; he moves his hand higher up my thigh and pulls my dress up a bit, stopping short of my panties and keeps his hand there. I start to feel myself get hot as I go to undo my seat belt, but the light turns green. He takes his hand back and puts it on the wheel again. I let out a laugh.

He pulls the SUV into the carport and turns it off. I rush to get out of the car and meet Mike on his side. Mike's town house is big, but not oversized. It's a lot bigger than what I was expecting. He grabs my hand and drags me to the front door. Fumbling for his keys, Mike drops them and immediately picks them up and opens the door. Mike gently lifts my arm over my head, twirling me around. A giggle escapes from my tipsy lips as I feel his colossal hands on the back of my thighs, lifting me up. As I lift his shirt over his head, I toss it off the railing. I run my manicured fingers through his hair. I take out his ponytail and put his hair up on top of his head into a bun.

He gently pushes me up against the wall and moves his lips down from mine and onto my neck. I let out a little moan as my legs fall to the wood floor. My five-foot-three stature stands no match to his towering mountain-man frame. He picks me up again and sits me on the table in the hallway, as if I weighed nothing. Mike reaches up my dress and grabs my panties, ripping them down my thighs. I start to go for his belt buckle and reach inside his pants; he's excited. He gently slides his hand between my thighs. I bite my lower lip as I reach for his boxers and pull him closer. My heart is beating as if it was trying to break free from my rib cage.

Mike picks me up again and walks me back into his bedroom, tossing me down on the bed. I come to my knees as I pull my tight black dress over my body and throw it off to the side, leaving me in just my lacey red bra. He crawls onto the bed and reaches behind me, and with the flick of the wrist, it's off and on the other side of the bed. *Witchcraft.* His pants are off. Mike reaches into the nightstand and grabs a condom and quickly slides it on. Within moments, he slides himself into my warmth. I dig my nails into his back, trying to get a grip on his tight muscular body.

"Harder," I whisper into his ear.

Mike pins my hands down on the bed. I can feel his breath on my ear as his breath quickens. He begins to grunt and moan, and I become even more wet than before.

"Oh, Maggie." He groans in my ear as he thrusts harder into me.

I immediately wiggle my hands from his grip and put one hand on his chest, pushing him away from me.

"Um, what did you just say?"

Mike looks down at me, baffled. "What?"

I push him off me. "Who the fuck is Maggie?"

Mike realizes he just fucked up. "I said Nevie, not Maggie."

I laugh. "No, you didn't. You most definitely called me Maggie."

Mike rolls over to the other side of the king-size bed, taking the pillow covering his manhood. "Shit, I'm sorry."

My mouth flies open in shock. "Are you fucking kidding me, bro? Is that your ex? Or current girlfriend?"

He rubs the bridge of his nose. "I have no idea why I said her name."

I get off the bed and begin the search for my clothes. "You have got me all the way fucked up, sir."

Mike sits up. "Wait, I can explain."

I hold out my hand. "Explain what, exactly? That you called another woman's name out while you were fucking me? Please, I would love to hear you try to lie your way out of this one."

I find my panties and slide them over my thick thighs. I hastily throw my dress over me. I quickly grab my bra and exit out of the bedroom. I see Mike jump out of the bed and follow me, jumping to put on his boxers on. Once I reach my phone, I immediately go for the Lyft app and request a ride. I don't even care how much it is. I request the closets ride and offer to pay double if it will break the law to get here faster.

I find my shoes on the stairs and grab them, not bothering to even slide them on my feet. As I reach for the door, I feel the rough hands of Mike grab my arm. I look at the hand and then back at Mike.

"I'm so sorry, Nevie. It just slipped out," he apologizes.

"It's okay, Mike."

"Really?" he asks hopefully.

"No, absolutely not. How would you feel if I yelled out an ex's name during sex?" I shake my head and open the door.

Mike follows me out into the hot summer night as I wait for my Lyft to arrive. He stands there, helplessly in his boxers.

"I am just so sorry. I have no idea how to fix this," he continues. "Please let me fix this."

"No, I shouldn't have come in the first place. I should have left you alone seven months ago. Honestly, I should have never talked to you two years ago. I think this needed to happen for me to see you really are just a piece of shit, my dude."

"I'm not a piece of shit, Neveahly," Mike protests.

I laugh. "I'm sorry, you're right, a turd sandwich."

Mike steps in my line of sight. "How can I make this right?"

"You can't? At all. You can't turn back time and not say her name." I see the Lyft pull up the curb.

Mike stands there, looking like a sad puppy as I turn into the ice queen. My veins run cold as my blood turns into straight icicles. I step to the side and inch my way toward the car. As I reach for the door, Mike makes one more plea for me to stay.

"If you get in that car, that's it, Neveahly. We are over," he threatens.

"Oh, well in that case." I open the car door and get in.

As the driver starts to pull off, I stare straight ahead to oncoming traffic, not giving Mike the satisfaction of looking back. You're not going to give me an ultimatum and expect me to choose you. I take a deep breath and allow myself to zone out to the sounds of the radio station.

CHAPTER 4

No words are being exchanged between the Lyft driver and myself. Five stars. I didn't feel like talking, and I don't feel like being entertained. I didn't even mind him playing a shitty music station. I just watch the cars zoom past us as he drove to the speed limit. I play on my phone for a bit and made sure that I delete him off every social media platform. When I'm done, I'm done. There's no going back.

Once we get into DC, we hit every red light. As soon as we crossed the line from Virginia to DC and got off 395, boom! Every fucking red light. We make our way to NOMA. NOMA is weird. You have your not-so-good areas, and then you have your super gentrified areas. You have the income-based housing, and right next to it, you have your high-rises. It was nothing like this when I was growing up. I feel like everywhere I turn now, a pop-up bar is on every corner. Slowly but surely, DC is losing its rich history every day and gains one new high-rise.

The Lyft driver drops me off in front of my building and takes off into the night. I can hear people on their balconies partying and drinking, and I much rather have had that over what the fuck happened at Mike's. I stand outside my building, staring at it. Gathering myself. I let out a deep, long sigh; grab my keys out of my purse; and enter my building.

Instead of taking the elevator, I decide to walk up the five flights of steps to work off the sexual frustration. By the time I get to the exit door for my floor, I can hear the music coming from our apartment. It's amazing how we haven't gotten kicked out yet. Our neighbors consist of people our age, but still. It has to get annoying after a while.

I can hear Tiffany's "I Think We're Alone Now" blasting. I smile. As I stand in front of the door, the aroma of the devil's lettuce hits my nostrils. My eyes roll into the back of my head and allow the smell to enter my nose and travel through my body. After the night I've had, I would love nothing more than to smoke a joint with my best friend. I can hear him singing completely off-key.

Slowly, I insert my key into the lock and gently turn the knob. I hold it and slowly push the door open. I walk in and see Will holding a wooden spoon, singing directly into it, with a face mask on, and Sharon with a matching mask. It's like they're having a girls' night. A part of me is a little jealous, I'm not going to lie, but I take in the scene of them eating pizza, cooking macaroni and cheese, and making nachos at the same time. Clearly, they have been smoking the whole night.

I carefully place my keys in the bowl, slowly place my heels down by the coatrack, and jump right in with them singing. Sharon jumps and slips in her socks, Will, who is so baked throws another wooden spoon for my mic. All three of us dance around the kitchen island singing to the late '80s song without a care in the world. For a brief moment, I am able to erase the entire night and enjoy the moment. I take in everything and accept that Mike is just a piece of shit. I needed this night to happen to know that it's over. I know. He knows. Closure.

As the song fades out, Will goes to the cabinets and takes out three shot glasses, a bottle of cheap vodka and fills the tiny beakers to the rim. In a matter of seconds, the cheap liquor burns its way down our throats. Leaning to my left side, I pull out the drawer where our emergency stash of hair ties are. I run my fingers through my long, thick, curly hair and place it in a messy bun.

"How was the date?" Will asks as he begins to roll a joint.

"Oh, who did you go on a date with? The football player? The stockbroker? The firefighter? I can't remember who you are dating these days," Sharon says, throwing some shade.

Be nice, be nice, be nice.

Will stops rolling the joint and looks at me. "Wait, there was a firefighter?"

"Briefly. It was fine." I lean further onto the island top. "Whatcha y'all doing over here?"

"Will's been trying to find inspiration for his script all night. So, he smoked pretty much all of his stash," Sharon informs me.

"Oh, really? How's that going?" I look over at Will and where he is in the process of rolling the joint. "Bro, can I see it? You're drooling all over it."

"Am not! I got this," he says, getting defensive.

I let out a sigh. "Please, dude? It's gonna be too wet to light, and then we're gonna have to roll another one. Actually, at this point, we're going to anyway."

"Fine, if you're so damn good at it," Will says, as he slides the Rick and Morty Rolling tray toward me.

I unroll the joint and empty it. I dash into my room and go straight for my nightstand drawer and grab papers out. I hop back on the stool and begin the process. Within five minutes, I've rolled three joints.

"I hate you," Will says.

"No, you don't." I smile.

"So, after all that shit over Twitter, Facebook, Instagram, and even Tik Tok, you still gave the football player a chance?" Sharon asks.

Nev, when they go low, you go to lower. Wait, no, you maintain your cool.

I shrug and take a long inhale. I hold it for a few seconds and exhale. "It wasn't a date. It's more like a friend buying me dinner."

Will takes a puff and laughs. "I could have done that."

I cough. "Trust me, no, you could not have."

Will sits there for a second and his face turns sour. "Ew, you fucked him, didn't you?"

"No, and if I did, it's none of your business," I say defensively.

"But if you're not ashamed of it, why are you getting so defensive?" Will probes.

"Since when is my love life on trial here?"

"Since college! You make horrible decisions! Not once have you made a good decision when it comes to men, Neveahly!" Will continues to smoke.

"I have had some bad ones, but they were not all that bad." I walk over to the fridge and grab a beer.

"Okay, let's start with the king of the lollipop guild," Will begins.

Sharon looks at me. "Who's that?"

"No one." I crack it open and take a sip.

"They dated or whatever for three months in college, and he completely ghosted her without any reason. Just stopped talking to her, and when that happened, every time she would get drunk, she would bitch and moan about him." Will puts out his joint.

"Not always!"

"You're right because then there was the rapper!" Will continues.

Sharon starts to laugh. "Oh, tell me you're joking!"

Will shakes his head. "I shit you not. Do you remember the movie *Malibu's Most Wanted*? B-Rad? Yeah, he was a better rapper than this fuckin' clown."

I walk to the doorway of the kitchen. "I would love to continue to listen to you bash all the guys I've dated, but I'm tired."

"Oh, Nev! Don't go!" Sharon begs. "I want to hear more!"

"G'night, y'all!" I give a half wave as I walk down the hallway that leads to my bedroom, gently closing the door behind me.

I don't even bother taking off my makeup. One night can't hurt me. It's not good for my skin, but it won't hurt me. I pull off my dress and throw it in the corner of my room and fall facedown into my pillow. I remember my phone is in my purse, which is in the living room. *Fuck.* I throw on a T-shirt and walk out there. I see Will and Sharon dancing to the beat of their own drum as I walk as quickly as possible, trying not to be spotted. I reach in my purse and grab my phone. I glide across the wooden floor quietly without being spotted, avoiding all human contact like the plague.

I fall on my bed, plug my phone in the charger, and drift off to sleep. I don't even bother turning on Archer for background noise. I just allow the sounds of cars honking and people partying lull me to sleep.

I wake up the next morning to the banging on the front door of our apartment. Our walls are paper-thin, and my door is no exception. I lift one side of my eye mask, which I don't even remember putting on last night. As soon as I come to consciousness, the banging stops. I figure it's one of Will's Grubhubs, and the guy has been banging on the door for a while. I pull the lifted part of my eye mask down and try to go back to sleep. Almost immediately, the banging starts up again. I hear Will's bedroom door fling open and hear him screaming he's coming. I completely remove my eye mask. *Okay, I guess I'm not sleeping in today.*

As I lie on my stomach, I start to hear voices. Will sounds utterly annoyed, while the other sounds somewhat upbeat and familiar. I can't place it, but to be honest, I'm not trying to. I'm only trying to figure out if I need to bring my bat out or not. I raise my body to a kneeling position. I look around the room in disgust: *a fucking pigsty. I gotta clean this up eventually.* Clearing my throat, I step around the clothes cluttering my floor and search for my *Bob's Burger* slippers. Before I can even slide them on, there is banging at my door.

"Just wait a fuckin' second," I say in a raspy voice.

"Uh, Nev, you need to come out here," Will says, annoyed. "Someone is here to see you."

I hurl it open, and to my surprise, Asher, my baby brother, is standing before me. I stare at him, wondering if this is a dream or not because I haven't seen him in over three years, let alone not having gotten so much as a phone call.

"Why hello, sister! I see the years have been treating you well!"

"What in the McFuck are you doing here?" I brush past him.

I make my way to the kitchen to work on my first of many cups of coffee.

I look at the microwave to see the time. "Jesus tap-dancing Christ, it's 8:47 a.m. Why are you even up this early?"

I flip on the Keurig machine and place a cup underneath and wait for it to warm up.

Asher sits on a stool by the island. "Well, I haven't been to sleep yet, sis. I just got in from the Virgin Islands, and I figured you would be my first stop."

"Mom didn't want you either?" I say, hitting the biggest option on the machine.

He narrows his eyes. "no, she did not."

Will walks up and stands by him. "And you thought we would want to you here? Bro, you are the definition of shit show." Will drags his feet over to me as I place the warm cup of coffee to my mouth and steals it.

"Okay. I guess I will make another one." I'm way too tired for this.

"Can you make one for me?" Asher asks.

"No," Will and I both say in unison.

"Also, what about Amira? You are a lot closer to her than me," I urge.

I go on my tippy toes for the next mug I can find. Will barely extends his arm and pulls it down for me.

"Show-off."

"Amira is on one of her benders. I don't know, she's off her meds again." Asher moves closer to me and places his head on my shoulder. "Please? It will only be for a couple of weeks?"

I laugh. "So let me get this straight. You want me to let you stay in our apartment, and I haven't heard or seen you in three years? Am I correct?"

"Yes," he says slowly.

"I should say yes to this because?" I demand.

"Because I'm your brother, and that's the sisterly thing to do," Asher snaps.

Will jumps in. "Okay, so it's not just her apartment. It's also mine, and I'm just confused on why you are showing up now?"

"So my boyfriend and I broke up," Asher begins.

"There it is." I turn the carousel of K-cups around looking for a flavor.

"Wait, let me finish. My boyfriend and I broke up, and I thought maybe this would be a good time to reestablish a relationship with my family," Asher explains.

"Okay, so start with, I don't know, insert whatever other sibling you have. Your biological dad was a notorious whore." Will offers.

"Easy," I narrow my eyes, "Look, I get it. I am a piece of shit, and I've been a piece-of-shit brother over the years. Let me try to make this up to you. I honestly have changed my ways, and I would love to show you that."

"Until another guy comes around?" I add.

Will and I high-five.

"I'm trying to be strong on my own here, Neveahly. So what say you? Will? Nev? Can I stay here?"

I look at Will. "I mean, we could use the help at the store?"

Will rolls his eyes. "Fine, but you have to be actively looking for a place of your own, and employment. You can't work for us forever. Got it?"

Asher gives me a big hug. "Thank you."

"Listen to me, we have worked really hard for this bookstore to be where it's at today. I swear on your life, I will end you if you fuck any of this up for us."

Asher laughs. "Okay. You act as though I have never had a job before."

I almost spit out my coffee. "Ash, dancing in cages and stealing rich guys' money is not a fucking job, little brother."

"I mean, I plan events for these rich people before I steal their money, Nev! Duh!"

"I'm starting to regret this decision already," Will says, walking back to his bedroom.

I walk back to mine as Asher starts to make himself at home on the couch.

By midday, Asher is already complaining about how hard it is to work. We only asked him to lift up a couple of boxes, and you would have thought we asked him to do some super-duty manual labor. Will and I shift gears and ask him to do something he might possibly be interested in, like setting up a display, but all Ash is interested in is playing on his phone.

By 3:00 p.m., I took his phone away and put it in a lockbox and told him he could get it by the end of the business day. Asher looks at me as if I am the devil incarnate.

Five p.m. flies in, and Asher wastes no time and starts to hit on our customers. Will and I meet each other's gazes as he spits his game and are actually impressed that he's succeeding in what is happening. They exchange numbers, and the customer goes on his merry way. Half an hour goes by, and we start to clean up the store.

As I begin to wipe down the windows, I see a woman barrel down the sidewalk on the opposite side of the street. I call over Will and Asher to see. Asher, Will, and I stand in the window display area and watch her.

"Jesus, I wouldn't want to be whoever is going to be on the receiving end of that," I crack wisely.

We all stare at her as she crosses the street. She didn't even look both ways, and cars come to a complete stop, honking their horns, cursing at her. This woman does not give one fuck, and she keeps on going.

"Oh, shit." Asher laughs. "This bitch is fucking mad."

She makes her way down the sidewalk and heads toward our store. I get a better look at her, and then I realize who she is. Mike's girlfriend, or ex-girlfriend; at this point in time, I have no idea what they are. The front door flings open; smacking the book carousel on the other side. We stare at her from the window display as she comes in acting like she is about that life. Will and Asher look at me as I hop down from the display. She looks around the store. As soon as she hears my feet hit the ground, she takes a swing and misses. I grab her arm and twist it behind her back. She yelps in pain.

"Are you gonna be cool?" I calmly ask.

She continues to struggle as I push her arm farther up her back. "Yeah, I'll be cool."

"You're not gonna take another swing at me, are you? Because I will hit you back," I respond.

She nods, and I let go of her arm. The young woman grabs her arm and gains perspective that there are other people in the store. Will and Asher look down; half-intrigued and half worried, both in protector mode, unsure if they should step in. I hold my hand down low to signal got this, well, for now.

"Did you see Mike the other day?" Maggie snaps.

"Yes, I did," I admit.

She laughs. "Did you fuck him?"

I roll my eyes. The word *fuck* lingers through the air. Such a dirty and filthy word when it comes out of her mouth.

"We had relations, yes," I say slowly, being careful how I navigate this entire conversation.

Maggie inches closer to me. "Oh, did you?"

I hold out my hands. "Look, before you get any ideas, he called your name out while we were banging. I put an end to it, and I said we were through."

"Wait," Will chimes in, "I thought you said you guys didn't bang?"

I snap my head. "Bro, this is not that time."

"You know we are still together, right?" Maggie insists.

I shrug. "No, I didn't. I just thought he wasn't over you, but I guess now I do. Honestly, why are you here? Do you want me to back off? Because if that's the case, I'm backing off. You can have him."

"Have him? He was mine from the jump!" she says defensively.

"Wow." I laugh. "Look, if you want to do this, we can talk like adults, but I'm not down with this high school 'you fucked my man' bullshit. You come into my place of work to start shit on something you don't know anything about for what? Clout?"

"Because you're fucking a man who is taken!" Maggie yells.

"Again, I didn't know you guys were together. If I did, I wouldn't have had sex with him. Why are you even coming to me at this point? If he's been creeping around so much, I'm sure I'm not the only one he's fucking," I yell, matching Maggie's energy.

"Did he tell you he has a daughter?" Maggie folds her arms across her chest. "Did he tell you that?"

"Nope. Nor did I ask," I say with no emotion.

"Wow, are you just a cold bitch, or do you just like ruining families?"

"Ruining families? No. Cold bitch? Absolutely. Again, is there a point to this visit, or are you here just to gain some followers?"

Will and Asher laugh.

"Screw you, that's not what I'm about," Maggie says defensively. "I'm just saying that maybe you should ask questions next time."

"That's not my job to ask questions. I go into meeting guys thinking there are no fucking strings attached. I shouldn't have to ask questions! Maybe, just maybe, he should have been up-front with me to begin with. I wouldn't have fucked around with him if he was seeing someone. I'm a shit bag, but not that big of a shit bag."

Maggie laughs. "Right. So what? You're going to leave him alone now?"

"Yeah, call me crazy, but when a guy moans a different name than mine in bed, it's a complete turnoff."

"Well, I don't want him either," Maggie says. "I don't even want our daughter to know he's her dad."

"Again, that sounds like a 'you' problem and not a me problem. So unless you're going to buy something from my store…" I start to trail off.

Maggie looks around the store. She sees a display and knocks it over. She has a shit-eating grin on her face and walks past me and out the door.

"Real mature," I call as she slams the door behind her.

Will and Asher come down from the window and help me pick it up. Books and pamphlets are everywhere as I pick up the cardboard cutout. No one says anything as we put it back together. I should be bothered by this whole encounter, but after what I've been through, I have become comfortably numb.

As we get into Will's SUV, we ride to the apartment in silence. No radio, no conversation, just the sound of the streets of DC's traffic and nightlife consuming the air.

CHAPTER 5

I immediately get into my oversized T-shirt and start drinking. It's going to be a night to myself: a stereotypical writer night: drinking, writing, and ignoring the world; well, an unhealthy coping skills writer night. I'm a young woman who lives in the city, and it's a Saturday night, but after the encounter I just had at the store, everyone can go kick rocks for all I care. I want nothing to do with the outside world. As a writer, you are essentially playing God, creating a world where you can control the chaos around you, where there can be a safe word when shit gets too real, or you can hit delete if you don't like the outcome of a situation. I need that right now, free from baby mama's and lying, cheating bastards.

"I'm here, if you want to talk," Will says as he seasons Sharon and his burgers. "Today at the store was intense. I know I talk a lot of shit, but this is not what I wanted to happen between you two."

I sigh. "I know. I appreciate that. I just need a night to write and relax. Maybe this could be the jump start to a new book?"

"What happened at the store today?" Sharon asks, walking up behind Will.

Will looks at me. "Nothing. It was just a tough day."

"Don't lie to her. Mike's girlfriend who is actually his baby's mama came in today to confront me and to tell me to back off. Well, that I could have him."

Sharon's mouth flies open. "I'm sorry, what?"

"Yup. Congratulations, I played myself this entire time." I walk over to the fridge and grab a beer.

"I mean, now you know he would make a shitty father. Just think if he were to have knocked you up. God, being stuck with a bastard child and a not so great football player?" Will offers.

Sharon and I look at him in disgust.

"Hey, I'm just saying, you dodge a huge bullet. You should technically send her a thank-you note, have it read, 'Thanks for saving me from your situation, and I'm still a single childless woman who does not have any responsibilities!'"

"So are you going to confront him about it?" Sharon asks, completely ignoring Will.

I shrug. "Eventually, or maybe never. I don't know exactly what I want to do with this situation."

"Well, you deserve better. Maybe you should ghost him. Sometimes, ghosting is completely acceptable." Sharon offers.

I start to walk back to my bedroom, saying goodnight to everyone. I met the minimum requirements for communication for this Saturday night. I close the door behind me and kick off my slippers. Reaching underneath my bed, I pull up my laptop and open up a Word document. I stare at the blank document for what seems to be an eternity and just watch the cursor blink. I can't think of anything to write except, "Fuck Mike," which I do, over and over again, until I fill up an entire page. *I can't let this man live in my head rent free like this.* I hold the Backspace button and watch the cursor remove the words on the page. I feel the tears fall from my eyes. *Puppies and kittens Nev. Don't do it, just think of puppies and kittens.* The rage builds inside.

We have been off and on for almost two years, and this is what happens? This is what it comes down to? A baby mama walking into my fucking place of business and trying to start shit? I should have left him alone. I give up on writing and allow the sadness to flow through my body. I turn it on Netflix and start to scroll.

Endless shows, and nothing to watch. How can this be? *When will they get newer seasons of* Pretty Little Liars*? How come only season 12 is the most recent season of* Criminal Minds*? Are there like sixteen of them? What the fuck is a* Grey's Anatomy*?* I continue to keep scrolling like this for another twenty minutes until I settle on a shittier version of *Get Out. Oh, I hope Jordan Peele sees this and sues the shit out of them. This is literally the same goddamn movie except much worse actors.* I can barely follow the story. I'm half paying attention and more focused on my mobile game. My game freezes as a phone call comes in. I see it's Mike. I contemplate whether or not to answer the phone. At the last possible second, I answer the phone.

"What could you possibly want right now?"

"Don't hang up. Can we please talk?" he begs.

It's really loud where he is I can barely hear him.

"Why? I'm pretty sure I said all that I needed to say when I left your house."

"No, but I can explain everything, and there is some more shit I need to tell you. Can I come over? Can we talk?"

I laugh. "What? No. I have to work, and my brother is in town, so I don't think it's best if you come over right now."

"Wait, you have a brother?" he asks.

"And a sister," I reply.

I go back to playing my game on my phone and put him on speaker.

He laughs. "Wow, I had no idea."

"Because you never asked."

I roll my eyes.

"That could be why. Please? Can we just talk? I promise it will only be for like ten to fifteen minutes? I won't even come upstairs!" he screams into the phone.

"Where the fuck are you? Why are you yelling?" I stop playing my game.

"I'm in the club. I'm like right down the street from you." He slurs his speech. "Please! Have a heart, woman!"

I look at the clock on my phone. The late-night hours are creeping upon us, and I can tell he's had way too much to drink. Clearly his girlfriend has not confronted him yet about what happened at the store.

"It's late, Mike. I've had a really rough day."

"I know. So have I. That's why you're like the one person I want to talk to right now. Can we please talk?"

There's silence for a brief moment.

"You have ten minutes, but that's it, bro."

"Okay, I'm coming over," he slurs.

"Okay, just—" Mike hangs up the phone before I can even lay down the ground rules for him.

Shit. I don't want to see him, but why am I drawn to him like a moth to the fiery flames from hell? I'm pretty sure that's how the saying goes. The rage that once subsided comes back. I close my laptop and swing my legs over the side of the bed. *All right, baby girl, this is it. This is the time to unleash the beast and say fuck you to Mike for the last time.*

"I thought you said you weren't talking to him anymore?" Asher asks as he creepily stands in the doorway.

I almost jump out of my skin. "What in the fuck, Asher! How long have you been standing there?"

"Don't worry about."

Asher comes into my room uninvited.

"Sure, come in."

He jumps on my bed. "So why are you even entertaining the idea to see him?"

"I'm not. Okay, I am, but I do have some questions that I need answers to. I thought you were out tonight?"

Asher shrugs. "I was, but the guy was boring, and all he wanted to do was talk about his dead wife. I mean, God! She's dead! Get over it already. Are we going to bang or what?"

I look at him in disgust. "Every time I think you turn a corner, it's like you stray further away from God."

Will comes in from the balcony carrying a tray of hamburgers and cheeseburgers. Asher immediately gets off my bed and walks over to the doorway.

"At least I'm honest with myself. Unlike how you're acting right now! Girl, this is not going to end well, at all. This is how it's going to go: he's going to come here, and he's probably drunk as shit. He's going to say something to piss you off, you're gonna come upstairs and cry, and then you won't come out of your room for a while. Am I close?"

I narrow my eyes. "No."

Shit, he kinda is.

Will stops in the middle of the living room. "What's not going to end well at all?"

"Mike"—Asher meets Will in the living room and drags him to my doorframe—"asking questions about his girlfriend."

"After what happened at the bookstore today?"

I say nothing. My room falls silent.

"Oh, goddamn it, Nev! You're better than this!" Will says, handing the tray to Asher. "What could possibly come out of this besides more heartache and disappointment?"

"Nothing," Asher says, taking a bite of a cheeseburger. "Now who's the disappointment?"

"Still you," Will and I say in unison.

I see my phone illuminate, and I look down to see Mike's name flash across my screen. Asher rushes over to the bed to take my phone away, but I grab it at the last second. We wrestle for the phone, before I have it in my hand fully. I stiff-arm Ash and send a text saying I'll be down in a second. Asher shoves my arm away and moves toward Will and they look at me with disapproval written all over their faces.

"Nev, I'm telling you," Asher warns, "this isn't going to end well."

I brush past him and make my way to the front door. I grab my keys, slide my flip-flops on, and exit the apartment.

I hear Mike's SUV before I see it, and I'm still in my building. A part of me is a little embarrassed. A grown-ass man blasting music as if he's in high school, trying to look cool, and I'm associating myself with him. *Good luck, Nev.* I stand at the door and take a deep breath the humid air hits my face, and I feel my skin start to dampen. I peer down at the bottom of the stairs and see him standing by the passenger-side door with two guys. An overwhelming sensation of dread and fear wash over me.

The two men accompanying him look older and look like they stepped out of a J.Crew catalog, reliving their yesteryears of coolness. The SUV blasts shitty techno music as I descend down the stairs. He sees me and turns around.

"Nevie," Mike's face is full-blown red from being drunk, "thanks so much for seeing me," is what I think he said. He is so drunk; I can barely understand him.

I frown. "God, you're really drunk. What does drunk Mike want to talk about?"

"Cool, do you wanna go back to my place?" he slyly asks.

I laugh. "Absolutely not. You wanna talk? So talk. Also, who the hell are those guys?" I ask, pointing around him.

Mike turns around. "This is Brad and Todd."

"Okay, well, I'm definitely not going back to your house with two extra guys. That just screams all types of rapey vibes."

Mike starts to laugh. "What are you talking about? No one is going to do that. C'mon, let's go." He goes for my arm, and I pull away.

"I said no."

Mike groans. "Is this because I said Maggie's name instead of yours? Babe, how many times am I going to have to apologize for that?"

"Oh my god, that's part of the reason, but I have some questions." I look at him.

Mike leans up against the car, unable to stand up. "What are your questions?"

"For starters, why didn't you tell me you had a kid?"

All of a sudden, Mike now has the strength to stand up.

"Who told you that?" his words become crystal clear.

I laugh. "Not so drunk anymore, are you?"

"No, seriously, did Maggie tell you that?" Mike's demeanor goes from playful to serious.

I back away. "Yeah, she did. She came to my store today trying to fight me."

Mike rubs his forehead. "Jesus Christ, what else did she do?"

"What else? Bro, is this normal for you? Because this is something I can't get down with. So I'm going to have to—"

"Hey, I gotta pee," Todd interrupts.

Mike turns around. "Not now, Todd!" he screams.

"Look, I can't do this anymore. It was fun way back when, but this is it for me, bruv. I wish you the best of luck, I really do, but this has run its course."

Mike lifts himself off his SUV. "So two years down the drain? That's it?"

Baffled, I look at him. "What the hell are you talking about? You were never mine. It was always you, me, and Maggie. It was never just *us*. Now there is a kid in the mix, and I don't even like kids, dude. So yeah, two years down the drain."

Mike turns around and kicks the tire of the SUV. "Don't do this, Nev. I need you."

I back away toward the steps and slowly scroll toward Will's name in my phone. I press the call button and let it ring a few times and hang up. Our SOS since college.

"No, I don't think you need me. I think you are just not used to this kind of rejection. I get it, though, Mr. Hotshot, now stuck with a baby mama and kid." I look around to see if anyone is on the streets, just in case if I need witnesses: no one. *Fuck.*

"No one leaves me," Mike threatens.

My eyes widen. "Hold up. Let's not turn this into a Lifetime movie special, my dude. We can end this and let everything go and go our own ways without anything else getting fucked up."

As soon as the words left my lips, I felt Mike's hands around my neck. I drop my phone on the sidewalk, and I hear it clash against the concrete. Mike pushes me up against the brick wall, lifting my small frame up and my feet slightly off the ground. I gasp for air as I try to grab my keys out of my shorts. I hear the SUV door open as Todd and Brad come flying out of the back seat.

My vision starts to get blurry, and my oxygen levels start to deteriorate. I hear Brad and Todd tell Mike to let me go as they try to wrestle him off me. I find my keys and stab Mike in the hand; he immediately lets me go. I fall to the concrete. I feel my way around on the ground for my phone and call 911. Before I realize what is happening, I see the SUV take off and Will come running down the steps with Asher and Sharon.

As I cough, gasping for air, Asher takes my phone and talks to the operator, while Will and Sharon try to read the plate number as the SUV speeds down the road. I try to steady my breathing, with my back against the brick wall, while all four of us wait for the police. I sit there, not even noticing that I'm crying as I feel Asher's arms around me. I hear his soft, soothing voice, telling me everything will be okay, as we hear moments later the sound of the sirens come screeching down the road.

A police officer and his partner exit their vehicle and approach us slowly. I never have had a good encounter with the police. As a matter of fact, nine out of ten times, I've had to run from them from a party, but this time, maybe they can help out in this situation. I try to stand up, but my legs give way, like a newborn calf learning to walk. I allow the two officers to approach me.

"Ma'am, can you tell us what happened?" the first officer asks.

"I was ending it with a guy I was seeing," I say in a raspy voice, barely able to talk.

"What is his name?" the officer asks as he writes down everything I say.

"Michael. Michael Washosky." I cough.

He stops writing and looks at me. "The football player?"

I nod.

"The tight end for the Bay did this to you?" the second officer slowly asks.

I narrow my eyes.

"Yes, he did," Sharon jumps in. "Is there a problem, officer?"

The policemen both exchange glances.

"No, there is no problem," I answer for them. "I'm assuming he's on one of their fantasy teams, and this would probably fuck this all up for them." I begin to cough.

"No, ma'am," the first police officer says. "I'm just trying to get this right."

"Do you need an ambulance?" the second officer offers.

I shake my head. "I'm fine. Nor do I want to press charges. I just want this night to be over and done with. I panicked dialed. Sorry I wasted your time, officers."

"Well, this is an assault, so whether you want to press charges are not, we are going to have to arrest him," the officer says.

I shrug. "Hey, you gotta do what you gotta do."

"Are you sure it was Michael Washosky?"

I roll my eyes. "I'm sure it was him. Now if you don't mind, I would like to go upstairs and get extremely fucked up and forget this night had ever happened."

I start to stand up slowly and sway a bit. Asher helps me up the stairs along with Sharon. Will gives the police officers a backward glance as we all make our way back into the building.

We say nothing in the elevator. I fucked up. I know it, Will knows it, we all know it. I stare at the elevator doors where I used to be able to see my reflection, now are dull. I cannot help but think how fitting is that a representation of my life right now. Once full of life and literally almost got the life choked out of me. A perfect ending for a relationship or whatever the fuck I had with Michael.

The elevator arrives, we file out; one by one, saying nothing. Making our way into the apartment, I go straight into our makeshift liquor cabinet and start to pour the cheap stuff. Will, Sharon, and Asher hang back and just watch me take shot after shot without saying a word. I can feel them judging me. I take two more shots before I have the courage to face them.

"What do you want to hear? That y'all were right?" I snap.

"No, Nev," Will says softly, "not like this."

I laugh. I skip the shot glass, take the cheap vodka, and start to drink it straight from the bottle.

"Well, you were." I feel the tears form in my eyes. "I'm fucking stupid. I know that."

"No, you're not stupid," Asher says gently, "just hardheaded."

"No, I'm stupid. I went downstairs, by myself, let a man get control of my fucking emotions, and I said something that could have gotten me killed. I'm stupid."

I take another swig.

"I'm going to bed." I start to make my way toward my bedroom. I stop at my doorframe, turn around, and face them, tears cascading down my face. "Thanks for coming down, though."

I walk into the room and shut the door. I take a long regretful swig and slam the bottle on the nightstand. I hear the door open again and see Asher walk in. I start to cry as he walks over and embraces me.

"I don't want to end up like mom. One abusive relationship after the other." I cry.

"I know," he whispers, "you won't."

Asher helps me onto my bed and tucks me in. He hops onto the other side and turns on the TV as I drift off into a drunken slumber.

Waking up the next morning, I try to pretend that last night didn't happen, but it keeps replaying in my head like a horrible movie. Over and over again, it's stuck on a continuous loop, hoping there would be a different outcome, but alas, there isn't. I roll over and stare up at the ceiling. Where do I even go from here? I'm damaged goods now. I wouldn't even know how to have a healthy relationship if I tried. I catch Asher's frame from my peripheral. Sleeping soundly. As much as we don't get along, we do come together when we need to. From the womb to the tomb.

I sit up carefully and make my way to the bathroom. I'm surprised I do not have a hangover. I look over to see the bottle of vodka that was once filled to the top is now half-empty. I decide to take a shower and try to wash off all of last night. I quickly turn the shower knob and slide it toward the middle and then toward the hotter side. I strip down and get inside. I stand under the showerhead, allowing the hard pellets of water to hit my skin and my curly hair. I stand there for what seems to be an eternity before I even start to wash myself. I get lost in thought. *What if Mike tries to contact me? What if he comes back? Should I get a gun?* The thoughts come and go, and I finally start to bathe. I feel so unclean. I scrub, and I scrub, and I scrub. Nothing seems to get the feel of Mike off me. My skin starts to look raw, and I realize it's time to get out before I do any more damage.

I sit on the toilet seat and start to dry off, gently. I brush my teeth and go back into my bedroom. I see Asher is not in the bed, and I throw my towel off and get dressed for the day. I walk into the closet and find a pair of shorts and my favorite band tee and slide it on. I let my hair air-dry and make my way to the kitchen for my first cup of coffee for the day.

To my surprise, Asher is already making coffee for us. I fight back the tears when I see him. I feel as though, even if he is my little brother, he was my protector last night, and I may be tough on him, but he does come through when I need him. I blink rapidly and clear my throat. Walking into the kitchen, I sit on a stool by the island and wait for a cup of coffee to brew. Asher slides a cup across the island and joins me. We sit there in silence. Just two siblings enjoying flavored coffee with an obscene amount of sugar and cream.

"Yesterday was fucking wild, ya?" Asher asks, breaking the silence.

"Yeah, sorry about that," I say slowly.

He laughs. "Sorry for what? How many times have you bailed me out of situations like that? It's the least I could do for you."

I shrug. "I know, but I should have listened to you guys. I shouldn't have gone downstairs."

Asher puts his hand on mine. "After work today, I'm going to take you somewhere."

"You're not going to kill me, are you?"

Asher laughs. "Trust me, I would have done it by now."

"Where are we going to go?" I ask as I take a sip of my coffee.

"You'll see."

Asher helps out more than usual today at the store. He doesn't complain once, and he's actually nice to most of our customers, offering little makeup advice to the ones who need it the most. Will, walking on eggshells with me today, offers to close for me. I tell him it's no big deal, but he insists. I let him close, and Asher leads us to the Metro.

Asher and I ride in an understanding silence most of the way. I take in the scene of different passengers riding with us. Majority of them are young tourists with families. I keep to myself and try not to say anything to anyone, but it doesn't matter on the Metro. People will talk to you if you have headphones on, and you could be reading a book on how to eat ass; they give no fucks. They will ask you if it's a good book even. Trust me, it's happened to me before. Not the book on eating ass. I was reading a gruesome comic book, and a lady's tits were out and vagina for the whole world to see, with headphones on, and this guy sits down next to me and asks me if the comic book was good. We ended up dating for two months. Great guy.

Asher studies my face as I haven't smiled all day. I start to notice that we have been on the Metro for a while and that I have no idea where we are going. The redline can only take you so far before you have to transfer.

"Okay"—I turn to him—"where are we going?"

The Metro stops, and Asher stands up. "Here."

I follow him out of the Metro car. We go up a flight of stairs, and we are met with the sun beaming down on us, not a cloud in sight. It's a gorgeous day, but it's so damn hot. Asher gets two water bottles from a vendor, and I take a look to see where we are. I smile. I see the merry-go-round where we used to come as kids. Our mom would take us here when we were sad, and we would run up and down the grass and play soccer.

"Surprise," he says as he flings his arms out.

I wrap my arms around him and start to cry.

"I didn't want you to cry. I just thought this was going to be a great place to come! To kind of get away and clear your head!"

I wipe my tears. "No, I'm not sad, I just think it's sweet you remembered that this is my favorite place in the world."

We start to walk toward the merry-go-round, and I can feel the excitement I once felt all those years ago start to form inside the pit of my stomach. The butterflies. We stand in line waiting to get to the booth to claim our tickets. The air might be thick with the humidity, but it's filled with laughter and joy. I look at the grass and see how green it is and remember how I miss playing soccer. I smile at the toddlers trying to kick a ball that is just as big as them. It's our turn to get tickets, and I pay for them. We have almost twenty minutes to kill, so I spot some seats, and I notice a concession stand that sells beer. It's funny the things you notice when you are of age to buy alcohol. I get one for Asher and me.

"I'm sorry Mike's a piece of shit," Asher offers.

I laugh. "It's not your fault I've got bad taste in men."

"That makes two of us." Asher takes a sip of his beer. "The guy I was with in the Virgin Islands was awful."

"Really? Not according to Facebook."

Asher looks at me.

"Okay, good point, Facebook is where you put shit on that you want us to see." I take another sip of my beer.

A warm gently breeze glides through the air on this unforgivingly hot summer day.

Asher sighs. "What is with us Walker kids picking the wrong men?"

I shrug. "I'm sure Amira doesn't have as bad a luck as we do."

"We don't know that." Asher polishes off his beer. "He was abusive, controlling, and manipulative. But I looked past that because he had money, and he funded every project that I did."

"Why are we like this?" I ask.

"I think we watched Mom go from abusive boyfriend to abusive boyfriend, and we just thought it was okay for the longest time. I think out of all of us, Nevie, you're the only one who's really doing okay."

"How am I possibly doing okay?"

Asher sits up and grabs my hands. "You have a business that Papa gave you, and you didn't run it into the ground like we all thought you were going to."

"I'm a little offended," I say defensively.

"I said, we thought you were going to. You are following your dreams and becoming a writer, and you're doing that with your best friend. Yeah, your love life is shit, but who's love life isn't in their late twenties? Our love life is going to suck, and if it doesn't, that means you are married and miserable."

I smile. "I don't want to be married right now."

"See! Who wants to? Not me! I mean, I'm glad I now have that right finally, but I don't want to right now. Mike is the worst. He plays like shit, loves like shit, and probably will end up being a shit dad, but think of it like this: you don't have to worry about him anymore." Asher leans over and takes a sip of my beer. "I'm giving you until the end of the weekend to mourn the loss of his baby dick, and then you're over it."

I laugh. "Okay."

Asher looks down at his phone and then at the tickets. "Shit, it's our turn!"

We race over to the merry-go-round, knocking kids over to get to the front of the line. I find my favorite horse, the one I've ridden since I was a kid, and get on. Ash rides next to me, just like we did when we were younger. The music starts, and the horses begin to move. Asher grabs my hand, and I reach for his at the same time. We laugh as the ride goes around and around. I feel myself morph back to a childlike state. I look at Ash and see him in his. I feel happiness and joy for the first time in a long time. I don't want this ride to end.

I look around to see the other children enjoying the ride and some kids who are petrified. Amira was always afraid of this. Asher or myself always had to sit with her, or she had to ride with us. The music fades out as the ride comes to an end, and I still feel the excitement that I did when I was younger.

Instead of taking the Metro back, I treat Asher to a Lyft. We talk about all the fun times we had in DC when we were younger, and all the times, we would drive our parents crazy, singing in the car, making them listen to the Spice Girls on repeat. It feels like no time has passed since I last saw Asher. I feel like I'm slowly getting my brother back, and he's forming into this amazing young man.

We get back into the apartment and see Will and Sharon are cooking again. They have set up four places, by the kitchen island. We sit down and eat as if we are one unit in this house.

CHAPTER 6

Summer is finally coming to an end. Tourists are going back to their respectable states, and school is starting again, and it's time for our end-of-summer bash. Will and I contemplate what our theme's going to be as we sit on the couch in our living room. Asher taps the pen on the notepad repeatedly.

"I will slit your face from ear to ear if you continue that," Will threatens.

"Jesus, dude, all you had to say was stop." Asher puts the pen on the coffee table.

I stand up and start to pace back and forth in the room. I take my stress ball and toss it in the air. It hits me in the face every time. A couple more times of pacing, and I give up and sit back down next to Will. I take my notepad and hit myself a couple of times in the face with it. I have no ideas, and I am completely stumped.

"Can I ask something?" Asher raises his hand.

"No," Will and I say.

"Okay, so I'm going to ask it anyways. Why is this such a big deal?"

I sigh. "So we throw this party, every year, to raise money for the bookstore and to say goodbye to the summer. Last year we did a *Hawaii Five-O*-themed party, and we got fucking crazy."

"Yeah, our landlord showed his dick to everyone, and we all got a month free of rent. It was awesome," Will chimes in.

"Okay, so," Asher starts to formulate, "why don't you do something that's trending?"

Will and I look at each other, confused. *The fuck does that even mean?*

"The fuck does that even mean?" Will asks bravely.

"C'mon, you guys aren't even that old. Trending, like on Twitter or Facebook?" Asher looks at both of us.

We shrug.

"I don't really care what's trending. That's the whole purpose of our bookstore. We sell old unique books and hard-to-find comic books," Will says.

Will gets up to get a beer.

"May I suggest a white lie party?" Asher offers.

"What the fuck is that?" I inquire.

Asher laughs. "It's a party where you put on a white shirt, and you"—Asher looks at both of us, bewildered—"are you kidding? I can't tell if you guys are actually serious or not. It's pretty straightforward. You write a white lie about yourself on a T-shirt. It's a great conversation starter and also a great way to pick up chicks and dudes. Oh my god, you guys are super old."

I glare at him. "You're not even a full three years younger than me. Humble yourself, sir."

"It's all over TikTok!" Asher exclaims.

"You mean the app made for children?" Will mocks.

"It's not for children! It's for like-minded people who want to share their creative—" Asher calms himself. "Nope, I'm not taking the bait."

Will and I laugh.

"You were getting really mad," I say, laughing.

"No, I wasn't," Asher says defensively. "Anyway, I think we should do this party."

"I think he's right, Will."

Will sighs. "Fine. White lie party it is."

Asher jumps up and gives us both a big hug. "Can I plan it? I promise I won't let you guys down!"

"Just don't steal from us. We aren't rich," I ask.

Asher and I notice Will has been acting funny as the week continues on. Asher keeps his distance as I keep an eye on him. Will isn't saying much, but his actions are. Slamming things down, getting irritated over the slightest thing, you would have thought he just quit smoking, and he's on day 2. His appearance starts to change. His hair, which is long to begin with, is kept in a messy bun, and his clothes are disheveled, like he hasn't done a load of laundry in a couple of weeks.

I let Asher go home early for the night so I can corner Will and finally ask him what is going on. Maybe he got Sharon pregnant? I hope not.

As I count the money for the night, I finally get the guts to ask him, "Bro, are you okay?"

He stops counting the money from the cash register. "Fuck! Now I've got to count all over again!"

I slide off the stool. "No, don't worry about it. I got this. You're acting weirder than usual."

He throws the money back into the register and goes to lock the front door. "Yeah, I'm fine. Let's just hurry up. We got a lot of shit to do before Saturday."

I laugh. "Okay, but Asher is actually helping us with a lot of it? And we can kind of relax for once." I throw my money down. "Stop. What the fuck is going on?"

He stops pulling the curtains down and turns to me. "Sharon asked me if I wanted to move in with her. She wants to take our relationship to the next level."

At least she's not pregnant. I force a smile. "Dude, that's it? I thought like it was something serious."

He frowns. "Did you hear what I just said? Sharon wants us to move in together? That's pretty serious to me. That's asking me to change my lifestyle around."

I turn around and walk back to the register. "Yeah, I heard you, but I fail to see the problem. Sharon is good peeps."

"We've only been dating like five months!"

I close out both registers. "I know, but love is love, dude."

He stops right in front of the counter, studying my face. "Okay, but I haven't said I love you to her yet."

I meet his gaze. "Then don't move in with her? I don't know what the right answer is here."

"What if we move in together, and it turns into a shit show? And then you get another roommate, and I'm left out in the cold?"

I laugh. "First of all, I'm not getting another roommate, and second of all, why are you expecting the worst? What if you guys get married? What if it works out? Why are you dooming this before it turns into something beautiful?"

"Because that's what I do, Nev! I don't get nice things." Will slides onto the counter. "I don't get girls like Sharon who are super nice and beautiful, who believe in me, and actually like me without a catch."

"So you want to ruin it, before anything begins?" I recap.

"No, I just don't want her to make a wrong decision."

"Why would she make a wrong decision. What if it turns out she's the monster?" I suggest.

"I'm always the monster, Nevie. I'm the one who comes in like a wrecking ball," Will says. He looks down at the floor, so defeated.

I roll my eyes. "Okay, Miley, instead of coming in like a wrecking ball, why don't you switch it up? Why don't you, I don't know any more of her songs, so insert a lady Gaga song in there."

Will laughs.

"Do you want to go grabs some beers?" I offer.

"Yeah." Will stands up and heads toward the back.

We take the Metro to Gallery Place-Chinatown and get drinks at Lucky Strikes. I order a pitcher of the cheapest beer, and we play a round of pool, poorly. The music is so loud we can barely hear each other when we talk. We decide to leave after an hour. Will and I head out down the escalator, pretty buzzed, toddling our way out the door. I check the times for the next Metro on the app and start dragging Will toward the west side of the station.

"Dude, don't you think it's too soon to move in together?" Will stammers.

I shrug. "I don't know. I mean I moved in with a guy in college after three weeks because I pitied him. I'm the wrong person to ask."

He laughs. "Oh my god! I forgot about that! What was his name again? Jared? Johnny? Jake from state farm?"

"Wow, Corey. Not even remotely close." I steer him toward the escalators leading down into the station. "How are you this drunk? I had way more than you."

"You're an alcoholic, and I am not," he slurs.

I hang on to him so he doesn't fall down the steep escalator. "Hurtful, but true. Anyway, if you like her, you like her. If you think it's going too fast, then pump the breaks. She'll understand. Just don't fucking lead her on, bro."

He leans on me. I almost lose my balance. "I mean, she's got awesome titties."

I look around to see some people staring at us. I smile. "Could lower your voice a tad bit?"

"She cares about me, she says I'm awesome, and she believes in me." He starts to lean forward. I grab his shirt.

"Dear God, I forgot you are literally the worst drunk," I say.

We reach the bottom, and I pull out both of our Metro cards. Once I scan both of them, I drag him toward our side of the track. We cross the bridge and go down another flight of stairs. I plop him down on the bench and quickly maneuver to the other side so Will doesn't fall over.

"Says the girl who calls random guys when she's drunk to get dick," he says loudly.

People start to stare. I can't help but laugh.

"I do, and it's great."

"So I should move in with her?"

Every part of me wants to scream no. I don't want to lose my best friend and get stuck with a ridiculously high rent, but who am I to stand in the way of love?

"Bro, sleep on it. All you have to worry about is our little white lie party on Saturday," I say.

I squint my eyes to see what time the train is arriving.

"I'm tired," Will says, resting his eyes.

"I know, buddy." I pat the top of his head.

Ten minutes go by, and the train pulls into the station. Will drifts in and out of consciousness, and I am praying he doesn't vomit on the train. I help him up on, and I sit him down next to me.

A brief struggle up the stairs and into the elevator, I shove Will in the corner. I grab his phone after I hear it vibrating and see its Sharon. I slide it to ignore the call and will tell him later about it. We get to our floor, and I throw his arm over me and drag him to the door. Opening the door, I throw him on the couch, and sit next to him. Asher comes out from the kitchen laughing.

"What did he have?"

"Half a pitcher of cheap beer and like four shots," I say, trying to catch my breath.

"What was the occasion?" Asher moves over Will's limp limbs and sits next to him, tuning on the TV.

"Sharon asked Will to move in with him," I say, kicking off my shoes.

"Shut up!"

I nod. I get up and walk toward my bedroom and turn around. "If he wakes up, tell him to call Sharon. I'm going to bed."

"Will do," Asher says as he watches TV.

I wake up and get dressed as fast as I can the next morning, knowing that I overslept. I took the morning off so I could do some errands for the party. I make a mad dash to the front door and see Will is still sleeping in the same place where I left him last night. Furious, I shake him awake.

"What? What's wrong?" he says, discombobulated.

"What's wrong is who the fuck is at the store right now? Why are you still here? Where is Asher?"

"He is at the store. I need to sleep this one off, Nev," Will says, turning over and pulling the covers over him.

I rip the cover back off. "Dude, get up! I had just as much as you, if not more! Get the fuck up!" I grab my purse off the coatrack. "Also, give me your keys. I need to go to the liquor store to get the kegs."

Will digs in his pocket, whips out his keys, and rolls over to go back to sleep.

As angry as I am, I realize I have stuff to do today. I call Asher and apologize that he has to be at the store alone and not help me with the errands. I tell him that Will should be there soon and to call me when he does so I can come pick him up.

By early afternoon, I acquire all the things I need for the party. It takes three trips for me to bring up all the stuff up to the apartment, and to my surprise, Will is no longer on the couch. I figure that Will needed Asher's help at the store, which is why I never got the phone call. I place all the bags on the beer pong table and by the sliding glass door. On the last trip, I kick off my flip-flops and fall onto the couch. I feel my phone go off and look down to see Asher's name appear on the screen. I immediately answer it.

"What's up?"

"Nothing. I was just wondering what time Will was getting here," he asks.

I sit up. "Wait, he's not there?"

"No, he's not here."

I get up from the couch and bust into his room. He's on his computer typing away, "He's here. I'll be there in like thirty minutes."

"All right," Asher says and hangs up the phone.

Will doesn't even acknowledge my presence when I open his door. He keeps typing away, like he's in a trance. I move in closer and see he's wearing headphones. I walk over to him and rip the headphones off his head.

"What are you doing?" I demand.

Will turns around. "What is your problem?"

"My problem is you're here and not at the store."

"Asher said that he's got it." Will puts his headphones on his shoulders.

I laugh. "You're joking, right? He was supposed to help me today! We had shit to do to get ready for the party! Where is your head, bro?"

"I mean, normally you do this stuff, so I thought he was fine at the store." Will goes back to typing.

I spin him around. "Look, I know you're going through some shit, but get it together. I'll go, but when I get back, your entire attitude better change."

I walk out of his room, slamming the door behind me. I slam the apartment door behind me as well. I feel an overwhelming sense of guilt. *I should be more understanding. He's going through some shit, and I'm acting like a total cunt. Although, even when I'm going through some shit, I do get it together.*

I speed over to the bookstore to see how busy it is. It's never been that busy, so I park the SUV in front and make a mad dash in. I see Asher at the register ringing people up and actually being pleasant to customers. He flags me down.

Asher waves me down. "I could use a little help here!"

I get behind the counter and start ringing up another customer. "What the fuck is this? Where did all these people come from?"

"So don't get mad. I made a TikTok about your store and how awesome it is, and two hours later, all these people started to show up," Ash says, sliding a card through the reader.

"So what are the flyers?"

"Okay, so really don't get mad." he hands me one. "They're for your white lie party. I figure you can make some money back from all the supplies you got, and then I thought, wait a minute! Some people might show up, and it could be a cool business opportunity for you to promote your career, and maybe one of these people could help Will too."

I look at him, and then at the flyer, and then back at him. "Wow."

"Wait, is that a good 'wow' or an 'I overstepped my bounds' wow?"

I reach over and give him a hug; I whisper thank you in his ear and give him a kiss on the cheek. We finish ringing up the customers in line and clear out the store. I must say, my baby brother is quite the thinker when put in a situation where money is to be made. I saw a side of him today, and I am proud.

Asher helps me close up the store, and we get back in Will's SUV and make our way back home. I hook up my phone to the Bluetooth, and we listen to songs from our childhood, starting with the Spice Girls. Of course, I had to sing all the parts Asher did not like, but it felt like we were back in our mom's car again, arguing over who got to be Posh Spice, even though Scary and Ginger were the better singers.

Getting into the elevator, Asher sees the guy he met from our bookstore when he first arrived to DC. They start talking, and Ash claims he lost his number. They exchange numbers again and say their goodbyes as we get off on our floor.

I haven't seen Asher's face light up like that in a long time. His whole demeanor changed. He starts acting like he's back in high school, and the captain of the football team is hitting on him, again. I told Asher we could order pizza, but when we came in the apartment, dinner was already waiting for us. Will made chicken cutlets with mashed potatoes with gravy and broccoli. An actual home-cooked meal. I throw my purse on the coatrack and walk into the kitchen.

"Wow, I'm surprised you cooked," I say.

I walk toward the fridge for a beer.

Will shrugs. "I owe you one. I'm sorry about today."

I tussle his hair. "Its coolies. Stop acting like a dick."

"Yeah, and don't leave me alone next time. I wanted to go on the errands with my sister," Asher chimes in.

"I know, dick move. I'm sorry." Will pours Asher a glass of wine.

"Why, thank you."

We sit around the island and eat dinner. Will tells us about how much he wrote today and how he feels like the writer's block is over. I am actually proud of him. Being a screenplay writer isn't easy; coming up with an idea that hasn't been overly done or played out is quite the challenge. As we are finishing dinner, there is knock at the door.

"That's probably Sharon," Will says, excusing himself.

Asher and I exchange glances.

"Do you think we should leave?" I whisper.

"Bitch, are you crazy? I'm not leaving for shit," Asher loudly whispers back.

"Do you not know how to whisper? It's a quiet act."

We go back and forth for a bit, and the door swings open. Sharon is standing there, smiling. Asher and I look a tad bit confused, so we smile back. There isn't a fourth plate, so I assume she is just coming from work, or she ate at her place. I examine her. She has an overnight bag, and that's it. Okay, off to a good start. Asher has been examining her too, and we both go back to eating as they walk over.

"All right, so I guess we'll see you in the morning," Will says.

I smile. "Okay. Sounds great."

"Yeah, sounds groovy," Asher adds.

Will looks at us suspiciously.

"Okay, sweet dreams!" I say in my sweetest voice.

Asher and I watch them disappear into Will's room. Asher turns around and laughs.

"Sweet dreams?"

I laugh. "I panicked!"

We both keep drinking and eating and talking about how we are going to set up for the party. I feel awkward and a little uneasy as well as guilty. This is something Will and I should be doing, but he and Sharon are closed off in his room. I want to go knock on his door, but the door is closed, and the air seems a bit stiff. Asher can tell I'm half paying attention, and he throws a piece of broccoli at me.

"I'm sorry, dude. This is what Will and I normally do," I confess.

I take a long swig of my beer.

"I know. I'm not trying to replace Will. I'm just trying to throw a successful party," Ash says. He offers a pity smile.

"Okay, well, I guess we are all set for tomorrow," I say.

I take my plate over to the sink and start to wash it out.

Asher follows behind me and hands me his plate. I take it from him, and he goes to the couch and watches TV. I tell Ash good night and go back to my bedroom.

I wake up and basically jump out of the bed; I am excited for today. I throw my hair in a messy bun and throw on some raggedy shorts and a crop top.

I dramatically fling my door open and skip down my hallway. I turn to see Asher is already awake and making coffee. Will and Sharon are sitting on the couch, looking despondent. I start to ask what's wrong, but I'm not going to let it kill my vibe just quite yet; I will be a good friend once I start drinking alcohol. I give Ash a kiss on the cheek, and to my surprise, he has everything mapped out where things should go on the rooftop. I look it over with him. I point over to the couch, asking what is wrong, and Ash just shrugs. We continue to talk about table placements and seating arrangements. I grab a copy, with two coffees and walk over to Will and Sharon.

"Good morning, Debbie Downers!" I say cheerfully.

I both give them a cup of coffee. Sharon offers a half smile. "Sharon, you're with me. You're going to down that coffee, and then I'm gonna give you a line of Adderall in my bathroom, okay? Will, you're with Asher."

"Oh, I don't do that," Sharon protests.

I laugh. "Today you do. Drink up, buttercup."

I grab a couple of bags over by the beer pong table and walk over to the front door. I slide on my flip-flops and open it.

I look at Sharon. "Are you nursing that coffee, or are you downing it?"

She chugs it. "Where are we going?"

"To the rooftop, duh." I start loading the bags on my arms. "Grab some bags by the pong table and meet me by the elevator."

I grab my keys, shove them in my front pocket, and head to the elevator. I hear the door close behind me, and a few seconds later, I hear it do the same thing. I can hear Sharon struggling. I turn around, go back, and help her. I grab a bag and place it on a free wrist and continue to walk toward the elevator. We walk in silence.

Saying nothing, we wait for the elevator. I can almost hear her weighing her options in her head if she wants to talk to me about whatever that's bothering her. I side-glance her and see her biting her lip, torturing herself. Whatever she is thinking about, I decide to let her marinate in her thoughts until we get to the rooftop.

The elevator comes, and we get on. I see the Adonis-looking model Asher has made friends with. He remembers me and asks if I need help. I lie and say that would be great, if he could just carry some of the bags up for us. He obliges with no protest. I'm taken aback by it; normally I have to threaten Will with his life or bribe him with weed or alcohol. He talks about his time modeling for Tommy Hilfiger and Armani, and I almost forget Sharon is with me.

If I hadn't caught her from the corner of my eye, I would have left her in the elevator.

I quickly introduce her, and she gives a polite smile and a hey. We get to the rooftop and set our things down. He finally introduces himself as Joshua. Not exactly what I was expecting. I was expecting something more along the lines of a Fynn or an Elias, something German? I don't know, just not that. Nothing so boy next door. Or if it was, I would have thought he would have changed it by now.

I take the sketched-out placement out of my back pocket and look on the back of the sheet for the layout of how the party is going to look. I start emptying the bags, dumping them out and scattering them on the ground by the pool. I finally sit down next to Sharon and decide to let her stop torturing herself.

"Okay, what's wrong?" I ask.

"What are you talking about?" She plays dumb.

She starts to unwrap the tea lights.

I look at her. "Really? You came in with a smile yesterday, and now you and Will are all gloomy today. Who shit in your coco puffs?"

She lets out a deep sigh. "I'm afraid Will and I are not moving in together."

I'm relieved and sad at the same time. "Oh, why is that?"

"He doesn't want too. He thinks we are moving too fast and that we should slow down. I mean, I get it. It's just that I don't understand where we go from here. I want our relationship to move forward, so I told him I loved him, and he said he didn't know if he was capable of feeling that way toward me."

I felt the words punch me in the face as if I were on the receiving end of it. "Oh, dude. I mean," I stop and think of something that could fix this but come up short, "I honestly have nothing I could tell you that could fix this, I feel like I would just make shit worse. I never know what to say in these type of situations."

She laughs as tear stream down her eyes. "I appreciate you trying, Nev. I thought if I came over last night and laid next to him, he would like the idea of being next to me all the time. I'm here always, and one would think that just us moving in together wouldn't be such a big deal. When I brought it up, he completely disengaged from the conversation and shut everything I said down after that."

"Will is complicated," I say slowly.

She laughs. "That's an understatement."

I let out a sigh. "So what are you going to do?"

"I'm going back to England. My contract is up, my lease is up, and I have nothing really keeping me here."

I shrug. "I don't blame you."

"I just thought he was the one. I mean, he is a tortured soul, and he is so smart and clever and witty, and I just don't know how to get through to him. He's a great writer," she says. She wipes her face.

"He's not a tortured soul. He's a fucking idiot. I love him to death, but if he can't see what an awesome person you are and that you're a beautiful, intelligent woman, then you really need to find someone who will," I try to empower her.

I stand up and start stringing the lights across the siding of the roof.

Sharon comes up and hugs me. She starts crying in my arms. I let her cry. She gets it together rather quickly, but I can still feel her pain. I hate that he did this. I hate that I'm in the middle of this. Sharon seems strong and independent; she will bounce back quick. *Hopefully.*

We set up the tables and put the white cloths on them. I put the flameless candles on top and the red solo cups facing down. Sharon goes around to the other tables and does the same. Asher brings up a keg and places it in the corner. Will follows behind him, one hand carrying a tub and the other hand carrying a bag of ice. The men use teamwork to put the keg in the tub of ice, and they go downstairs to get the second and third one. Will and Sharon say nothing to each other.

"I'm sure there will be other guys at the party," I suggest.

"I know, but they are not Will, and I'm not trying to look for a hookup." She starts to tear up.

I go over to her side of the rooftop and comfort her. I place my hand on her back and go in for a hug. She again wipes her tears and goes back to work. Sharon takes a seat on a pool chair and starts blowing up small pool toys. I join her to help. I stop after three and toss them into the pool. She tosses hers in and stares out into the water. I look at her and see how sad she is. We've spent the whole day together, and I have nothing to offer her to take away her pain.

"Wanna go get fucked up while we get ready?" I offer.

She laughs. "Alcohol isn't always going to be the answer, Neveahly."

"You're right, but it is right now." I grab her hand and lead her back to the elevator.

"Wait, we need to finish cleaning up," she calls.

I press the down button. "What? No, let the guys do that. We just spent the entire day making this place look fucking amazing. If you don't want to get fucked up, let's get buzzed at least and listen to awesome nineties pop music."

"Okay, you win." She throws her hands up.

"Yay! Thanks for letting me get you drunk!"

It is easy to get Sharon to come over to the dark side. A little bit of Jameson and a little bit of tequila can make anyone say, "Fuck morals." I don't think I've ever seen her like this before, and I am loving this free, fun-loving Sharon. She throws on some short shorts and a white tank top. We blast some boy band music as I put on her makeup and crimp her beautiful blond hair. We take two more shots of tequila.

Will and Asher sit in the living room playing *Mario Kart 7.* Already dressed in all white and looking pretty good. Asher throws the controller down, and Will laughs.

"You cheated!" Asher screams.

"How? How could I possibly cheat in *Mario Kart*?"

"I don't know. You just did!" Asher looks at us and smiles. "Well, well, well. Hello, ladies, don't you look pretty."

Will gets up from the couch and walks over to us. He smiles at Sharon. "You look great, Sharon."

Sharon sways a little. "Not great enough to keep though, huh?"

"She has had a couple of shots," I say in her defense, "so let's get this started, shall we? Remember the rules: nothing too hurtful, and this is supposed to be a conversation starter and not something that can ruin someone's night."

"Yeah, because I'm going to fuck every guy I see tonight," Sharon slurs.

"Easy, tiger." I pull her back.

Will grabs the Sharpie off the countertop and writes something on my shirt, and Asher begins to write something on Sharon's. The men hand us the pens. We all take a picture with our phones and look at what they put on our shirts.

"Will, what the entire fuck is this!" I yell.

I look and zoom in. "I drunk-call guys for emergency dick appointments?"

Will breaks out into laughter. "I mean, do you not?"

"I fall in love easily?" Sharon says, looking at Asher.

Asher shrugs. "I'm sorry. I don't really know you, but you look like the type."

Sharon laughs. "I mean, you're not entirely wrong, but I do find that offensive that you were able to peg me for that type."

"I'm not a lightweight," Will says.

"I only date rich men?" Asher asks defensively.

"From what I heard, that's all you do." Sharon laughs.

We all laugh and start to make our way to the rooftop. Sharon and Will stand on opposite sides of the elevator as Asher and I drink from the flask I brought from the apartment. We get to the top to see some people are already in the pool and drinking.

Music is blasting, and everyone is getting drunk and having a good time. I think more water is outside the pool than inside. I have lost more Sharpies than I can count, but at least we got them from the dollar store, so it's not a complete loss. Sharon did her first keg stand for thirty seconds and now holds the record. It's packed up here, and Will and I are beaming with joy. I go off and search for Asher and find him in a corner with Joshua. I smile, and let the two be.

I circulate around the party and talk to people. I see more people from the store than I have seen in a while. A couple of regulars who don't seem like the party type ended up coming. I down the rest of my red solo cup filled with rum and Coke. I turn and run into someone. I go to apologize and realize it's Mike. Immediately I become disgusted and walk away from him; he follows.

"This is the only way I can see you! You won't return my calls!" he screams over the music.

"Yeah, normally people would take the hint."

I continue to walk away from Mike, but he follows me around like a lost puppy. I scan the party for Will or Asher: no luck.

"Can you just talk to me?" he begs.

"Are you going to put your hands around my neck again?" I ask.

Mike hangs his head down low. "I'm sorry. I was super drunk."

I laugh. "When I get drunk, I don't choke people out."

"I know the cops came, and I got hit with a citation."

"That's it? A citation? Yeah, sounds about white." I roll my eyes.

"C'mon, Nev. I said I was sorry. It won't happen again," he begs.

I face him. "How did you find out about this party?"

He holds up the flyer. I grab it from him. "When did you go to the store?"

"I don't know, a couple of days ago?"

I scream in anger and continue to walk to the other side of the party. Mike grabs my arm. "We have officially broken up," he screams over the music.

"Oh, really! That's great! We can finally be together! I've always wanted to be in a violent domestic partnership!"

"Seriously?" he asks with a hint of hope in his voice.

"I was being sarcastic! At no point in time do I ever want you to touch me again. How clear do I have to make that?"

"You don't mean that. You've said that before, and then you were at my house two days later." He grins.

If I didn't want this drink so much, it would be on him.

"I was young and dumb." I spot Will and flag him over.

"Do you need help?" he asks, looking at Mike.

"Yeah, I do." I say, looking at Will.

"I'm leaving." Mike throws the beer down at my feet. A few people turn and stare as they watch the tall muscular man leave. Asher comes over to where I am standing.

"You okay?" he asks, worried.

"Yeah, I'm fine. Next year we're having security guards, okay?" I look at both of them.

Sharon comes stumbling over. "Oh my god, was that him? Let's go egg his fucking car! Oh, better yet! Sugar in the tank!"

I laugh. "Let's get her downstairs."

Will grabs her hand. "I got her."

Sharon pulls away. "I don't need your fuckin' help, ya nob. I met someone." She looks over at some homeless-looking guy. We all stare at her.

"I'm pretty sure he's homeless, Sharon," Will screams over the music.

"No, he's boho. You wouldn't know a thing about being up with the times!" Sharon starts to sway.

The man starts pissing in the corner.

"No, I'm pretty sure he's homeless. Let Will take you down to the apartment. You don't have to sleep in Will's bed, but crash on the couch?" I suggest.

Sharon grabs my face and kisses me on the lips. "You know, if I played for the other team, you would be my teammate."

"Okay, she's done for the night. Thank you so much for the compliment. I would probably bang you too if the setting was right, but it's time for you to sleep it off."

Will helps her toward the door. She is wobbly on her feet, and Will steadies her.

Just one night where Mike doesn't fucking ruin it. No, I'm not going to give him that power tonight. I go over to the bar and ask for another rum and Coke and pound it back. A couple of people come up to me and start a conversation, but it doesn't last long once they realize how hammered I am. I think I'm able to have a conversation with people, but what comes out of my mouth are not words but are, in fact, quite literally, loud noises.

I see Asher and Joshua talking and becoming cozy as the night goes on. I can see a relationship forming in front of my eyes, and I think Joshua is a perfect match for him.

The party slowly comes to an end as the sky goes from midnight-black to Mayan sun. I am the last person standing. Well, sitting in this case. Sharon and Will have already gone downstairs, Joshua and Asher have been gone. Here, with a bottle of Jack Daniels with a straw in it, sipping it slowly as I watch the sunrise over the buildings of DC. It's beautiful. Drunk doesn't begin to cover how I'm feeling. I stand up and manage to make my way to the elevator. Everything seems to be going slow and fast at the same time, and yet I'm not moving at all. I make it to the apartment and drag my body into my bed, fully clothed. I situate the bottle of Jack Daniels on my nightstand and go to sleep. I kick off my shoes and let the alcohol-induced sleep wash over my body.

CHAPTER 7

I'm 100 percent sure there is a mariachi band in my head right now. My mouth is filled with sand from exotic lands, and I fell down a flight of steps at one point last night, or I was used for a test dummy in one of those car collisions to see if the airbags deploy. Everything hurts, and I have no idea what exactly happened. The last thing I recall is Mike showing up and starting shit and him throwing beer at my feet. Sharon got super hammered; Asher is somewhere with Joshua. I rotate to the other side of my bed. Good, no one is there, so it wasn't a night of superbad decisions. I feel the urge to vomit and make the sprint across my room, dodging the items that are lying on the floor.

Pure liquid. *Did I even eat anything?* I grab the porcelain throne as I wretch everything in the depths of my stomach. I feel the snot slowly descend from my nose and the tears come from my eyes. Crying and vomiting are not a great mix. After a few minutes, of spitting into the bowl, I realize I'm done and cower into the fetal position. I feel the beads of sweat form on my forehead and the coldness take over my body. I lie there, begging for sweet death to take what is left of my body and soul. I don't even remember getting this hungover in college. *Am I really getting that old where a hangover can cause death? Is sweet death going to be my release?* How I beg for the sweet release. I imagine death in the form of an angel in black who kisses me gently on my lips, and my body gives out.

I realize I've been lying on the floor for quite some time, and the wave of nausea and sickness have passed. I roll onto my stomach and slowly come to my knees. Using the wall, I let it guide me and help me stand up right. I walk carefully and slowly out of the bathroom and into my room. I go in search for sunglasses on the dresser and find a pair. I slide them onto my face and exit the room. I stand in my doorway, one hand on the wall. I walk toward the kitchen. *I just need the hair of the dog to get the day started.*

Steady as she goes. I pace myself. The room begins to spin as I get to a stool by the island. Beads of sweat drip from my face. I spot a somewhat clean glass in the sink and brace myself to get up and get it. *I know we have Bloody Mary mix in the fridge. I just need to mix them both, and I will be fine.* As I stand up and get the glass, I fill it halfway with vodka and halfway with the Bloody Mary mix. I stare at the mixture.

"Bloody Mary full of vodka, blessed are you among cocktails," I say.

I take a long sip.

I hear a moan come from the couch.

"Who goes there?" I demand.

"Will. What happened?" He groans.

"I don't know. I didn't think I got that fucked up, dude," I say.

I slowly walk over to him. The room starts to spin again, and I speed up and sit on the empty side of the couch.

"I'm sweating alcohol." I take another sip.

"You basically had an entire bottle of Jack Daniels to yourself last night," Will says.

"Where is everyone?" I start looking around.

"Sharon slept in my bed and just left like an hour ago."

I take another sip. "Did you guys work it out, or is it over, over?"

Will sighs. "No, it's over, over."

I hand him the glass of Bloody Mary. "Take some. You probably need it more than I do."

Will swings his feet on the ground. "I thought we could work it out, but I just don't want to take that step of moving in. I like having my own place, you know?"

I lean back on the couch. "I get it. So are you guys still friends, or do I have to unfriend her on all social media accounts?"

Will laughs and then winces in pain. "Don't make me laugh, dude."

I grab my head in agony. "I honestly want to die. Everything hurts, and I want to die. Did Mike show up at the party, or did I fucking imagine that?"

Will's entire mood changes. "no, he unfortunately did. He also tried to start shit with everyone there. We had to call the cops."

My mouth drops. "Are you serious? Where was I?"

"Getting chocolate-wasted, my dude."

I groan.

Will goes back to a lying position on the couch. "I mean, it can't be worse than the stalker back in 2012. He will cool his jets and forget about you and move on to his next victim."

I frown. "That doesn't make me feel better at all, dude. That somehow makes it worse."

Will leans his head up. "Just sleep this one off. Don't worry about it until you have to."

I get up from the couch with my Bloody Mary and go back into my room. I chug the rest of it, pop two Tylenol PMs, down a bottle of water and go to bed.

I sleep for what seems to be two minutes, but when I woke up, five hours has passed. I feel a little better but not much. At least the room stopped spinning, and the cold sweats have gone away, for now. It's still light outside, so I still have some of the day. I grab my phone and see if I have any missed calls. Quite a few. None from Asher, all from Mike. After what Will tells me about last night, I don't know why he would even want to talk to me right now.

I entertain the thought if I should even look at the messages. It's adding fuel to a fire that's already spreading like crazy. I don't want to give him false hope, and I damn sure don't want him to think this behavior is remotely okay to display to women. I delete everything without even looking at it. I go on all social media and start deleting him one by one. Luckily, there are no pictures of him and me on any accounts, so it's rather easier to get rid of him.

I hear a knock at my bedroom door, followed by it being opened. I see Asher, Joshua, and Will standing there, looking at me in all my hangover glory. I throw the covers over me and pray they all go away.

I hear one of them walk over to me and pull the covers from over my head. I see its Asher. I let out a groan.

"I'm glad you're okay, but what do you want?"

"Let's go to brunch. That café across the street," Asher says, looking back at Will and Joshua.

I look back at them. "Okay, but I'm not even dressed, nor do I have plans on even looking presentable today."

Asher laughs. "Since when did that ever matter before?"

I throw a pillow at him and start to get out of bed. I toss on some jean shorts and a tank top, and we all make our way toward the café.

The sun beams down on us on this gorgeous September day. The air is blowing, and the clouds are moving, giving us a break from the yellow ball of fire. We opt to sit outside on the patio and people-watch. I still wear my shades over my face. I cannot stand the brightness of it all and still think the alcohol is trying to kill me as it slowly works itself out of my system.

Everyone orders a mimosa, and the smell of it makes me wretch in my mouth. I swallow it down and try to take a sip of the drink. I stare at the side of the road and watch people come and go as the conversation continues around me. My mind wonders, *Why would Mike even show up? I mean, you choke me, you leave me shitty voice mails, and then you think I'm going to come crawling back? No way.*

"Nev? You listening?" Asher asks as he waves his hands in front of my face.

I shake my head as I try to join the conversation. "I'm sorry, what did you say?"

Asher laughs. "Where did you just go?"

I take a sip of my drink, "I don't know, I just zoned out."

"I think she's thinking about why Mike even showed up to the party last night and the fact that she even dated slash fucked him? Am I warm?" Will chimes in.

I roll my eyes. "You don't know me that well. I was also concentrating on trying not to die, dickhead."

"If it makes you feel any better, he's not even cute," Joshua offers.

I smile. "It doesn't."

We all sit in silence as the food is being placed on the table. I don't even remember what I ordered. I stare at the eggs Benedict and home fries with a side of grits. I offer a kind smile to the waiter as he leaves. We all eat with no words being said.

It's hard to enjoy your food when all you can focus on is not dying, but somehow, I manage to power through it. I'm sure conversation was had, but I offer none on my end. I sit there, reevaluating every decision I've ever made with alcohol up to this point. I must be getting older; no way a hangover has had this effect on me. We finish our meal and leave the café. As we head back to the apartment, Asher informs me he has booked an event in LA, and he leaves tonight. Me, still being completely hungover and confused to when he exactly booked this said event gives him a big hug and tells him he can come back anytime and that my door is always open.

Will and I decide to play a little *Mario Kart* and smoke for the rest of the day to relax on such a beautiful Sunday. Game after game, we continue to play as if we are in college dodging writing a paper or procrastinating going to a lab, avoiding all responsibilities. We don't get days like this like we used to, and I treasure them when we do.

The sun slowly starts to set, painting the sky cherry red. The day sped up and slowed down all at the same time. We both look awful and like we haven't showered in days, but in reality, it's only been a couple of hours.

"Are you feeling less hungover?"

I shrug. "Yeah. I feel less like shit and more like myself, if that's what you mean."

He hits me with a red shell, knocking me back into third place.

"Goddamn it! No talking, it's distracting!" I scream.

I feel my phone vibrate in my pocket. I unfold my legs and quickly take it out of my shorts to see who it is. *Maria? I haven't talked to her in almost two years.* Will's phone starts to vibrate too. We both decide to pause the game.

"Who does yours say?" Will asks.

"Maria, Nick's mom. Who does yours say?"

"Jon."

Our whole demeanor went from relaxed to worry within a matter of seconds. I slide the phone over immediately and answer. I put her on speakerphone.

"Hey, Maria. How are you? It's been a long time!" I try to sound cheerful.

"Hey, Neveahly, I've had better days." Her thick accented voice trembles.

I look at Will. "Is everything okay? How's Nicki?"

She begins to sob. "Not good, my love, not good."

"Well, where is he?" I pry.

There is a long silence over the phone. Will and I look at each other. I pick up the phone.

"Where is he?" I ask again.

The silence turns into sobs. We both immediately knew what had happened. We knew this day was going to come. We just thought we had a little more time.

"He's dead. I'm so sorry, honey, but he died a week ago, and it took me forever to find your number, and Jon's." Her sobs become heavier.

"No, no. Don't be sorry. I'm so sorry we couldn't stay in contact over the years. It's just after the last intervention—"

"I know, I know." She softly whimpers.

She continues to cry over the phone as Will and I sit there taking in the information.

"So is there a funeral or any type of service?"

"I don't know if you guys can make it, but Tuesday, there is a service. I cremated Nick. You know he loved the ocean, and at Cocoa Beach, we will place the ashes in the water."

I look at Will. "We will be there."

"Okay, good. I gotta go. I wish I could stay and talk to you longer, but I have to call more people." Maria hangs up.

"Jon, did you know?" Will's voice starts to break.

"She called me and I wanted to call you guys, but she beat me to it. I'm leaving tomorrow," he says softly.

"So are we," I reply. "We just need to call and make some arrangements for the store, and we will see you tomorrow."

"All right." Jon hangs up the phone.

Will and I sit in silence for a moment. Without saying a word, Will gets up and goes to his room and gently shuts the door behind him.

I call the agency that we work with that helps us when we have emergencies like this, and they spring into action. I tell them where they can find all the instructions on how to open and close the store. I get us a nice resort, and reserve us a Villa as well as two airplane tickets so we can leave early tomorrow morning.

The word *dead* follows me around like a thought bubble. I am numb, and it hasn't sunk in that he is gone. I want to crawl into my bed, but I cannot shut down yet. I have to pack. I feel myself losing control over the situation. *Clean, Nev.* I color-coordinate my closet, and before I knew it, it was pushing 11:00 p.m.

Shit, I need to go check on Will. I open my door and see him sitting on the couch. I walk over to him and just see him staring at a blank TV screen. Nothing is on. No music; nothing. He is just sitting there. I sit next to him without saying a word. I've never seen him like this: sad to the point where he's not even crying.

"I got us airplane tickets for tomorrow morning at eight a.m."

He nods his head.

"I also got us a nice villa at this resort on the beach." I turn my head to look at him. He sits there with no emotion.

He nods his head again.

"Can I make you something to eat? Do you want a beer?" I offer.

"No," he says quietly.

"Okay, so I guess I will see you in the morning?"

He nods one more time.

I get up and walk back to my room. This time, I keep my door open, just in case he wants to come in and talk.

CHAPTER 8

We sit there quietly; just Jon, Will, Maria, and I sitting there, waiting for Nick to come in. I keep jiggling my leg, while Will and Jon sit on the couch, reading over what they have on notebook paper. Maria, who tries to wipe her tears away, cannot stop crying. We've done this time and time again: asking Nick to stop using. Nothing seems to work. Not his mom's tears, not the fact that he's killing himself, or he is wasting his talent.

I can't sit still. I start pacing the hotel room. I feel Will's and Jon's eyes follow me as I continue to walk back and forth, wearing down the dingy carpet on the hotel floor. I stop and look at them.

"What if this doesn't work, again?" I ask.

"What if this does?" Jon counteroffers.

I throw my hands up in the air. "Maria, you have got to stop enabling him if he doesn't stay in treatment."

She nods her head. "I know, Nev. I know. It's just so hard. He's my only child, and I don't want to lose him.

"We know," Will says, glaring at me. "I think what Neveahly is trying to say but not so eloquently here is that after today, we can't help him anymore." Will gives me a look that says: what in the hell is wrong with you? This woman is begging for our help to get her son off drugs and you do this? I don't know what's wrong with me. I've done this so many times, I just don't know if I can do it again.

The lock on the hotel room beeps, and I jump. I go back and sit down in the chair and wait for the door to open. We all give one another looks as if to say, "Stay strong no matter what." We see the door fly open, and Nick isn't alone. He has some girl hanging on him, she looks worse off than Nick. Nick, who once had an athletic build, is skinnier than I could ever imagine. He's just skin and bones and looks like he hasn't bathed in weeks; he smells how he looks.

Nick looks at us; he's high. On what, I don't know, but he's flying. He flashes his big toothless smile gears up as if he is about to give the performance of his life. None of us are amused. I went from worried to pissed off in two seconds flat. The woman starts looking around the room and starts to get paranoid.

"Nicki, please, come sit down," Maria begs.

"Ma," Nick draws out. "Mama, you're here. Did you fly down here all the way from New York City?"

"Nicki, we are all here because we love you," Maria begins, "but we see you have an addiction. We have asked you over and over again to get help, and we miss the old you. I miss my Nicki with aspirations. I miss my Nicki where we used to go to Yankee games. I miss my Nicki who used to call me all the time and tell me he loved me for no reason. Now when you call, all you want is money."

"Mama, that's not true," Nick says defensively.

"Please, Nick, we want you to go get treatment," Maria finishes.

Nick goes and sits on the bed; the woman continues to stand at the door.

"Nick," I begin, "stop torturing your mom, and us, and go get help. You turned into a total dick bag, and no one likes the person you've become. You used to be this guy who made the best movies and had dreams, and now you're an absolute shithead. Go get help or get fucked."

Will stares me. "Really, Nev?"

I shrug. "What? Oh, I love you, and you're better than this. Sorry I couldn't see that part. It was written so small."

"Nick, we all want the same thing for you: to go get help. We all love you and don't want to end up going to your funeral when we are in our twenties. Please?" Jon begs.

Nick looks at us. "Can I ask you all a question?"

"Sure, Nick, anything," Maria says with hope in her voice.

"Have you ever danced with the devil by the pale moonlight?" Nick starts to crack up.

I throw my piece of paper away. "Okay, he doesn't give a shit. That line is from fucking *Batman*. He is high as fuck right now."

"Nev, don't—"

"No, Jon," I interrupt. "I had to go through this shit with my mom and watched her almost kill herself, and I'm not gonna watch my best friend do it to himself." I walk over to Nick and grab his face. I take in the stench and all. "You see her." I point to Maria. "She is begging you to get help. You see those two guys. Those two men would die for you." I look him dead in the eyes. "You see me, right?"

Nick nods his head as he keeps laughing.

"I would die for you, but I'm not dying for you if you are going to keep doing this shit." I push him back on the bed. I walk out of the hotel room; Jon follows behind me.

"Wait, Nev," Jon calls behind me. He catches up to me and grabs my arm.

I turn around. "What?"

Jon grabs me and wraps me into his arms. I struggle to get away. I thrash in his arms, and he doesn't let me go. I start to sob uncontrollably as he holds me close. I fall to the ground in his arms as I continue to cry, and Jon holds me. He knows the anger is misplaced.

*****

I lie in bed, staring up at the ceiling as my alarm continues to go off. I've been up since three this morning. I don't think I actually slept. I keep replaying the last time we saw each other in my head over and over again, and I get mad at myself again. *How could I have been so insensitive? Why was I so fucking angry?* I feel the tears escape my eyes and touch down on my pillow. I grab my phone and end the alarm and spring out of bed. I go into the dresser drawer full of shorts and put a pair on and a long-sleeve shirt. I grab my luggage and roll it out to the living room.

Will sits in the kitchen by the island, cupping his coffee mug and staring off into space. The overhead light illuminates only his face and just the table. I don't think he even noticed me when I came out of the room or when I stood in front of him. I even had to say his name a couple of times for him to snap out of it.

"Hey, you okay?" I ask.

"No. Who is ever going to be okay burying one of their best friends?"

"Good point," I say, sliding onto one of the stools.

I grab his cup of coffee and take a sip. It's extremely sweet. "Jesus, what's in this cup, diabetes?"

"With a little coffee."

I slide it back to him. "We have to get going." I order us a Lyft.

"I know. This just sucks, man. I wish he just got his shit together." Will wipes a tear away.

"I know. God, poor Maria."

"Losing your only child, can you imagine?" Will chugs the rest of his coffee.

We go downstairs and wait for our Lyft. The ride to Regan National Airport was quick. No traffic for a Monday morning is highly unusual. Checking in was rather quick too. We sit at our gate and wait for our boarding section to be called.

The flight to Florida is a little over two hours. With a little turbulence and a lot of alcohol, it was a smooth flight. I wake up, and we have already landed. I completely forgot we have to ride a train to get to the main terminal and that there are so many frickin' kids excited to see Mickey Mouse. I feel the effects of alcohol starting to wear off as well as the Xanax.

We grab our bags from the carousel baggage claim and make our way to rent-a-car. We got a nice upgrade because of the long wait. Will and I piled all our luggage in the car and drive the hour and one minute to Cocoa Beach. Will and I don't talk the entire time. Instead I just hooked up the Bluetooth and listened to the sweet sounds of Paramore.

I pull into the resort. Our villa is on the beach, and it is beautiful. The interior is pretty big. Two bedrooms with a full kitchen and dining room area, as well as a living room. *Maybe Jon can come over tonight? Catch up on old times. Even Maria if she's up to it.* Will, who has been knocked out this entire time, I shake him awake and tell him we are officially done traveling for the day.

As we unpack the car and head inside, Will and I claim our rooms, and I start to unpack my luggage. The realization that Nick is gone still hasn't hit me yet. I feel as though Will and I are on an impromptu vacation meeting Jon. As I finish, I sit on the bed and look at my phone. I struggle whether I should call Jon or not. I end up doing it anyway.

A couple of rings in, he picks up. "Just the person I want to hear from."

My heart flutters a little bit. "Oh, is that so?"

"Yeah, how are you, Nev?"

"I'm good. Well, as good as one can be who is about to bury a good friend. How are you?"

"Uh, about the same." He lets out a little chuckle.

"So I was thinking, would you want to come over tonight? Maybe we have dinner with Will and possibly Maria?"

"That sounds great," he answers immediately.

"Oh," I say, taken aback. "I thought I would have to do a little convincing, but that's great."

"Why?" He laughs. "I haven't seen you in a year. I would love to see you."

I feel my cheeks get hot, and a huge smile creeps across my face.

"And Will of course," he adds.

"Oh yeah." For a second, I completely forgot about him. "So let's say eight thirty?"

"Sounds great!"

"Cool, see you then." I hang up.

I leave the room and race over to Will's. No answer. I bang on the door again and still no answer. Finally, I bust open into his room and see that he is passed out, half-naked on his bed. I go over and shake him awake.

"What?" He groans.

"Jon's coming over for dinner," I say, excited.

Will lifts his head up, with his hair going all over the place. "Why do you sound so excited about it?"

I tone it down. "Because I haven't seen him in a year, that's why. I'm gonna call Maria and Google where I can find a Publix."

Will puts his head back on the pillow. "Okay."

I call Maria, and she accepts the invitation. She offers to bring a dessert, and I tell her to just bring herself.

I hop back into the car and type in the nearest Publix, and the GPS finds one about ten minutes away. I get there in five, with all the green lights on my side. It's good to see nothing has changed about this beach town. Jon, Nick, Will, and I used to come here when we skipped class. Nick would insist we would come here because the waves were better. I came here because the guys were hotter, and there was less of a chance we would see someone from our college.

I find one of those frozen lasagnas, something that can go into the oven, and it's easy. I grab a salad and some garlic bread. I also grab some nice-looking throwaway plates and some utensils. I double back to the wine aisle and grab a couple of bottles and two cases of beer. I check out and head back to the resort. The dinner should cook in under two hours, so I heat up the oven and guess that it's probably not a good one and give it a little more time than it should.

After putting in the lasagna, I start to get ready. I take a nice long shower and wash the airport off me. All the people coming from all over, I just imagine that everyone doesn't shower and scrub down as much as possible. I settle on a nice pair of shorts and a halter top. Shoes don't really matter, and we can always go walk on the beach. *Maybe Jon and I can go walk on the beach. Wait, where did that thought come from?* I put some nice makeup on and a little bit of shiny lip gloss and go back to the kitchen.

Will, who is finally up, is sitting in the living room, just watching TV. He has already made it to the fridge to get a beer. I let my hair air-dry as I put gel in my curls to make them extra curly. I feel them bounce around as I walk from one side of the kitchen to the other. Will comes into the kitchen for another beer.

"Why do you look so nice?" he inquires.

I shrug. "Am I not allowed to look nice?"

"I just think it's kind of funny, you wanting to look nice. You never cared how you looked around us before, and all of a sudden, you want to look nice."

I look inside the oven to check on the food. "I did sometimes."

He cracks open a beer. "No, you didn't. Not once did you care how you looked around us guys."

"Okay, so I'm getting older, and now I want to look nice." I close the oven and walk over to the salad.

Will's eyes follow me. "And you don't cook."

I let out an annoyed sigh. "I do, too, cook."

Will takes a sip of his beer. "You like Jon."

My mouth flies open, trying to cover my smile. "What? No, I don't. I mean, I do. He's one of our best friends, but not like that."

"You're trying not to smile, which means you're lying." Will walks out of the kitchen. He goes back to the living room and continues to watch TV.

I follow after him. "Why would I like him?"

He raises an eyebrow at me. "I don't know, you tell me?"

I laugh. "After all these years, now would be the time I start liking him?"

"Why are you getting so defensive?" Will grins.

"I'm not!" I raise my voice.

Will starts to laugh. "Yes, you are."

There is a knock at the door. *Just in time, right before I was about to lay into Will and how I would never ruin a friendship.* I walk over to the door and see Jon and Maria standing there. I am overwhelmed with so much joy and sadness at the same time; it's a stupefying sensation. Tears start to come from my eyes before I even realize myself what is happening. Maria wraps her arms around me tight and gives me a kiss on the cheek. Jon gives me a tight hug.

I move over so they can come into the villa. Will sees who is at the door and gets up from the couch. We all hug one another and stand there and, without saying anything, acknowledge why we are all here. The reason why we are all together. Although he is gone, he has brought us together.

"Would anyone care for a drink?" I finally offer. "I got wine and beer?"

"Wine would be nice," Maria says.

"I'll get a beer," Jon says as he walks into the kitchen.

I pour Maria a glass of wine, and we all sit at the dining room table. We exchange glances, unable to start the conversation. What is there to say? Sorry your kid is dead? Sorry we failed you for saving your son? No one wants to be the first one to apologize, so we all just sit there. We stare down at our glass and canned beers until Maria is brave enough to break the silence.

"You guys don't have to feel bad or sorry for me," she says, "or feel like you failed me or Nick."

Jon, Will, and I quickly glance at each other.

"We all tried our bests," she continues. "In the end, Nick failed himself. The disease got him, and the demons inside took control of him and got the best of him." Maria polishes off the rest of her drink. "So I don't want you to think you failed in any type of way."

I grab her hand. "I still feel like shit."

We all laugh.

"Oh, Nevie. I still feel like that day, you were the only one who kept it honest with him. He was acting like a shit bag."

We all laugh again. It's funny hearing that phrase muttered or said out loud with this small Dominican woman who is a true Catholic.

"Is there anything we can do?" Jon asks.

"Just live. Be happy." She gives us all a motherly look.

We all nod our heads in agreement.

"Well, Nev, what about dinner? I'm hungry." Maria looks at the oven.

"Oh, shit!" I rush to the oven just in time. Nothing burned. *Sweet.*

We enjoy our meal together, and it felt like Nick was sitting there with us. It is hard to push out the last memory we all have of him, but it's easy to tell a story of him being Nick. It's hard to push out a time where he called you to ask for money, but it's also very easy to remember a time he was there for you. That's the thing about addiction; it's a cruel, cruel mistress that has you on this leash and diminishes every last shred of decency you ever had.

As we finish dinner, Maria thanks us all for coming down and doesn't know what Nick would have done without us in college. To be honest, Nick was the one who brought us together. Technically, Will and I were already friends, but Nick was the element that we needed in order for us to actually keep us together. Maria gets in her car and leaves, leaving Will, Jon, and I to our own devices.

"Well, I'm going to bed," Will says as he stretches.

"Are you serious?" I ask, completely shocked. "It's only ten!"

"Yup! I'm tired. Have fun, you two. I will see you guys in the morning."

"Um, okay," I say as I watch him go into his bedroom.

Jon and I both laugh and sit there at the table awkwardly.

"Do you want to go walk on the beach," I suggest, "or are you tired too?"

"No"—he laughs—"I'm not tired."

We step outside the sliding glass. I leave my flip-flops back at the villa. I see Jon taking off his shoes and leaving them at the back porch. We walk on the bridge leading us to the beach. It's a narrow walkway, but once we figure out how to navigate it, we see open sand and hear the ocean waves crashing down upon each other.

Jon and I walk a little bit away from the water but close enough for the waves to touch the sides of our feet. We say nothing as we start our walk, but we enjoy the sound of the water and the smell of salt in the air. The night sky is blacker than the blackest of nights but clear enough to see the stars and moon. I stop and look up.

"God, it's so pretty," I gush.

Jon looks up. "It really is."

"In the city, I can't see shit like this. I would have to go to my parents' house. Even then, I would have to go toward the woods." I keep looking up.

A shooting star flies across the sky.

"Oh! Make a wish," I say.

I close my eyes as I did when I was a child. With my eyes closed, hearing the water crash into itself is so calming and soothing; now I know how people fall asleep to this shit.

I open my eyes.

"Did you make a wish?" Jon asks.

"I did." I smile.

"What'd you wish for?"

"Well, if I told you, it wouldn't come true." I grin.

"If I guess it, would that taint the wish?" he asks.

I shrug. "I actually don't know what the rules are."

Without warning, Jon's lips are on mine. His soft warm full lips create goosebumps on my arms. Jon slowly pulls away.

"Okay, well, technically, my wish came true," I joke.

I get closer to him and kiss him again. I feel his tongue dance with mine. His strong arms pull me closer to him. My heart feels like it's going to beat its way outside my chest. His lips start to move from mine down to my neck. I bite my lower lip. His lips move back up to mine, and he slowly moves away. Our foreheads touch each other's as our breaths begin to quicken.

"So I'm gonna assume that was your wish?" I playfully ask.

He laughs. "I mean, I did tell you we were going to do this back at graduation."

I let out a chuckle. "That you did."

He moves his head away from mine and grabs my hand. Our fingers intertwine together. "Yup, one day."

I kiss him again. "Do you want to go back to the villa? Or is that too forward? Am I being too much of a whore? I can slow down. I'm sorry."

Jon laughs again. "No, we can go back. We can do whatever you're comfortable with."

We hightail it back to the villa. Jon and I tiptoe to make sure not to wake up Will, and close the bedroom door, quietly. Jon gently pushes me up against the door and picks me up. I wrap my legs around his torso as he takes me to the bed. We fall onto the queen-size mattress together; I take off his shirt and see his six-pack that I was not expecting. Jon reaches for his belt and slides it off and unzips his pants. I go for my shorts and slide them down toward my feet, with my panties. We slide back to the head of the bed as our lips are magnets to each other.

I lean up so he can undo my bra, not as fast as Mike, but it comes off eventually. I toss it off to the side. I lie back on the pillows and feel Jon on top of me. He places his member between my legs and slowly slides it in. I wasn't expecting the girth of it; it hurt a little but felt good all at the same time. He moans as he grabs my breast and starts to get the rhythm going. I can feel myself becoming more wet as he starts to pick up the pace. As he moans more, he moves faster. He moans my name, and I feel myself about to climax. *That's a first. Me finishing first? That's never happened.*

I feel my toes start to curl as the pleasure starts to intensify. He stops and flips me over so I'm on top. *Okay, who knew Jon could get down like this? Not I.* I keep the rhythm going and grab the headboard for some grip. He grabs my ass and pushes me on his member deeper and deeper. I bite my lip, trying not to scream in pleasure. The last thing I want to do is wake up Will and let him know I'm banging one of our friends. I can feel him climax inside of me, but he keeps pushing me on his member. I don't stop moving my hips. I climax and cannot possibly continue. I fall next to him.

I look at him, and he moves closer to me, stroking my hair. I kiss his lips. He wraps me up in his arms and continues to stroke my hair. He kisses me softly again as we lie there.

"So I know it's kind of crazy, but it is kind of late. Do you just want to crash here?" I offer.

Jon smiles. "Yeah, I mean, that would be nice."

I turn off the lights.

Waking up the next morning was bittersweet. I woke up in the arms of someone whom I've had a crush on since college, and we give our friend to the ocean, the place where he truly belongs, and say goodbye to him forever. I wake up first. I go into the drawer and put on an oversize T-shirt and tiptoe out to make some coffee for all of us. I keep the door crack and try to walk lightly.

"Late night?" Will calls from the couch.

I jump, almost falling over. I grab the counter and try to act cool. "What? No, I'm just making coffee for everyone. Us. You and me."

He gives me a deadpan stare. "Jon's car is still here."

Fuck. "Is it? Did he get too drunk to drive home last night? We were really throwing those bottles back."

"Okay, so if I go in your room, he's not going to be sleeping in there?" Will asks, getting up from the couch.

"Nope," I say casually.

Will starts to walk toward my bedroom, and I jump in front of him. "Okay, he's in there. You caught me."

Will starts to laugh hysterically. "Why lie? He's liked you since college!"

I shift my weight, feeling uneasy. "I don't know. It's weird? Is it weird? I feel weird. It feels kind of wrong. Who bangs someone at a funeral?"

"It's like the number one place to get pussy or dick. Everyone is grieving, and getting a piece is the best way to grieve," Will reassures me.

I go into the kitchen and start to make coffee for all of us. I figure out how to work the ancient pot, and it starts to brew. I stand in front of it and watch it slowly fill. Will comes in to join me.

"Nev, he really likes you," Will says.

"I like him too," I reply.

"I know you do. I'm saying this so you don't fuck this up. Don't push him away. Don't play any fucking games. He's the real deal. He's not Mike, or those other fuck boys you're used to." Will stares me down. "I'm serious."

"I know, dude. Last thing I want to do is hurt him or get hurt."

Jon comes out of the bedroom as Will and I stand next to the coffeepot, watching it brew. Will smiles at him and knows what's up.

"I have another shirt for you, dude," Will offers.

"Thanks, man." Jon grins.

"What time is the service today anyway?" I ask, looking at Will and then back at Jon.

Will shrugs. "I think at one p.m.?"

I look at the clock on the stove, and it's already 11:00 a.m. Luckily, the resort is a couple of blocks away from where we need to be. It's walking distance, but we do this every time. A major event, and we always wait till the last hour—well, in this case, two hours before we need to get ready.

I pour cups for everyone and get the last cup for me. I make mine the strongest with little creamer. Jon and I go back to my room, and I start pulling out outfit ideas as he continues to sit on the bed. There isn't the awkward, clumsy morning after; it's more of the "we've been dating for a while." Actually, we probably should talk about that at some point, but not before we throw our friend's ashes into the ocean.

I finally settle on a yellow sundress. Maria said no black last night, and we all agreed to honor her wishes. I hop on the bed with Jon, continuing to be perplexed at the fact that he now has a six-pack.

"So do you want to shower first, or should I?" I ask.

"Ladies first," he offers.

I kiss him on the cheek and hop in the shower.

I take a quick one; rinse off, knowing sand is about to get everywhere regardless; and hop out. I scrub my face and reapply my makeup. I put my dress on in the bathroom and let Jon go next. I wait for him outside in the living room where Will sits with a beer in his hand. I like his idea and grab one from the fridge.

Jon takes a fast one as well and walks out topless. Can't say I hate the view. Will throws a shirt to him and a beer, and we all sit on the couch with forty-five minutes to spare. The TV isn't on; we just sit there, gathering our thoughts and grasping the fact that today is happening no matter if we like it or not. I'm the first one to get up. I grab my oversize bag and slide on my white flip-flops.

"Guys, we gotta get going," I say.

Will chugs his beer. He goes into the fridge and grabs three more and puts them in my purse. "Take these."

I glare at him. "Are you going to carry my purse? This shit is gonna get heavy after a while, my dude."

"Also, are all those yours?" Jon asks.

"Did you guys want one as well?" Will asks as he heads toward the sliding door.

I roll my eyes and make my way toward the door. I feel Jon reach for my hand. I look down and then at him. I smile, and he returns one. We walk on the beach, and we can spot where the service is taking place. It's not extravagant, but big enough to see that Nick was loved. There were two rows of chairs and a walkway. At the end of the walkway was a picture of Nick: a high school senior picture of him. I smile.

We walk down and see Maria sitting in the front row. She turns her tiny frame, and reveals a small cardboard box in her lap. My legs grow weak. *Nick.* Someone who is over six feet tall is reduced to a cardboard box. I was not ready for that sight. I don't know what I was ready to see, but that was not it. I feel my knees buckle, and Jon catches me. I've never done that before. I've seen my friends in urns and grandparents in caskets, but seeing Nick in a cardboard box really did something to my soul.

I feel the tears stream down. *Get it together, Neveahly. This woman just lost her child. She doesn't need to comfort you or anybody else right now. That's not her job to make you feel better.* As we get closer, I stop walking. Jon looks back.

"Just give me a second," I whisper.

"You okay?" Jon whispers back.

I nod my head in fear that if I answer aloud, I will lose it. I count to ten in my head and swallow whatever I am feeling down and get it together. I walk up to Maria and give her a hug. She sees that the tears have already started, and she wipes them away with her thumb. She whispers it's okay, and somehow that made it worse, and I really start to cry. Jon and I sit down next to her while Will gives her a bear hug. A hug only a son would give his mother. She starts to whimper in his arms. Will holds her until she can compose herself. Nick's mom is like our mom. We will do the world for her, and it breaks our heart to see her like this. *It shouldn't have ended like this.*

Maria lets out a loud sigh and stands before the misfits. Majority of the people are from our college, but a handful of them are from Nick's life after college.

She looks out into the crowd. "I know it's a Tuesday, but to Nicki, it's Taco Tuesday: his favorite day of the week." Everyone laughs. "It's good see some of Nick's friends who stuck by him and some new faces. This is not a day for mourning. This is a day for remembering. I want you to remember Nick before the drugs, not after, not during, but before." She starts to tear up and clears her throat. "I want to keep this short because we all know Nick hated long-winded speeches, but to end this, I want to play Nick's god-awful favorite song."

Maria takes out a speaker with an old iPod and begins to play "Bad, Bad Leroy Brown." We all start laughing. I begin to tap my foot to the song, and everyone starts to sing along. Nick told me he loved this song so much because he remembers whenever he was sad, his mom would drive him around, and this was the only CD that wouldn't skip in the car. I don't know if he ever shared that story with anyone else, but I was grateful that he shared it with me.

"And meaner than a junkyard dog," the song ends.

Maria picks up Nick's ashes that sit next to her. We all get up and walk to the section of the beach that is closed off just for us. Will, Jon, and I walk next to Maria as she carries the ashes. Our feet touch the water, and we descend into the waves.

"May you rest easy, my love. May you find the peace in death that you could never find here on earth." Maria lets go of the box.

The box gently drifts into the water and gets taken away by the current. We walk back up to the beach. I put my arm around Maria as she puts hers around my waist. We meet the rest of the funeral service attendees.

"If you would like, there is a bar that Nick loved so much that I reserved a couple of tables. It's buy-your-own-booze, but that's where the after-party is going to be," she addresses everyone.

I give her a hug. "You okay?"

Maria nods. "As okay as I'm going to be."

"Fair enough," I reply. "Do you want us to wait for you?"

"No, you all go ahead. I'm actually going to head back to Orlando to catch my flight back to New York."

We all whip our heads around.

"What? I feel like there is so much more to catch up on," I protest.

She grabs my hands. "Nevie, go enjoy the party. Thank you for a lovely evening last night. You have my number. The next time you're in New York City, call me!"

She kisses Will and Jon on the cheek. She heads toward the street and gets in her car. We stand there, dumbfounded. We watch her drive off. We say we are going to call, but we all know we will lose contact. It will become too hard to hear our voices, and the memory of it all will be too much. Death can bring friends closer and can also be so painful that it can rip everyone apart.

"So let's get schwifty." Will grabs a beer out of my purse. "I'm going to drink until I can't feel feelings and possibly make some bad decisions tonight."

"It's not even three p.m. yet," I remind him.

"Says the girl who literally started day-drinking after she got out of a six a.m. lab one day." Will starts to walk toward the bar.

We get inside, and it's mostly the funeral guests and some vacationers. Jon, Will, and myself sit in the back, staring at everyone, laughing and having a good time as we grasp the fact that everything is completely different now. I down my dirty Shirley, and Jon grabs me two more. I'm drinking as much as Will is, and so is Jon. I may have made fun of Will, but none of us wants to feel feelings right now. Alcohol isn't the answer, but it sure feels like a cheaper coping mechanism right now.

Will slaps me on the shoulder. "Isn't that Mark?"

"Ow, asshole." I look up at the bar. I instantly hang my head down and let my curls swing in front of me. "Maybe if I just stop moving, he won't see me."

"Holy shit, that is him! The king of the lollipop guild himself!" Will raises his voice.

"Please, could you possibly shut the fuck up," I beg. I start to move behind Jon.

"Hey, let's call him over here," Will suggests.

"Hey, let's not at all do that and keep drinking like adults."

"Will, don't," Jon protests.

Mark spots Will and Jon and books it over to us. His five-foot stature is so off-putting it truly makes me wonder how desperate I was in college.

"Will, Jon! Oh my god! It's been like what? Eight years since I've seen you last? How are you guys?" Mark starts to pull up a chair.

Please go away. Please go away. Please go away.

Mark starts to realize I'm behind Jon. "Is that Neveahly?"

"Ah, there it is!" I pretend to find something behind Jon. "Oh, Mark, what are you doing here?"

"I heard about Nick through the grapevine, so I decided to come and pay my respects," he says with some decency. "Are you guys okay? I know you guys were like super close."

I glare at him. "I don't know. I guess we are. It's kind of hard seeing your friend reduce to ashes and then those ashes being released into the ocean, which eventually are going to be shit out of a whale."

Jon chokes on his beer and laughs, sending it flying. "She's still having a hard time with it."

"So, Mark, what are you up to these days?" Will asks.

I continue to knock back my dirty Shirley, and then I take Jon's and drink his. "Can I have some more?"

"Oh, I work for our college now. Yeah, I teach and try to get those kids excited about digital photography," Mark says excitedly.

"Oh, how cool," Will says and turns me. "He's a teacher at our school, Nev."

"I heard what he said, Will," I snap.

Jon comes back with our drinks.

"Nev, what are you up to these days?" Mark asks in a smug tone.

"I own a bookstore with Will in DC." I chug my drink.

"How retro, that's such a dying business! That's so cool!" Mark slyly says.

Okay, he's got five seconds to remove himself from this area before I punt him across the table for a field goal.

"Well, actually, Nev and Will have been helping me out with a lot of projects. There is so much political shit in DC and so little time. It's the best when they can come and help with shooting and with small projects." Jon saves the day.

I have never wanted this man more than I do now.

Mark's grin slowly fades. "Oh, well. That's cool. You guys still do film."

"Yup, it's cool you still take pictures for a living," I respond rudely.

"Well, I teach," Mark retorts, "and I edit as well."

"I wish we could stay, but we really need to get going." Jon again saves the day. "Take it easy, man."

I slide off the barstool. "Take it sleazy." I pat him on the shoulder.

Mark grabs my hand. "Say, would you be interested in some dinner?"

I look at his hand and remove it from mine. "I am going to have to pass on such a great opportunity."

We settle our tab and stumble onto the boardwalk. The sun is slowly setting as we lean on the fence, watching the last of the beach-goers grab their stuff and head back to their hotels. Will heads back to the resort and says he may or may not catch up with us later. Jon and I stand there, looking out onto the water.

"I probably should go back to my hotel tonight," he says as his eyes continue to connect with the water.

I grind my teeth as I continue to smile. "Or you can check out early and stay with me?" I blurt out. "Us. I mean, us."

He turns and looks at me, shocked. "Really?"

"I'm not gonna lie to you, bro, we aren't getting any younger, so beating around the bush thing isn't my style anymore," I confess. "So if you want us to be a thing, I kind of need to know now."

Holy fuck, did those words come out of my mouth? Is this liquid courage? Or am I just running off the confidence of turning Mark down?

Jon kisses me. "Do you want us to be a thing?"

I roll my eyes. "Don't do that. Tell me how you really feel."

He takes a deep breath and smiles at me. Jon places his hand against my cheek.

Brace yourself, Nev. It could be something you don't want to hear. This could have been a hit it and quit it. He might have just wanted a piece.

"I like you. I've liked you since I first laid eyes on you, and I really want us to be a thing."

I look into his eyes. "But?"

He shakes his head. "No buts. I want us to be a thing."

"So the distance: me living in DC and you in New York City. That doesn't bother you?" I raise one eyebrow.

He shrugs. "It's a four-hour train ride and a little over an hour plane ride. When it comes to us figuring out on who needs to move where, we will figure it out."

I smile. "I like the way you think, kid."

He kisses me again. "I'm going to go check out of my hotel, which is two hotels down from you guys." Jon pulls me close and kisses me deeply.

Time stops when I'm with Jon. Literally. It's as if we are caught in a freeze-frame shot, and the only thing that matters is us, even though such a horrible event brought us together. He did say back on graduation night that we would be together. I just didn't know the liquid courage from me would be the one to get us together. I knew he wanted to do traveling, and I knew that if we tried back when we were younger, we probably wouldn't have worked out.

The nightlife on the boardwalk is still alive, even for a Tuesday evening. Children gallivant, bobbing and weaving through the sea of people as their parents fill their tiny bodies with sweets and junk food. The fluorescent lights of the carnival games and the arcades that are rigged against you, and you spend more money than you intend to. With my flip-flops in my hand, I witness the innocence of it all.

I slide the heavy glass door open and struggle to pull it behind me. Will sits on the couch, playing on his phone with the TV on. As he hears the sound of the glass closing, he takes a break from the game and looks up. He acknowledges my presence and reaches for my purse. I completely forgot there are a couple of beers left in there. I shudder at the fact they are probably warm now, but he doesn't care and cracks one open. Proximity over coldness at this point. I grab a cold one out of the fridge and sit next to him.

I flip through the channels, endlessly trying to see if there is remotely anything interesting to watch, and come up empty. I hear a knock at the back door, and Will gets up to let Jon in. All three of us sit on the couch and stare at the TV as I flip mind-numbingly through the channels to find something for all of us.

"Do you think there was anything we could have done to save him?" I ask as I stop changing the channels.

"No, he didn't want to be saved," Will says, grabbing the remote.

I grab it back. "What makes you say that?"

Will sighs. "He just didn't care in the end, Nev. Rejection after rejection gets to some people, and he just couldn't take it anymore."

Jon and I turn to him.

"What are you talking about?" Jon asks, leaning over to see Will.

Will turns to Jon, shocked. "You didn't know? He kept submitting script after script, concept after concept, and he never got picked."

"We all do that, and we never get picked," I reply.

"I know"—Will sighs—"but he would do drugs to get one idea and do heavier drugs for another. I don't know. He thought he could be more creative if he just kept doing drugs, and then he just stopped creating all together."

Makes perfect sense now.

"Jesus," Jon says softly.

We continue to sit in silence as the TV fills the air. I don't know what we are watching, but Jon, Will, and I stare at it and pretend to care. I think it's something along the lines of *Bridezilla*. I begin to get sleepy.

"All right"—I start to get off the couch—"I'm going to bed." I head toward the bedroom.

"Night," Jon and Will both say.

I pull my dress over my body and toss it in my luggage. I throw on a tank top and some short shorts and begin to pack. I leave out an outfit for tomorrow and get into bed. Jon comes in shortly after I do and climbs into bed with me. Falling asleep in his arms for the second time, two nights in a row, is pure bliss.

Nick might be gone physically, but he will always be the glue of our group.

CHAPTER 9

Leaving today is hard. I hate it here in this godforsaken state, and all it does is bring back horrible memories, now adding on releasing the ashes of one of my best friends into the ocean but also leaving with a significant other. I haven't had a boyfriend in almost three years. Although leaving Jon does suck, I see him again on Friday. My birthday is Saturday, so it's just one day of not being together really, and I call that the Neveahly mind trick.

The plane ride back is brutal. We have nothing but the Disney crowd, and that is the fucking worst. I don't know which *is* the worst Disney crowd: adult Disney or kid Disney. Kids, you can give them a pass because they're young and dumb, but adult Disney goers are truly stuck in some loop. I assume it's due to the trauma they endured at some point in their childhood and they associate Disney with some good part. Anyway, I am stuck next to this woman who thinks I absolutely give a shit about her time in the parks, and I do not. I care about this rum and Coke and the Xanax that I want to kick in.

An hour into the trip, it does. The Xanax, it kicks in. I zone out and fall asleep. I'm not used to having a guy sleep next to me, so I didn't get the best sleep with Jon; not saying I hated it because I certainly did *not*. I'm just saying it's going to take some time to adjust to having another person on the other side of me.

The wheels touch down on the tarmac, and I feel my body bounce up and down. I quickly come to and realize we are back in Virginia. *Hurray.* I'd rather be here than in Florida, but Virginia is *almost* as bad. The flight attendant comes on and uses his Donald Duck voice to say he can't wait to see us again in his hometown.

That's why I hate flying from Orlando, and the fact that Disney isn't fucking in Orlando; it's in Kissimmee, which *is* a forty-five-minute drive from Orlando, but I digress.

Will, who is two rows behind me, starts to grab his luggage from under his seat. I stand up and clear the sleep from my eyes. The woman continues to talk about herself, and I swear to you she sounds like the teacher from the *Peanuts*. It probably is the Xanax I took or the two rum and Cokes I down at five in the morning. We will never know. I give her my card and tell her if she is ever interested in buying unique books to come by my store. Anything, *anything*, to shut her the fuck up. Also, never miss a chance to plug your business.

I was able to put my luggage in an overhead bin this time, so I grab it, and we make our way to the terminal. *Wednesday.* It doesn't feel like it. Time stops when someone you love dies, and yet you are expected to go on and continue with everyday life? It's so hard, and yet we are supposed to make it look so easy. I order a Lyft to our store so we can just go straight to work. Will says he needs a day and goes back to the apartment. He takes my luggage with him.

I arrive at the store to see it's still there and not on fire. *That's always good.* I walk in to see more traffic in there than usual in the morning. I look at the employees who have been helping out for the last couple of days and give them a wave. I walk over to them and introduce myself.

"I'm Mickey," the girl says, all bubbly.

Holy shit, it is too early for this.

"I'm Michael," the guy says.

"Cool. I really appreciate you guys coming and helping out on such short notice. I'm going to the back and doing some inventory," I say.

I turn on the computer and just stare at the loading screen. *I'm exhausted.* I didn't realize how tired I was until I sat down. The numbers start to float off the screen, and I can barely focus. I rub the inner corners of my eyes and try again. *I need coffee.* I get up quickly and walk to the café to pick up three, maybe four, cups of coffee. *Maybe five. I can give two of them to Mickey and Michael and keep three of them.*

I end up getting five coffees. I give Michael and Mickey one and take the three back with me to the office. They exchange glances, and I already know they are judging me, but I could care less at this point. First cup down, and I feel like I can focus. I run the numbers for the last two days, and everything has been going well.

Second cup down, I go through the boxes of books that have been donated. I deem what is sellable and what needs to be thrown away. Some of these books are worth thousands of dollars, and some of them are worth five cents. I price them out online and see what a fair price is. The ones that are super valuable I put in the special shelf that is locked.

By the third cup I was able to talk to customers. Some of the regulars have asked where Will and I have been, and I told them the truth. A lot of them know of Nick but don't know the *story* behind him. I give little detail and just say it was a tragic accident. Of course, you have some people give you their condolences, and then you have others who are fucking nosy. Those are my favorite. I try to think of the most uncomfortable story possible, which leaves us both there and them thinking, *Wow, I probably should have left it at "I'm sorry for your loss."*

Four p.m. rolls around, and I tell Michael and Mickey they can leave. I give them the money I owe them for three days with a little untaxed money on the side. I thank them and ask if I could call them if I ever needed their help again. Of course, they said yes. They were great. It's hard to find good workers who don't steal shit from you these days.

I close up the store and wipe everything down. I look down at my phone and see I've gotten text messages from Jon. I feel like I'm in high school all over again. I go back and forth on what I should text him back. *It's really not that serious. We were friends first.* It's different now; we've seen each other naked. After struggling with what to say, I finally send one back. We go back for a while, and then he calls.

"Hey," I say, trying to sound not so excited.

"Hey, so about Friday," he begins.

Shit he's going to cancel, I knew it. God, I should have known. I never should celebrate my birthday; nothing ever good comes out of it.

"It's okay if you can't come." *Ha! I beat him to the punch.*

"What? No, that's not what I was going to say at all. I was going to say that my train is an early one."

"Oh." *Way to go, Nev.*

He laughs. "Relax, Nevie. I'm not missing your birthday."

"No, I know. I just don't have good luck with my birthday," I confess.

"I am aware of that. You never let us celebrate it back in college," he reminds me.

"Yeah, because the one time we did, what happened?"

"Okay, the cops showed up, but we did throw a massive party and fireworks in September off a rooftop. Probably wasn't the best idea," he admits.

I laugh. "See!"

"Okay, so my train gets in at three. Is that okay?" he gently asks.

"Of course!"

"Okay, I'll see you then! I gotta go. I'm filming a music video, and I just wanted to hear your voice."

I'm not smiling. Okay, I am. That was super sweet. I want him to do things to me that are probably illegal in some countries.

"Okay, text me later." I hang up the phone.

I finish closing up. I come home, and Will is yet again passed out on the couch. I bring home some Cava for him and place it on the coffee table. I take mine to my room to eat it and call it a night.

Thursday comes and goes like the wind, and Friday shows up in all its beautiful bodacious glory. *Jon comes today.* I can barely focus at the store as Will rings up customers, and I am talking a mile a minute. I feel like I just did a huge line of coke, followed up with taking two Adderall pills.

We close early and hop on the Metro. I'm not even trying to hide my excitement anymore. I'm full-on kid in a candy store mode. Will, on the other hand, is back on Tinder and ready for action. He's been scrolling since him and Sharon broke up with no luck. He's gotten a couple of hits, so I wouldn't say it hasn't been a complete bust, but nothing has stuck. As I continue to try to hold my bones inside my skin, Will finally gets a match on Tinder.

"Hey, I got a match!" Will says, hitting my shoulder with excitement.

I grab my shoulder and rub it. "Jesus, okay?"

He shoves his phone in my face. She is really pretty. Light-brown hair, green eyes, and of course, her tits are out in the picture. Her name is Samantha. I scroll through her profile, and she seems pretty cool. A couple of quotes from Kevin Smith's movies—Will's idol—and references to *Pulp Fiction*. She also has a couple of pictures in costumes and onstage, so I assume she's into theater. *Great, an actress. This should be interesting.*

"She's pretty. An actress even," I say as I hand him back the phone.

"Cool. Can I invite her over to the apartment for your birthday dinner?"

I look at him, shocked. "What? Um, sure. I guess? I mean, don't you want to go out or something? Like maybe to dinner first?" I suggest.

"Meh, I figure why beat around the bush? If she doesn't pass the best friend test, she's not worth keeping around."

Awe, that's sweet.

"Okay," I cave, "but make sure she doesn't steal anything, or if she's super weird, can we come up with some kind of code to get her out of here?"

He nods in agreement. "God, she's hot." He keeps scrolling through the pictures as we continue to ride. "Oh, I cannot wait to hit this."

Gross. The thought of him clapping cheeks with someone is absolutely gross.

We finally arrive at Union Station, and I yank Will off the train and drag him through the crowd. I look on the board to see what gate Jon is coming from and grab Will again and book it through the station. I find two empty seats; we sit there and wait. I'm not the most patient person, so I get up and start pacing back and forth. Will continues to scroll through Samantha's pictures.

The train is on time, and I stop pacing as I watch people come out of the gate. Will could care less as he looks at his phone. *Jesus, dude, she could be catfishing you! It's my birthday weekend! Stop worrying about pussy! I mean, I'm not the type of person to be like, "Look at me. It's my birthday," but hey, it is my birthday.* I smile as I see him walk out, rolling his luggage and a bouquet of flowers in his free hand. Lilies, to be exact. My favorite. *I don't think anyone knows that lilies are my favorite flowers except him. I remember telling him that one night when we were drunk and on the roof of someone's house party.* I feel my face get hot, and my smile widens. Jon comes up as he lets go of his luggage and wraps his free hand around me and kisses me.

Will stops scrolling on his phone long enough so he can greet Jon and give him a hug.

"Happy birthday, beautiful." Jon hands me the flowers.

"Holy shit, you got flowers? Nice move, man."

"Thank you! Are you ready to get this weekend started, fellas?" I ask.

They both nod in agreement. We start to walk toward the west entrance of the Metro. Will tells Jon about his Tinder match and how she will be joining us for *my* birthday dinner at the house. Jon holds my hand as we walk and listen to Will as he talks about the bodacious babe. We get on the Metro and basically have the entire car to ourselves.

We all settle down around the kitchen island to start drinking. As the drinks start to flow; Jon and Will start talking about a script they can make come to life, and I sit there with Jon's hand on my knee, which is slowly moving up my leg. I try not to react. *I like this game.*

We order pizza and bring out Ol' Bessie out of retirement and begin to take bong hits like we did in college. As the night continues, we bust out our Nintendo Switch and play *Mario Kart*. As usual, I always forget which side of the screen I'm on and end up running into the wall the entire time. I think I'm doing so well, but in reality, I haven't even left the finish line. I cannot possibly think of a better metaphor for adulthood. The boys laugh, and I join in with their laughter. Will announces that he is going to meet up with Samantha for drinks tonight, and that he's going to get ready. He leaves the living room. As soon as his door closes, I leap on Jon, kissing him.

"We have some time before he comes back out here," I say.

I hear Will turn on his shower, and I go back to kissing Jon. I straddle him, with my hands on his cheeks. I feel his strong hands on my thighs slowly move toward my ass, pushing me closer to him. I can feel he's hard even through his jeans. I slowly move my lips down to his neck. Jon lets out a little moan. He pushes me off him and onto the couch and climbs on top of me. *It's like we are horny teenagers.* He lifts my shirt up and moves his hand up it, cupping my breast inside my bra. I hear Will's shower turn off, and I immediately push him off me; our foreheads meet, causing a loud thump.

"I'm so sorry!" I say, grabbing my forehead.

He laughs. "It's fine. He's leaving soon anyways."

I smile and kiss the top of his forehead.

Will's doorknob turns, and he walks out of his bedroom. I must admit, he looks pretty good. His hair is in a low ponytail, a collared shirt, and some dress slacks. I don't know why he's going all in on for some girl he hasn't even met yet, but I'm all for it.

Will does a turn and throws his arms out.

"You look great, dude," Jon says.

"Yeah, you look amazing," I add.

"Okay, so don't wait up. Happy early birthday, and I will see you guys tomorrow," Will says. He grabs his keys out of the key bowl and walks out of the front door.

We both let out a sigh of relief.

"I was for sure thinking he was going to say something about us being this close together. At least a joke or something," I say, looking at Jon.

"Yeah, I know," he agrees.

Jon and I explore each other's bodies in my bedroom over and over again throughout the entire night. I know we can't see each other every weekend, so I might as well get it in while I can. I fall asleep in his arms. At some point during the night, I realize I have all the covers. I unselfishly give some to him and scoot over and wrap myself back in him. I slowly adjust to having someone sleep on the other side of me. I can't even remember the last time I enjoyed waking up next to someone and not regretting it the next morning or praying my period would come.

I wake up the next morning to sounds of laughter as the front door opens. A woman's laugh, and Will's laugh. I think it's a part of my dream until I see the clock on my nightstand. It's not even 8:00 a.m. yet. *It's way too early to start my fucking birthday.*

I sit up in bed. I look at Jon lying in bed, sleeping soundly. There's no reason for both of us to be up this early. I gently lift the covers off my body and slide my feet into my slippers. I tiptoe out of my bedroom and see Will and Samantha drunkenly stumble into the apartment. *What the entire fuck is this?*

To my dismay, Samantha actually looks like her picture. Perhaps even prettier. Intoxicated is what they were when they probably left the bar; they are completely shit-faced right now. They have not even noticed me as I walk through my hallway and stand by the kitchen entrance. Will is raiding the fridge, while Samantha stands behind him, making another drink. Will turns around and drops the food in his arms when he sees me.

"Goddamn, put a bell on this chick," he slurs.

"Are you seriously just getting home, dude?" I ask.

"Is this"—Samantha stumbles closer to me; she does the one-eye blink—"is this your wife? You told me you were single?"

Okay, so she's not a good drunk, good to know.

Will walks over to her and throws his arm around her. "Nah, baby, it's all cool. This is Neveahly. My best friend."

Samantha starts to laugh. "Oh, shit, I am so sorry. I'm Samantha." She starts to extend her hand for a handshake and falls over a bit. "Gravity is so hard to figure out."

I ignore her and look at Will. "So you guys have fun last night?"

Will fist-pumps the air. "Oh, we went to this club, and then this after club, and I am not sure what happened after that."

Jon comes out of my room wearing his boxers, half-awake. "What's going on?"

"Jon," Will stammers, "how are you? Are you glad you finally hit it?"

"Okay, buddy," Jon completely ignoring the statement, "maybe your lady friend should get a Lyft, and you both should sleep this off."

"Are you guys gonna get married now? Oh, you are so gonna get married now!" Will starts to come from behind the island and loses his balance and falls over. He starts to laugh uncontrollably.

I go over to help him up. "Dude, seriously? Could you not be a sloppy drunk on this day of my birth?"

"No, seriously, Nev. He has wanted to wife you up *so* bad!" Will says.

"I honestly should let you just die here," I mutter. "C'mon, fat ass." I try to pull him up, and he just lies there singing "If I Could Turn Back Time" by Cher.

Jon walks over to Will to help him up. "C'mon, dude, get up."

Will gets up. "You guys are gonna have beautiful mixed babies. Wait, if Nev is mixed, is it like super mixed babies? How does that work? Or does it all cancel out and become like white babies?"

I laugh. "I hate you. Let's go, asshole." I start to help Jon get Will to his bed.

"If I could find a way," Will sings off-key.

Jon and I place Will on his bed, with his clothes on, and Samantha stumbles in and plops right next to Will. Jon and I walk out of his room and gently shut the door.

"Well, that is an interesting way to start a birthday," I say.

Jon kisses my lips gently. "Has he always been this bad of a drunk?"

Jon starts to walk toward my bedroom.

I laugh. "Do you not remember the girl from college? I think her name was Jody or something? She like broke his heart, and we went to iBar, and he got so hammered we had to haul him back to the apartment."

Jon and I get dressed for the day and make our way to the bookstore. I have to do a couple of things for the day even though we are closed. We always close on our birthday; we consider it a national holiday, to be honest. I get us a Lyft; I'm too afraid to go into Will's bedroom and look for his car keys in fear of what I will walk in on, and I am not in the mood to wait for the Metro. On the weekends, the Metro takes forever and a day to come.

Riding in the car, Jon and I go over possible ideas of what to do for the day. I tell him we don't really have to do anything but hang out and chill, but he really wants to make this special. *Okay, twenty-nine might be a good year. My last year of my twenties could possibly not suck.* I tell the driver to pull around back. The alarm system is there, and it's so much easier than making a mad dash back to the dial pad to key in the code before the security company calls, and I have to give them the code. It is nice the company is on top of things, but it's also a pain in the ass sometimes.

I unlock the back door and start to head for the security system, but the alarm doesn't go off. *That's weird. Maybe I forgot to set it when I left last night.* I walk farther in and see dozens of vases and balloons and flowers in the store. Red and white roses. My heart skips a beat, and I've never been so swept off my feet before. I turn around and kiss Jon, nearly knocking him over.

"When did you do this?" I ask.

He laughs. "I wish I could take credit for this, but I didn't do this."

I step back for a second and look at him to see if he's joking.

"Wait, seriously?"

He shakes his head no.

I go to the front of the store, toward the cash registers, and see a note resting on the biggest centerpiece: "Neveahly, how can you stay mad when you know I have this much love for you? Happy birthday, beautiful. Mike."

I crumple up the note. I realize my hands are shaking, and I try to steady my breathing. *Do I call the police? How the fuck did he even get in here?* I feel so violated. I look around the store and see all the roses and balloons and suddenly feel so sick to my stomach. I feel Jon touch my shoulder, and I jump.

"You okay?" he asks.

I come back down to earth. "Yes, I'm fine. Can you help me take all these to the dumpster out back?"

Jon's face goes from worried to confused. "Okay, so what's going on?"

"I just need to get rid of all this shit."

I walk to the back door and find the big cinder block and prop the door open. As I walk out, I lift the dumpster top open. I start to take the vases of flowers and toss them into the trash. I pop the balloons and toss them in there as if they are leftover favors from a party. *He must have spent a ton of money. Heh, what a waste.* Jon steps in my path.

"So do you need help?" he offers.

I smile. "You know, I bet this would go a lot faster if the both of us did this."

Without questioning who the grand gesture came from, Jon helps me toss everything into the trash. It didn't take long before everything was out of the store and every trace of Mike was gone, but I still feel violated. I walk to our cleaning closet and start to take out products to scrub down the counter and everything the vases touch. Jon takes a brush and a pair of gloves and helps. I turn on some Bruno Mars as we clean down the store, and before you know it, under an hour, we were done. I completely forgot why we were there in the first place.

As I put the stuff back in the closet, I feel absolutely gross. *Ugh, I need a shower. Perhaps a couple of them.* This time, I made sure to lock everything up; I even triple-checked to make sure that *no one* could get in. *I gotta call the security company tomorrow. We also probably should get cameras installed after this.* The Lyft meets us in front of the store, and we ride back to the apartment.

By the time we get back to the apartment, it's early afternoon. Will and Samantha have stirred from their drunken slumber, and they are sitting on the couch watching TV and drinking already. *Not sure if I'm going to like this Samantha chick.* Jon and I are surprised that they are even up. Samantha is extra cozy next to Will when we walk in.

"I'm surprised y'all are even up," I say, walking in.

I throw my keys into the bowl and kick off my flip-flops by the door.

"Yeah, it was pretty brutal last night," Will says in a raspy voice. "What's on the docket today, birthday girl?"

"Booze cruise! Pirate booze cruise!" Jon says excitedly.

"Shut up!" Will leaps up from the couch, almost dropping the beer in his hand. "There's an actual pirate booze cruise?"

"Yes! And it leaves like in an hour! I have to get in the shower, so can you be ready by then?" I shoot daggers at Will, knowing he takes forever and a day to get ready.

"For a fucking pirate booze cruise? Hell yeah, matey!"

Will puts the beer down on the table.

"I don't know if I want to go," Samantha whines. "I don't have anything to wear, and it's kind of chilly outside today."

We all look at one another as if she thought she was invited to this event.

"You don't have to come," I abruptly say. "Pirate shit isn't for everyone." I start walking to my bedroom to get in the shower.

"I mean, it seems kind of childish," she mocks.

I stop in front of my door and turn around. "I don't know. Johnny Depp was a pirate, and he's an adult, and alcohol isn't childish. Like I said, you don't have to come."

Tension fills the air as I stare down Samantha into her soul.

"Will, do you have to go?" Samantha puts a pouty face on.

"Yeah, it's Nev's birthday, and it's a fuckin' pirate booze cruise!" he says without missing a beat.

Samantha rolls her eyes. "Fine, I guess I'll go. Is there like a shop I can go to?"

"Google. It's this cool thing that every phone has now." I close my door and get in the shower.

I put on my Supergirl dress and my Vans with my jean jacket and head out to the living room. Jon sits in the kitchen, far away from Will and Samantha. I walk over to Jon, trying to steer clear from Samantha because I know I can't be nice right now.

We all are ready and head down to the front of the building where a Lyft waits for us. I swear, we keep this company in business. Jon and I have a row to ourselves while Samantha and Will have the back. They bicker the whole way there. It's like they have been dating for a couple of years, and I'm not talking a good couple of years. Jon and I try to stay positive the entire way there, keep engaging with the driver, but Samantha's high-pitch whine is deafening.

We get to the docks fifteen minutes early. The sun hides behind the clouds briefly, playing a game of hide-and-seek. The wind slightly picks up as we near the water, and the complaining coming from Samantha starts immediately. Samantha finds a little shop on the docks where she buys a different shirt and some shorts. *I mean, she could have gone home and not come. That would have actually worked out better, yet here we are.* We board the ship, and the crew is really into their roles. We adore it. Snapping pictures left and right and meeting other people.

Jon and I buy a bucket of beers to share with Will and Samantha as we find a seat on the big vessel. My curls bounce around in the breeze. I laugh as Jon runs his hands through them. We share kisses and ignore the negativity that Samantha spreads through the entire trip.

"This wind is so fucking brutal to my hair," Samantha complains.

"Really? I love it," I say as it blows through my curls.

Everyone grabs a drink and raises it to the sky.

"Cheers," I begin, "to a good birthday and to a hopefully amazing year. My last year in my twenties!" Our long neck bottles gently crash together.

"Jeez, you're twenty-nine? Not married and no kids?" Samantha makes a face. "That's my goal."

Lord, protect this woman from my wrath. I will break the end of this bottle and smash the remains of it against this bitch's head.

"I don't know," I say, taking a sip. "I want to travel the world and see other things before I have kids."

"So, like, what did you do in your twenties then?" she rudely asks.

"I ran a business," I snap.

"Oh, I mean, like, who reads books anyway?" Samantha shrugs.

"Everyone," we all retort.

"I don't," she says confidently.

"Why would you admit to that?" I genuinely ask. "Honestly, why would you think that's sexy?"

"No guys like smart girls," she honestly admits.

I look at Will. "I mean, I can see that."

As our trip nears the end, the boat glides into its designated spot. The four of us, a little tipsy, make our way down the ramp. Samantha says she has to go home, and I've never been more grateful to see someone go. The shrill of Samantha's voice alerts us that she will return for the birthday events for the evening. *Damn, so close. Maybe it's not too late to uninvite her?* Will gives her a sloppy wet kiss, and we take the escalator down to the Metro. Jon and I look at Will.

"What?" Will asks.

"Dude, really? I'll give you a week before you get sick of her." Jon laughs.

"Yeah, man, she's kind of a cunt."

"You don't like her." Will's face sours.

"Let's just say the thought of me pushing her off the boat, did cross my mind," I realize my tone was on the harsh side, I try to find a better of way of saying *hey, this bitch has got to go*. "She's not Sharon. I still have high standards with you after Sharon."

Will nods. "She is definitely not Sharon."

"She is like Caroline. Remember her?" I remind him.

"Who's Caroline?" Jon asks.

"You don't remember? Oh my god, from advanced lighting? She had jet-black hair, and her tits were like super big yet super fake and literally was dumber than a bag of rocks. She kept calling me mixed Barbie. I punched her in the face in the middle of lab. How do you not remember that?"

"Oh shit! I remember!" Jon exclaims. "Dude, Caroline was the worst! Wait, you dated Caroline?"

Will sighs. "Yes, not my proudest moment. Also, thanks for ruining that one, Neveahly Skye."

I put my hand over my heart. "I humbly accept your thanks, sir."

We get down to the Metro in time and barely make it. We slide through the doors and trek our way back to the apartment. A couple of stops later, we make it back and start to set up for the birthday celebration. I order pizza and get the beer pong table ready and put on the '80s playlist and roll a couple of joints.

I change into my Yoshi onesies for the night's shenanigans. Jon brought his Mario onesies, and Will has his Luigi's. We are all set for tonight's festivities when Samantha knocks on the door. *Fuck. I completely forgot about this bitch.* I prepare myself for what is on the other end of the door, and slowly open it. Sam gives me the once over and starts to laugh.

"I wasn't aware this was a costume party," she mocks.

"And yet here you stand in complete drag," I reply.

Her face stiffens. "So we are not going out?"

I shake my head. "Nope, this is what we do on my birthday." I move over so she can come inside. "Are you coming in, or are you just going to stand there?"

She side-glances me and comes in. Jon and Will are already warming their beer pong arms. Samantha looks completely disgusted by tonight's events. *Sorry we like to get wasted, smoke weed, and chill for my birthday. That's how I roll.* Seconds later, the pizza guy knocks on the door. I damn near push Samantha out the way. I am more excited to see Scott, our regular delivery guy, than I am to see her. I grab the three boxes and carefully place them on the kitchen island and give Scott a big tip. He wishes me a happy birthday and leaves.

Jon, Will, and I head toward the kitchen island and spark the traditional birthday joint.

"Nev, another year you are here, and I am somewhat happy for it," Will says, playfully tussling my hair. "No, seriously, we bury a friend and celebrate the birth of one in a span of a week. To Nev!"

I pour four shots for all of us. I take a long hit off the joint, throw back a shot, and exhale. I feel the alcohol and the purple haze fight over who will take control over my body; I haven't done that in years. Jon does the same, then Will, and of course Samantha just throws back the shot. She doesn't smoke. Which is cool, more weed for us.

"Beer pong?" I ask everyone.

We head to the table and take sides. Jon and me versus Will and Samantha. Will and I do the eye-to-eye shot, and I make it. Jon and I have the balls first. The apartment is filled with laughter from the original gang, but Samantha stands next to Will, trying to bring the mood of the party down. Jon and I both make it; we keep making it, and at this point, the game isn't really a game. It's a slaughter.

Will is super competitive, and Samantha is starting to see that. She is not even trying, and I see Will's face go from playful to irritated.

"Look, Sam, you can't keep moving your elbow that far over the line. The shot's not going to count," he reminds her.

Jon and I start laughing.

"Okay, well, it's just a stupid game, Will," she whines.

Will turns his head and looks at her. "It's not just a stupid game, Samantha."

One thing you should know about Will, Ms. Samantha, he takes pong very seriously. We win. Thanks to Samantha giving up and Will losing his cool. We move on to *Mario Kart 7*, and Sam doesn't even play, which is fine because we don't have four controllers. This time, I have the better controller, and we put it on "the stay on track" mode. I did not know there was even such a mode until now.

Samantha sits in the kitchen, playing on her phone, being standoffish from the group. *Okay, this isn't going to last.* I pause the game and get us all beers.

"Do you want a beer?" I ask Samantha.

"No, empty calories," she replies.

I roll my eyes and go back to playing. Three championships later in *Mario Kart*, and I lose every single one of them. Will breaks out the *Rock Band* instruments. Samantha finally decides she wants to join, but only if she can sing. We comply with her demands with protest and let her sing.

We should not have complied with her demands because this bitch cannot sing whatsoever. Her singing is what they probably played at Waco to torture those people. Luckily, we put it on no fail for her because I trusted my gut and went with the theory; she could not carry a note. She couldn't carry a bucket full of water if instructed to.

Before I could even notice he was gone, Jon places the delicious looking cake on the island with the numbers two and nine strategically placed on it, illuminating the phrase "Happy Birthday, Bitch." I smile. Of course they would choose this phrase. As the two somewhat drunk men stumble through the birthday song, I close my eyes and blow out the candles.

Samantha begs Will if they can go out for a couple of drinks with her friends, and I tell him it's okay. *Anything to get her out of the apartment, I'm cool with, my dude.* As the night starts to wind down, Jon and I clean up as I start to play my birthday playlist.

As we finish throwing the plates and red solo cups away, Jon grabs my hand and spins me around; we begin swaying to the rhythm. The soft mellow voices of Daryl Hall and John Oates float through the air as the song "Sara Smiles" fills the room. I look up and smile. *Damn, this would be a lot hotter if my name was Sara. The fuck was my mom thinking about when she named me Neveahly?* He leans in to kiss me.

Every part of me is tingling. *Could it be the amazing pot we got from the dispensary? Possibly. Or could it be the fact that I'm actually dating someone I like for the first time in a while? That is another possible answer.* I feel his body heat rise as the song ends. *How do you put this song on repeat? Oh god, please be another good one!* "Purple Rain" comes on. *Was this my birthday mix or my banging mix?*

Jon grabs my legs and lifts me up. I wrap my legs around his waist, as we make our way to the couch. *Nothing gets anyone hotter than Prince himself.* He gently bites my bottom lip and starts to unzip my onesie. I start to unzip his. I pull his down as I fight to get mine off. *God, why are these things so hard to get off?* We finally win the battle against the Nintendo onesies. Jon moves his soft full lips down to my neck, as I slide my panties off. Reaching down for his boxers, I remove them. Jon pulls me down further on the couch and inserts himself between my thighs. I moan loudly. Jon whispers my name as he starts to push deeper into me. I run my nails down his back, gently digging them in his skin. *Shit, that's probably going to leave a mark.*

I'm about to say, "Fuck everything in DC," and leave. Will's got this. I know he's about to explode, and when he does, I hear the key turn in the front door. Jon pushes himself off of me and leaps to the other end of the couch, as Will and Samantha come catapulting through the door. *Goddamn it, dude. Way to be a fucking actual cock block.* Drunk, they hurl themselves through the living room and into the kitchen. Jon and I sit there on the couch watching them start to demolish the leftover pizza.

"Oh my god! This is so good." Samantha moans.

"So good," Will agrees.

Will picks up the box and heads to his bedroom with Sam, ignoring Jon and I on the couch. He shuts the door.

"Shall we take this to the bedroom?" Jon suggests.

I grab his hand and drag him back to the bedroom; we finish what we started on the couch.

The sun spills into the room through my *South Park* curtains. I wake up covered in my blankets, with my Yoshi onesie on top of the comforter. Jon's Mario hangs on the dresser drawer, half in. I realize I have no top on and pull the sheet close to my chest to cover my breasts. *As if being modest counts now. Jon's seen every part of me.* I roll over to see Jon scrolling through his phone.

"How long have you been up?"

He puts his phone down and smiles. "Not too long, I had to check some emails." He kisses the top of my forehead. "I didn't want to wake you up."

I roll over and grab my phone to look at the time. "Jesus, it's already twelve o'clock?"

He nods. "Yeah. My train leaves at two, today."

I make a sour face. "Why did you let me sleep so late?"

"Because you look so pretty when you do."

"Creeper," I tease. "Do you want to do anything before you leave the District of Columbia?"

He shakes his head no. "I'm here with you. That's all I want."

"Awe, how cliché." I lean up and kiss him. "Have you heard Will and the wicked witch of the district yet?"

He laughs. "No, but I really hope she's a phase."

"Oh my god, me too. I cannot stand her." I scroll through my apps to see which food service to order from. "What do you want for brunch?"

"Actually, why don't we get something from Union Station?" Jon suggests.

"Good idea," I agree.

I get out of bed and hop in the shower. To my surprise, Jon joins me. *I haven't done this in a while without it turning into sex; it usually ends with me taking a shower only fit for Satan and the guy complaining.* Jon didn't mind the hotness of it. It's very rare that you're able to find someone who enjoys extremely hot showers, and in this case, I have found my person.

We hop out, and I find an extra towel for Jon. As we dress for the day, I put a little bit of makeup on today; even if it is for the next two-ish hours. As we make our way out into the living room, Will and Sam sit on the couch, still in yesterday's clothes. The whole area reeks of alcohol and stale cigarette smoke. It hits me, almost making me gag.

"Oh, Jesus," I mutter, "when was the last time you showered, dude?"

Will, who looks like he's been partying all night, turns his head. "Uh, I guess a couple of days ago." He looks at Jon and his luggage. "Are you leaving, dude?"

"Yeah," Jon says slowly. "No need to get up. I'll catch you next time."

Samantha says nothing.

"I'll be back." I grab my keys and head out the door with Jon.

As much as I hate riding the Metro on the weekends, I don't mind too much when it comes to spending more time with Jon. We sit in the half empty car, holding hands, gushing over each other. At the top of their lungs, my insecurities wash over me as I try to enjoy the rest of the time with him. *He's not like other guys, Nev. Let those defense guards down.* As the short ride to Union Station comes to an end, loneliness overcomes me. I force a smile as I suggest we eat at Johnny Rockets.

We opt to sit at the counter. Conversation is scarce as we dig into the pancakes and eggs. I am also fighting back tears. *It's not that serious, Neveahly. You'll see him mid-October, and you'll talk on the phone every night and be in constant contact with him. You're just going to have to work at this relationship; that's all that is different.* The thought that I am falling for him faster than I am expecting hits me, and my heart starts beating faster. I get lost in my thoughts, and I don't even realize that Jon's been talking to me.

"Where are you?" he jokes.

"Sorry, I have no idea. I think I really did drink and smoke too much last night," I admit.

Jon finishes the last of his coffee. "Not more than the rest of us."

"What were you saying?"

He puts his hand on top of mine. "I said everything will be fine. October will be here before you know it."

I smile. "I know. It just feels so far away."

"I know," he agrees.

I pay the tab, and we walk to the gate. I sit next to him, trying to not be a Debbie Downer. I don't want him to leave, and I also don't want to come off as a stage 4 clinger. As the time comes to board, Jon slowly gets up; I go on my tippy toes to give him a kiss goodbye, and try to make a quick exit. *Ha! Can't feel feelings if you just quickly leave.*

He quickly grabs my hand. "Don't do that." He kisses me deeply.

I allow myself to be swept away in his embrace. *Let this good thing happen.*

"I'll call you when I get to my apartment," he says. He gives me one more kiss and starts to get in line.

Do I stay and watch him get on the train? Do I leave? Is it a dick move to leave? I should stay. I watch him disappear into the sliding glass doors and get loss in the mass of people. I feel the tears blur my vision and sting my eyes as I start walking to the Metro. I catch the train just in time before I had to wait another twenty minutes. I sit in silence as I ride off into the dark tunnel.

Walking up to my building, I realize my emotions are all over the place. I'm excited that I have Jon in my life and had a successful birthday for the first time in years, but now I have to go back to an empty bed, which is saying a lot because I enjoy sleeping alone.

I turn the corner abruptly, and I see Mike sitting there on the steps in sweatpants and a tank top. Rage consumes my body. I go from, "I am quite possibly in love" to "I'm a teen titan, and my name is Raven. I'm getting ready to summon my father from the nether realm, and the demons are about to take over my body, and I will not be capable of owning up to my actions right about now." I'm not sure that reference is entirely accurate. I never finished the comic book or the TV show; it got kind of confusing.

"So you are alive," he snaps.

"Why wouldn't I be alive?" I match his attitude.

"I don't know. You didn't call me and thank me for the flowers or make plans with me for your birthday?"

I laugh. "Thank you for committing a crime and invading my privacy and not accepting the fact that I no longer want to have anything to do with you anymore. How's that for a fucking thank you?"

I start to walk up the steps right past him. He grabs me. "I didn't invade your privacy. The door wasn't completely closed."

There are too many witnesses out here, Nev. "I'm not sure if that will hold up in a court of law, but I'm like hundred percent sure that you should leave. I literally have no desire to interact with you or want to entertain the thought of you being in my life anymore, Michael."

"Look, I lost my cool, and I said I was sorry. What the fuck else do you want from me?" he yells.

People walking on the sidewalk slow their pace to turn and look at us.

"Mike"—I get closer to him—"let's go to the rooftop and talk, okay?"

He agrees. We get in the elevator and stand on opposite sides of the car. It seems like an eternity to get up there, but when we finally make it, we sit in front of the pool. The entire rooftop is empty.

"I thought we we're going to work this out?" he asks.

I sigh. "Do you just hear what you want to hear? Or have you just never been rejected by a girl before? Because this is starting to become pathetic at this point. At no point in time did I ever say I wanted to work this out."

He narrows his eyes. "I just think that sometimes you get irrational when you get mad."

I laugh. "Irrational? Bro, I had to bury one of my best friends and celebrate a birthday in a span of a week. I'm not irrational. I'm just going through some shit, and since I'm going through some shit. You have been the cause of nothing but fucking drama, dude."

He puts his head down.

"Did you ever think, Gee, Nev never calls me to tell me anything personal. I wonder why. Because you are just unreliable. I never trusted you, and I never will. This"—I point back to him and then myself—"will never work out. It was never just us."

He snorts. "So that's it? Two years and just like that, poof! Done?"

My eyes widen. "Two years of what, Michael? Fucking? Because that's all we were doing. There was no relationship. I never met your parents. I don't even know who your friends are. You only know Will because he's my business partner as well as my friend!"

"So that night at the club, you felt nothing?" His voice grows angry.

I laugh. "Are you dumb? Stupid or dumb? We were drunk. I honestly thought it was going to be a hit and quit it, and it just lingered on for two fucking years. Sprinkle a little bit of a crazy psycho girlfriend who still came to my place of work."

Mike gets up, frustrated. "Jesus, how many times do I have to apologize for that?"

"It's not about being apologetic. It's about the fact that it fucking happened."

"You're right. I should have said something. I was an asshole back then, and I—"

I jump up. "Please do not finish that sentence. Do not justify being an asshole. You were and still are a whole-ass man. Are you joking? Are you serious?" I study his face. "It's one thing to be a teenager, but you are well into your thirties." I sit next to him. "I'm sorry, bro. Your character is officially getting written off *The Neveahly Show*. You should have been a one episode type character, but it turned into a love interest storyline that should have never left the writers room."

He looks at me and studies my face. "So what? You're fucking someone new now?"

I start laughing. "And if I am? Also, hakuna your tatas. Everyone is replaceable. Even me."

He licks his lips. "You are seeing someone."

"First of all, it wouldn't matter if I was or was not because we would still be having this same conversation, and second of all"—I get right in his face—"I could fuck your entire football team, and it still would be *none* of your goddamn business."

I hit a nerve. Oh, I hit a nerve. I shouldn't have said that. Mike looks like he's about to drown me in this pool. Mike's face gets fire engine red, and I see his fists clench up into a ball. I see him eyeing the pool and then back at me. *Goddamn it, Nev. You gotta stop going places alone with this dude.*

Mike brushes past me. "What? Does he buy you nice things? Does he take you places? Would he put roses in your shop? Would he buy you anything you want?"

My mouth drops. "I don't need a man to finance my lifestyle, sir. I have my own business and my own money. Whatever a man can offer me after that is a bonus, not a fucking requirement. I'm not one of your goddamn groupies or one of your many girlfriends who need money in order for them to love you. Get so fucked, Mike."

Holy shit, where did this come from? A girl who went from a spineless cunt into a ferocious tiger.

"Let's get one thing clear, shall we? I've never *ever* asked you to finance anything of mine, and I never will. I think that's what really is the problem here is that you can't get what you want, and you're acting like a child, Michael."

I shake my head, "It's sad, really. We could have maybe been friends at one point, but now I want nothing to do with you."

He releases his fits and sits back down. He puts his head in his hands and looks defeated.

"So this is it?" He looks up at me, eyes red. "Because I'm not coming back anymore after this, Neveahly! I swear! I will never call you again!"

"Yeah, you said that last time, and yet here we are, having this same conversation. Please, stop. No calls, text, pigeon carrier whatever. I never want to hear from you again."

Mike stands up and flings the chair into the pool. I don't flinch. He looks at me, waiting to see if I react, but I look him dead in the eye.

Mike walks toward the rooftop doors and slams it behind him, almost shattering the glass.

I wait until there is no chance of him coming back and fall back into the chair. I've reached the boiling point of anger. I get up and fling the rest of the chairs on the deck into the pool. I scream as loud as I can at the top of my lungs. My legs give way, and the grounds beneath me.

Tears begin to blur my vision, causing my contacts to float around. I blink several times, and steady my breathing. *It's over, Nev. It is all over.*

Goddamn it, why do you let him do this to you again? You let him get so far under your skin that he made you into this monster of distrust, but no more. I watch the chairs sink to the bottom of the pool. I bring my knees to my chest and just sit there and let the wind blow my curls around and dry the tears on my face. I haven't had a rage session in so long.

I allow myself to get lost in thought for hours as I watch the pool water move with the wind. This alone time is what I need.

CHAPTER 10

After the rooftop run-in with Mike, it's been radio silence, and let me tell you, it's been fucking amazing. A couple of weeks of normalcy is what I need. September flew like a bat out of hell, and October comes in like a witch on a broom. A perfect way to introduce poetry slam for our bookstore. It's been bringing in a new type of foot traffic for Wednesday, and it is making our profits skyrocket. That is, when Will doesn't bring Ms. Samantha. Goddamn, we all thought this shit was going to be a fucking phase, but she is still here two weeks later and at the apartment every other day. Will occasionally will bring up that maybe she should move in, and I shut that shit down faster than a trip to Epstein's island. No, sir. I don't think so, sir. Not a chance in hell, sir.

It's the perfect storm when she comes through the store. Calm at first, pleasant even, and then *boom!* Will or I say something to trigger her, and she fucking flips out on one of us and storms out. The constant arguing, though, is such high school bullshit. It gets so old so fast I'm out of the apartment more than I'm in. I thought about even getting a small cot for the back office so I can sleep there.

Jon is dropping not so subtle hints for moving down here and us getting an apartment together, and at this point, I'm all for it. Will may be my best friend, but with Samantha being there all the time, she can have my room. Or they can make it her acting studio.

I can hear them bickering as I log the numbers into the computer from the back office before; he should be getting ready to set up for the Poetry Slam. I try to ignore it. Luckily, the store is closed, so no can hear them except me. Perhaps people who are walking outside, mostly me though. As I try to finish the Excel spreadsheet, the voices get louder and louder. I finally say fuck it and walk out see what exactly they are arguing about.

Jesus, please be something of importance and nothing absolutely dumb. I come out as Will is counting the money and closing out one of the registers.

"I'm just saying, if we do this piece together, it would be great!" Samantha begs.

I roll my eyes. *Okay, this is great. A stupid piece that shouldn't even be read. This is about original poetry, but go off.*

"Look, poetry slams are about original poetry. This isn't even original. It's from Shakespeare," Will protests.

I walk over to the closet and start grabbing folding chairs and set up for the event.

"You never want to do anything I want to do!" she protests.

"That's all we do!" he screams.

Finally, a fucking backbone, my dude. Welcome to the land of the living.

I start to create a row of three; Will does the same. Will and I start to create an aisle so there is room for people to walk around.

"Hey, can you help me set up the stage?" I ask Will, completely ignoring their fight.

"Yeah," he agrees.

We walk back to the storage room together. I look at him and shoot daggers into his soul.

"Bro, I know." He looks down at the floor.

"Fucking, do you? She's driving me crazy! All you do is fight! Fuck and fight! C'mon, can she go somewhere else tonight?" I whisper.

He nods. "I'll give her some money. Maybe she'll get some food and go back to our place."

"Doesn't she have a place of her own?"

He laughs. "Yeah, she just likes ours better."

I sigh. "Oh my god! Just because no simp September is over doesn't mean you have to go back to being one! Grow a pair, and stand up to her! She's got great tits, and that's it, my dude."

We pull the stage out and wheel it over to the clearing. Samantha sits in the front row, pouting. Will helps me unfold the stage; we continue to ignore her. Sam starts to make noises as she pouts, Will turns to face her, but I have had enough.

"Okay, that's it." I turn to Sam. "You're a whole-ass, grown-ass woman, so act like it. If Will doesn't want to do the fucking poem, he doesn't have to. Also, it's *original* poetry. Not being able to memorize and recite shit. Anyone can do that, Samantha. I don't know how else to explain this shit to you. This isn't even about you. You shouldn't even be allowed to do this. My god! Grow the fuck up! I know you are younger than us, but seriously? This is getting old real fast."

The face of Samantha, who thinks she is America's next sweetheart, turns completely red. She looks to Will for help, but he stands there and says nothing. *Don't look at Will, sweetie. He knows I'm right.*

"Excuse me?" Samantha stands up.

"I'm not a parrot. I'm not repeating myself. Either you help Will and me set up this fucking stage or dip out. I'm over this princess act. All you do is cause shit when there is no need for it." I stand my ground.

Will turns to me with pleading eyes to beg me to take it back.

Samantha starts to bring on the tears. When she sees it doesn't work on me, she storms out of the store and slams the door behind her. I lock the stage and grab the mic and set it up.

It's exhausting dealing with her. I sit down on the edge of the stage. Will joins me, with his head hanging low. A man who is losing the battle, and the war. "I'm telling you, dude, break up with her before she pokes holes in the condom," I plea.

Will looks down at his phone and sees Samantha calling him. "Can you just apologize?"

I laugh. "For what? Telling her the truth? Stop bending to her beck and call. No pussy is that good."

Will picks up the phone and leaves the store.

"You better be back before the show starts," I scream before the door closes.

I pull out my phone and see Jon is calling me. I answer it.

"Hey, you just missed out on an epic tantrum," I tease.

He laughs. "Let me guess, Sam?"

"You would be correct." I stand up and start to lock the mic stand in place.

"Jesus, again? What about this time?"

"I may have told her that she needs to stop being such a princess."

Jon sighs. "I mean, you're not wrong, but I'm assuming you did not say it in a nice way?"

"You would assume correct, sir," I hop off the stage and slide into a folding chair. "She's just such an awful cunt. I cannot outwardly express that enough to Will anymore."

"You could, but I don't think he cares anymore," Jon replies. "I hate to make this call so short, but I have to get back to set. I just wanted to hear your voice before it got too late."

I smile. "You are just really crushing it with the good boyfriend points."

"I miss you, and I'll talk to you tomorrow."

"I love you and miss you too. I'll talk to you tomorrow, babe," I hang up the phone.

Oh shit. Did I just say I love you? He's never said that. I just said that now. I didn't mean it. I mean, I did, but if he doesn't feel that way, then I don't. Fuck. Do I call him back? Do I say, "Just kidding?" Oh, fuck me. I stand up and start to pace back and forth between the chairs. *Oh no, I blew it. Way to go, Nev. You moved too fast, and you said the* L *word so early into the relationship? You have known him for like eight years though. I should call him back. No, that's going to look super desperado. Okay, just say there was a cross-connection, and the FBI agent that listens to your phone calls said it. That's totally believable.* I start biting my nails, completely forgetting that I painted them. I spit blue chips out of my mouth.

I don't have time to worry about this. I look down at my phone to see if he called me back. *Nothing. Okay, that could be good. He could easily not have heard it. That would be swell.* I go on and finish setting up the speakers. *I should call him back. Maybe I should explain myself and how I got caught up in the moment and that I didn't mean to say it, but I feel it, and I completely understand that if he doesn't feel that same way yet, it wouldn't hurt my feelings.* I grab my phone out of my pocket, and Will is calling me.

"Where the fuck are you?" I demand. "We open in like forty-five minutes, and you just run out?"

He sighs. "Look, she's really upset, I'll be there in twenty. Can you stall?"

"Stall? Stall? Are you mad? Bro, you got ten to get your ass down here." I hang up the phone.

I go into the employee lounge and grab the cheese tray and five bottles of wine. I double back for the cups and arrange them nicely on the refreshment table. I see Mickey and Michael at the door, ready and willing to help. I am so relieved; I unlock the door and let them in.

"Hey, guys, I'm so glad you can come out and help us," I say graciously.

"Yeah, man, no problem," Mickey says, giving me a big hug. "Where's Will?"

"Calming the District's princess down. You know how that goes. We open in"—I look down at my phone—"shit. I'm going to call Will until he picks up. Everything is all set up."

I excuse myself and go in the back to call Will; it goes straight to voice mail. *I don't have time for this. We are just going to have to go on without him.* I walk to the front of the store, and I see him, with Samantha. She's smiling wide and has a smug look on her face. Will looks defeated, and I cannot help but realize, something went down between wherever they were and when they arrived back here.

"Oh, I'm so glad you could make it to the poetry slam," I say sarcastically.

"Samantha wants to read her poem," Will says while looking at the floor.

"No. I said no before, and I'm saying no again."

"It's an original poem this time," she smugly says.

I roll my eyes. "Fine. Look, I don't have time for this, nor do I care." I get behind the counter. Gently putting the record on, I slide the needle onto the vinyl and the soothing voice Ms. Lauryn Hill floats through the air.

More people turn out than we expect. The poets come in and give a little bit of their soul to the crowd. It's so beautiful hearing different bits and pieces of everyone. As each poet takes the stage, you can feel their words flow into your soul. You empathize with their pain, their beauty, their story. Then there's this bitch Samantha. Her rhyme scheme all over the place and fitting words just to fit words. I don't even know what the poems is about really.

As she comes off the stage, a smatter of applause is given. A woman, a familiar woman, comes on after her. It takes me a few moments to recognize her, but it's Sharon. I have never been more excited to see an ex of Will's. My face lights up, and I turn to Will. His face turns red. Her poem is so raw and bold: beautiful. Sharon was the last one onstage, and you can tell that she has been through it after Will. Sharon's words may have spoken to pain, but her poise, and new demeanor screams I'm stronger.

After all is said and done, people start to leave the store, but Sharon sticks around. She changed her hair, she dyed it red, and it looks good against her pale skin. She's lost some weight and has even changed her style. I must say, she looks great. I walk up to her to say hi and notice she's with another man. A handsome rugged man, the exact opposite of Will.

"Sharon, I didn't even recognize you," I say, giving her a hug.

"Neveahly. Yeah, I dyed my hair and changed a bit. How are you? Will never brought me to the store. This is so quaint! I love it!"

"Yeah, this is it. I'm great."

Will comes up slowly, like a frightened child. "Hey, Sharon," he says softly.

"William, it's good to see you." She politely gives him a handshake.

She hit him with a William and a handshake. I don't know why, but I cannot help but get a little bit of satisfaction out of this. I feel as though this is payback from when he flagged down Mark at the bar in Florida. I shouldn't enjoy this, but I do.

"This is Claude, my fiancé," she says, introducing him.

My mouth drops. "Her fiancé, Will." I look at him.

"I heard her, Neveahly," Will snaps.

Samantha walks up to Will and throws her arms around his waist. “Babe, I'm hungry,” she whines. She looks at Sharon. “Who are you?”

“This is Sharon,” I say proudly.

“Oh, hi.” She turns back to Will. “Can we go get some food?”

Will looks at Samantha. “Yeah, sure, we can go. It was good seeing you, Sharon,”

“Yeah, you too, William. Take it easy.” She turns to me. “It was lovely seeing you, Neveahly. Maybe we can do brunch sometime?”

“That would be amazing,” I say cheerfully.

Sharon gives me a hug. I see her peer over to see Will. She looks as though she wants to say something, but she grabs her fiancé's hand and quietly leaves. Will stares at me with hateful eyes. “What?” I ask.

“Did you invite her?” he demands.

I laugh. “First of all, I didn't even know she was still in the country, and second of all I cut all ties with her when you two broke up. No, I didn't invite her.”

“Why are you so mad?” Samantha asks.

“I'm not. Let's just clean up, and then we can go get something to eat,” Will says with an attitude.

It takes less time to disassemble the structure and put the chairs away than when we put it up in the first place. Will drives us all back to the apartment. I can feel the tension in the car. I know he's absolutely angry that Sharon has moved on, but what did he expect? For her to be miserable for her entire life?

As we enter the apartment, I can see the wheels turning in Will's head on how his life would have turned out if he stayed with Sharon. I hope that goes to show him that he can do better. I warm up some dinner for the rest of us as we sit in the kitchen silently. I crack open a beer and enjoy the silence. Will still hasn't really said anything since we got home, and Samantha keeps poking at him to see what's wrong.

“I just don't see why your entire attitude has completely changed since you got home from seeing that girl Sharon,” Samantha whines. “Who cares? If she is just some girl, why does it matter? It's not like you guys dated or anything.”

Will's and my eyes meet. He gives me the "don't tell her" stare to avoid a fight. I say nothing, but Sam sees the look we give one another. After a few moments pass by, she puts the pieces together.

"Oh my god, you guys did date!" she exclaims.

Will puts down his fork. "It wasn't even that serious."

"How long did you guys date for?"

"Like five months," Will mutters. "And we broke up, and now I'm with you."

"Who broke up with whom?" Samantha demands.

"She broke up with me," Will confesses.

"I should go." I start to get up and clear my plate.

"No," the both say in unison.

I sit back down. *So I can be an accessory after the fact? Cool.*

"So what? I'm like some rebound chick?" Samantha asks.

I mean, that's what you started off as, yet here you are.

"No." Will grabs her hand. "No, you weren't some rebound chick."

"How long did remain single before you started your Tinder account?" Samantha removes her hand from Will's.

"Like a week."

"So I am a rebound chick!" she screams. "Do you still like her?"

Silence fills the room. *Damn, homie. Now's not the time to be silent. But also, this would be a great time to break up with her.*

"William!" Samantha slams her fist down.

"No." He stops for a second. "No, at least I don't think I do."

Samantha starts to cry. "So what am I? Just someone to kill time with?"

"Okay, so I really think this conversation should be had in private, so I'm just gonna tiptoe on outta here." I grab my beer and start to leave.

"No, it's okay, Nev. I'm leaving." Samantha starts to head toward the door.

Will goes after her. *Dude, let her go. This is your chance.*

My phone begins to violently vibrate on the table. I see it's Will's mom, Ellen.

"Hey, *Ellen*," I say loudly, trying to get Will's attention. "What's up?"

Will stops at the door and turns around.

I put her on speaker. "Not much," she says. "Is Will with ya?"

"Yup, he's right next to me. You're on speaker."

"Hey, Ma, why don't you ever call me? You always call Nev first," he complains.

"Because I like her more," she jokes.

"Ha ha. Very funny. What's going on?"

There's a brief moment of silence. Samantha comes back from the door to see what's going on. I look up at Will and then back down at the dark screen.

"Ma, what's going on?" Will says in a worried tone.

"It's your father. He's dead," she finally says.

"Oh. When did he die?" Will asks nonchalantly.

"Like a week or so ago," Ellen matches his tone.

"Mom, and you are now telling me this? That your husband, Jay, has been dead for about a week or so?"

"Ya, there was no rush. It's not like he's going anywhere," she jokes.

Will and I both start to laugh.

A horrified look creeps across Samantha's face.

"So I'm gonna have him cremated, and I figured you would want to say goodbye or whatever," Ellen continues.

"Ya, I guess. When do you need us up there by?" Will enquires.

"Well, he's due to get burned up by Friday, so if you could get here by Friday or Saturday, that would be great," Ellen suggests.

"Okay, Nev and I will leave Friday," Will says.

"How are you holding up, Mom?" I ask. "I hope you haven't partied too hard yet."

She laughs. "No, I'll just wait for you guys to get up here."

I laugh. "Okay, see you Friday, Ma!"

"Bye, love you both!"

"Love you too," we both say, I end the call.

Samantha stares at us in horror.

Will looks at her. "Do you want to come up to Syracuse for a funeral?"

CHAPTER 11

Instead of calling the agency, I call Michael and Mickey and ask if they are willing to work for us. Might as well at this point. I explain we have another funeral to attend, and they accept the informal offer and agree to come in. I am happy they are able and willing to because I need a vacation. Not saying this is a vacation, but I need to get out of DC for a bit. I feel the area itself is sucking away my potential, and I need to breathe some new air. I call Jon and let him know what happened.

"Jesus, seriously?"

"Yeah. I feel like I should have a to-go bag ready at this point. People keep dropping like flies," I pull out my suitcase from the close it and start to throw items in.

Jon laughs. "I know how you feel."

"Oh, yeah, how was California?" I ask.

He sighs. "It was okay. Just wannabe Spielbergs with a cookie crumb budget. It was worth it though. I miss you."

Okay, he hasn't brought up the "I love you" thing.

"I miss you too." I grin.

"I also love you too."

I chuckle. "Oh, so you did hear me yesterday?"

"I did, loud and clear." He laughs. "I figure you were going to do your Neveahly thing and sweat it out for the entire night."

"I did. I really did." I sigh.

"I don't know why. You should know that wouldn't scare me away."

God, he's such a good man.

"Okay, I gotta get packing, I'll talk to you tomorrow."

"G'night, babe. I *love* you. There, I said it first this time." He laughs.

"Ha ha. I love you too." I hang up the phone and toss it on the bed.

I smile. I throw a couple of more things in the suitcase and call it a night.

Will was able to get all three of us tickets at a cheap rate. Well, his was cheaper because he can prove his is a death in the family, and the rest of ours were somewhat cheap. Samantha, not being the morning person she claims to be, is super bitchy at 4:00 a.m. Will and I go about our early morning routine.

Alas, Samantha cannot leave it alone. She keeps poking, and prodding, but Will offers no explanation, or shows any emotion. Will puts on his headphones and ignores her. I honestly think the only reason he brought her is because she was standing right there and didn't want her to feel left out. She had the nerve to bitch and complain that we were not sitting in first class. Lookee here, baby girl, until you can pay for first-class tickets, you're sitting with us peasants in economy business.

We arrive at Hancock Airport at 10:00 a.m. I did not prepare myself for the Syracuse cold. The only thing somewhat appropriate for the weather are my Ugg boots and possibly my long-sleeve shirt. Not my see-through sweats that leave nothing for the imagination, and definitely not the fact that my coat is in my suitcase. We grab our luggage from the carousel and wait on the curb for Ellen.

"What are we looking for?" I ask Will as I shiver down to my core.

Will shrugs. "I don't know. Maybe the truck?"

I laugh. "I'm surprised she didn't torch it by now."

"It's so cold. Why can't we wait inside?" Samantha whines.

I pull out a couple of tiny bottles of Jack Daniels and hand her one. "Here. Be an adult and drink." I throw one back.

"It's not even noon yet." She looks at me with disgust.

"Okay and? There are no rules when someone dies." I grab another one out of my purse and take that one back as well.

Will grabs one from my purse.

"There are healthier ways to cope with loss, guys." Samantha looks at us with seriousness.

Will and I burst out into laughter. I almost fall off the curb.

"Oh, sweet naive Samantha. One day, you will lose that innocence, and alcohol will be your only friend,"

A red 1957 Bel Air Chevy comes whipping around the corner. My mouth drops. It's the most beautiful car I've ever seen. It's my dream car. I've only wanted two cars in my life: the Bel Air Chevy and a Hummer. Two very different cars, but I love them both. People turn their heads as the car slowly approaches us. Ellen pops up from the driver's seat.

"Did you kill him just for the car, Ellen?" I joke.

Cherry-red interior, with a cherry-red steering wheel. White trim inside, I would most definitely kill someone for this car.

"No, but I can keep this beauty. Will, you like my new ride?"

Will is as speechless as I am. "I don't know what to think except—"

"Shotgun!" I scream.

"Goddamn it! My dad is the one who's dead!"

I shrug. "You're the one who brought extra baggage with you," I point to Samantha. "It's rude to leave it unattended."

Samantha narrows her eyes.

"Who is this?" Ellen asks, pointing and grinning at Samantha.

"Hi, I'm Samantha Honey Mayweather." She extends her hand to shake Ellen's.

I laugh. "Your middle name is Honey?"

"Nice to meet you. I'm Ellen Hope. Will's mom."

"Yeah, uh, this is my girlfriend, Mom," Will says slowly.

Ellen meets my gaze to gauge a reaction. I shrug.

"I'm starving. Let's go to that Diner by the house!" I beg.

"Oh god! I haven't been there in so long. Probably not since you guys have been up here last!" Ellen starts to open the trunk.

"No, Ma. I got it," I say, throwing my bags into the back. I take Will's and throw them in there. Samantha hands me hers, and I stare at her. "Is something wrong with your arms?" I walk to the front and pull the seat back so Will and Samantha can get in.

Samantha puts her bag in the trunk and walks over to my side of the car. She glares at me as she slides into the backseat. Will hops in after as I slam the seat back. We all buckle in and take off.

Ellen, Will, and I start talking about all the times we have been up here, and the last time we were up here was to see *The Book of Mormon*. Will surprised me for my birthday. It was such a great present, and we all got hammered at the Diner. Samantha, unable to come to terms with how none of us are upset, just sits in the back quietly.

We arrive at the whole in the wall establishment and sit at our favorite booth. Rita is surprisingly still working here; she remembers us. Well, me, because there are not a lot of biracial people in this area. She flashes her toothless smile as she sees our familiar faces.

"Well, well, well. Aren't you guys a sight for sore eyes," Rita says.

"I'm surprised you're even here, Ms. Rita." I grin. "I would have thought by now you would've run off with that cook you were talking about."

She laughs. "Edwardo? Nah! He was just being friendly! Let me guess. You want loaded fries, beers all around, and sliders?"

"Damn, that is just a fucking memory of yours!" Will says, highly impressed.

"Actually, do you have like a house salad?" Samantha chimes in.

"We sure do, hon. I can get you that." I see Rita scribbling our order on her pad as she begins to walk back to the kitchen.

"So let's just address the elephant in the room. Why wait so long to call us?"

Rita comes back with our drinks. I grab the cold bottle and place it to my lips. I intended to take a short sip, but I damn near finished the bottle.

Ellen looks at hers. "I don't know. It's not like he was lying in our bed for weeks. He was just lying in the morgue. Plus, it takes forever to get the paperwork in, and there was no point for you all to be up here for that long."

"I know, but we could have been here to help you through this," Will says, reaching over putting his hand over hers. "I hated him just as much as you did. Probably more, to be honest here."

Ellen lets out a laugh. "I know. But what's done is done. Oh, before I forget, we need to go to the funeral home after this. Wrap up the last bit of signatures needed to burn his body."

"Okay," Will says. "I mean, do we get to watch the body burn?"

Samantha nearly chokes on her beer. We all look at her.

"You okay?" I ask.

"Yeah." She starts to clean up her mess. "Fine."

We finish our food and drinks and head to the funeral home. I didn't even want to get out of the car. *Can you be in love with an object? Of course, you can. They make shows about it.* I let Will sit in the front seat this time so he can be next to Ellen. They need each other right now. Being strong for so many years can run you down till you are nothing but the former shell of yourself; but now, I see two former shells coping, trying to break free from the harden cast. Samantha and I sit in the back seat, having no conversation whatsoever. She tries to, but I ignore her. I'm not trying to purposely make her feel uncomfortable, but she immediately goes into talking about herself, and I have no interest in hearing about her nana or her poppa. I don't even want to know about her sorority sisters. I care none about any of that shit.

Will lets Samantha and me out of the back when we arrive at the small funeral home. It's a house. It reminds me of the movie *My Girl.* We walk in and a petite woman steps into our line of view to greet us.

"How may I help you?" the young woman asks.

"Hello, we are here for Jay Hope," Ellen says softly.

"Yes, are you Ellen Hope?" she asks gently.

"Yes, I am. This is my son, Will Hope."

"I'm Samantha, Will's girlfriend." Samantha forces her way in.

"Hello," the woman politely says. "If you all would just follow me this way." She leads us into a large office.

We all take our seats. Samantha scoots her closer to Will's. Forcing herself between Mother and Son. *Pathetic.*

"I have been made aware that you have opted for a cremation. Is that correct?" the woman says, looking down at her paper and then back up at Ellen and Will.

"Yup," Will says in a monotone.

She pulls out a binder with different options for urns. "In this binder, you will find—"

Will pushes it back. "No need. A cardboard box or a plastic bag will do just fine."

The woman's eyes widen. "Sir, I'm sure you would love to put your loved one in something less—"

"Lady, all we are going to do is throw him in the trash. We don't need to spend any money on memorializing this asshole."

The blonde hair, blue eyed director was not ready for Will's bluntness.

"Okay, so the cost of cremation in the state of New York is two hundred and fifty dollars without funeral services."

"Jesus, lady, I can start a bonfire in our backyard for free and burn him that way," Will responds.

Samantha gets up and leaves the room.

"Fine, whatever, I'll pay it." Ellen gives her a card. "Just, I don't want a fancy urn. I don't need a box. Just give me a bag. That's it."

Dumbfounded, the woman runs the card and gives Ellen the receipt. "Well, since all the paperwork is in order, and you've already spoken to everyone, we can give Jay to you by tomorrow."

"Thanks. Call me when his ashes are ready." Ellen gets up, as we follow behind her. Sitting in the Bel Air, no words are exchange. Silence fills the beautiful antique car, as we drive back to the house.

I help unpack the car and take the luggage upstairs. I claim my usual room. Will and Samantha stay in his childhood room. After placing the suitcase next to the bed, I feel a wave a nausea come over me. *Okay, that's weird.* I shake it off and slide down the banister to meet Ellen who is already waiting with an open bottle of wine in the sunroom. I plop down next to her as she starts to fill my glass.

"So do we like Samantha?" Ellen asks me softly.

"No, we do not. We are praying she is a phase." I take a sip of my wine.

After Sam and Will settle in, they decide to join Ellen and I. We go on as though nothing has happened. I crack a tasteless joke and Samantha has had enough. She stands up and looks at us in disgust.

"What is *wrong* with you people? Who laughs and carries on like this when someone dies? Who doesn't want to keep a little bit of someone even if they don't like them? If it wasn't for him, Will, you wouldn't even be here!" She snarls.

Well, Sam, it was nice knowing you.

Will starts laughing. "You're right, Samantha. How unbelievably cruel of me to make light of a situation such as death"—he puts his beer down on a coaster—"to be absolutely relieved that a man has tortured me for twenty-eight years of my life..."

Samantha shifts her gaze in my direction. She knew she has fucked up, royally.

"Has told me that I would never amount to anything except being a loser. I listened to him every day saying how much he never wished I was born, and after a while"—Will begins to laugh again—"it kind of wears and tears on your soul so much you start to believe yourself you wish you were never born."

"Will, I didn't—" Samantha begins.

"Know? Of course, you didn't," Will interrupts, "because you always seem to side with the person who is not of mine. One time, my father looked at me when I was a kid and said, 'God you're ugly, just like your mother,' while my mother was standing right there. He mentally abused us for years and years and years. So no, we are not sad he's gone, as a matter of fact, I wish I was standing over his body before he died just so I could see the life drain out. Knowing that when he was leaving this world, no one, not one person was going to give one fuck that he was gone, because that's how much of a horrible person he was."

"I'm sorry," Samantha says softly.

"Are you?" Will mocks using a baby voice. "You're sorry because you got caught for being dumb?"

"Okay, Will," I step in.

"No, fuck you, Nev," Will snaps. "Fuck him, fuck you. Fuck everyone. Fuck him for never being proud of me. Fuck him for never having one kind thing to say to me. Fuck him for not once telling me he loved me, fuck him for thinking the world was out to get him and always playing the god damn victim." Will leaves the sun room and walks out of the front door.

We follow behind him, stopping at the front door frame. Will stands in the yard for a brief moment and then makes his way toward the street and finds a heavy rock. Picking it up, Will walks back to his father's truck and smashes the driver's window in.

"Oh, stop!" Samantha says, trying to run out after him.

I stop her. "Unless you want to be on the receiving end of that, you need to let this happen, my dude."

He walks around and goes to bash the passenger-side window in, sending shards of glass everywhere. Pulls the tailgate down, gets in the bed and starts smashing the back window. Glass flies everywhere. Will finds a crowbar and starts to hit the top of the cab. Neighbors start to come out of their houses. I slowly move from the doorframe into the grass, carefully trying not to step on any glass. Will hops out of the bed of the truck and starts to hit the sides, denting every inch of the blue Ford.

Every ounce of pent-up rage, every year of pain is let out onto this truck. Nothing is safe from Will's wrath. Next are the taillights. Gone with the flick of the wrist. One, two. Gone. Headlights. One, two. Gone. Windshield, with all his might, he climbs on the top of the hood and goes to town. Kicking and bashing it as hard as he can with the crowbar. Screaming at the top of his lungs until he cannot scream anymore.

Jumping off the blue Ford and sees the spectacle he has caused. "The fuck is you staring at, Gary? Jay has banged your wife so many times her vagina looks like Arby's meat!" Will tosses the crowbar at the neighbor; luckily, he misses.

Will starts to walk through the grass and collapses. With all his might, he lets out an animalistic scream. The screams turn into whimpers. I slowly walk over to him as he wails on the lawn, like a lost child, looking for his mom. I sit in the grass, carefully approaching the wounded man. Will places his head in my lap and grabs my thighs and continues to cry. I stroke his long hair and try to ease his pain.

"Why didn't he love me, Nev?" He cries over and over again.

"Because he was an awful man," I offer, "a miserable, awful man."

"I don't want to be like him." He cries. "I don't want to end up like him."

Ellen comes from the doorway. "All right, shows over. Go back inside your houses." Ellen comes and sits next to Will and me.

There is nothing one can say to a friend when they hurt like this. I want to take his pain and make it mine, but it just doesn't work like that.

I hate Jay. I truly do. He broke a boy before he became a man and damaged a great person. Who does that to a child? If he wasn't dead now, I would kill him myself.

He gets up from the grass and acts like nothing has happened. We go back to the sunroom and continue to drink. Samantha calls it a night and goes up to the bedroom where she and Will are staying in. I can't imagine what the two endured over the years, the bond they have formed in order to survive the hell that Jay has created for them.

I excuse myself. As I ascend up the staircase, for the first time ever, I hear Ellen cry.

"He's gone now. He won't hurt you anymore," I hear Will say in a soft tone.

I pass by Will's room and hear soft little whimpers coming out. *It could be a trap, Nev. She could have heard you coming up the steps and started crying. Don't fall for it. Then again, she could really be hurting right now.* I outweigh the bad and gently tap on the door.

"Oh, come in," Samantha says.

Be cool, Nev. Don't be a dick, and don't be a cunt. You could have kept walking and let her cry this shit out.

"Are you okay?" I gently ask.

Samantha wipes what appears to be a genuine tear. "I think I really fucked up."

I open the door wide enough so my body can fit through. "I mean, yeah. Yeah, you did. I don't know what would possess you to think that was okay to say even if that's not how you grieve."

Samantha looks at me and starts to cry more. "I didn't know, Neveahly. I just thought it was sick that you guys were so happy."

I walk in and sit on the bed next to her. "Imagine being brutality raped. I'm talking over and over again, then imagine your rapist dying. Would you be sad, or would you be elated?"

Samantha's eyes widen. "Oh god, did Jay rape Will?"

I smack forehead on my hand. "Jesus, no. It was a hypothetical. Keep up, Sam. I'm saying this, imagine someone being so horrible to you for so long, and they just die, and the torment stops. They aren't sad, and they don't have to be."

"Oh." She finally gets. "I mean, I guess I can see that."

"Yeah, and then you come in and tell them how to feel? That's not exactly right, is it?" I suggest.

She shakes her head no. "I guess it is rather rude of me."

"Yeah, it is. So not right now, but tomorrow, you should go apologize to Ellen. Will isn't ready for the apology. He probably won't ever forgive you, but Ellen will."

Samantha looks down at the carpet. "So it's probably over between Will and me?"

"I can't say for sure, but I wouldn't hold your breath either," I say honestly. "Just be there for him and stop being so judgmental."

She leans over and gives me a hug. "Thank you," she whispers.

I push her off me. "Yeah, and don't ever do that again." I force a smile as I leave the room.

See, I did a nice thing for someone, and it only cost me a hug. I go into my room and turn off the lights. For the first time in a while, I turn on some background noise, Archer, and fall asleep to the sounds of Mallory Archer barking orders at her team.

I wake up early afternoon. It's the first time in a long time I've slept this late. It wasn't the alcohol because I didn't have a lot of it, but I wasn't feeling that great. I feel kind of sick. I sit up and slowly place my feet on the carpet and get my bearings. I take deep breaths in and out in order for the room to stop spinning. I open my eyes as the room seems a bit brighter than I remember it had been all those years before and blink a couple of times. As I stand up, I feel a wave of nausea hit me like a sack of bricks and make a daring dash to the hall bathroom. I almost knock over Samantha in the process. I barely make it. I'm talking photo-finish-type make it.

With my head in the toilet, and one hand holding my curls back and the other grabbing the bowl, I heave everything that's in my stomach into the water. The blowback hits me in the face and makes me cringe. I gag a little and vomit some more. I hear a light knock on the door.

"You okay, champ?" I hear Will call from behind the cracked door.

"I'm fine," I reply. "I must've eaten something gross." *Shit, what did I eat yesterday?*

"Okay, well, Ellen has some pancakes for you downstairs if you want some," he calls from behind the door. "Do you want some ginger ale?"

"Water would be great," I call. More vomit spews through my mouth.

"All right, well, Jay's ashes are ready. I was just about to wake you up. We are leaving in like an hour. Is that enough time for you?" Will opens the door. "Jesus, you don't have any pants on!"

I close the toilet seat down and flush. "No, I literally just woke up and ran in here. I'll get in the shower, pass on the cakes."

Will scans my body. "Are you sure you're okay? You look like shit."

I flip him off. "Thanks, bro."

He shrugs. "You do."

Will leaves the bathroom and closes the door behind him. I turn on the water full blast and just jump right in. I barely turn on the cold water as the hot steam makes me feel better. I do a quick rinse and clean. I hop out, get dressed quickly, and meet everyone downstairs. Ellen is smiling while she and Will talk; Samantha sits quietly in the corner, watching TV. I kind of feel bad for her now. *Kind of.* I offer her a smile, and she smiles back.

"So how does this work? Do we go over there? Do they just throw them away for us? What?" I ask as I go to the fridge to get some water.

"Unfortunately, we have to go there and pick him up," Ellen says.

"Even in death, he is still an inconvenience." Will rubs the sides of his head. "Goddamn it, are you guys ready?"

"Yup, let's go!" I say as I sip some water.

As we get the bag of ashes, we all just stare at it. When Will and I saw Nick, the emotions were hard-hitting and raw. I had an out-of-body experience; it didn't feel real in any way. Now as we stare at this plastic bag of ashes, I feel nothing. I almost feel disgusted. It looks like kitty litter. Maybe we should make it kitty litter? I probably should bring that up, but Samantha is already having a rough go of it right now; the last thing she really needs to hear is that we should let an animal shit on this man's remains.

"Do you want to keep it, Ellen?" I gently ask.

Tears form in her eyes. Wiping them away, she laughs. "God no, Nev. You know what I want to do? I want to get rid of all his shit upstairs and put it out on the curb."

Will looks at her. "You don't even want a tax break for goodwill?"

"Why would I subject those people who are in a financial crisis already to his shit?"

We all laugh, even Samantha.

"Do you have black trash bags?" I ask.

"Yup, underneath the kitchen sink." Ellen replies.

I shrug. "I'll get the bags and the beers, and let's go to work."

"You know, I think I'm going to stay down here, if you don't mind," Ellen says as she turns on the TV.

I smile. "That's fine. Do you want us to keep anything?"

"Not a fucking thing." She grins.

I head toward the kitchen sink and grab the trash bags, and Will and Samantha grab the beer. We race up the steps and dart into the bedroom.

I fling the door open, and it's kind of a mess. His shit is everywhere on his side, while Ellen's side is immaculate. There is order to this chaos. I take out a trash bag and start putting all his belongings into it. Without even thinking, just putting shirts, jeans, everything into the bags. I even put his pillows into the bags. Toothbrush? In the bag. Everything.

Will did the same. I turn on some music to make the atmosphere a little lighter. Nineties pop music. I know Will is going to give me some shit for it, but he ends up bopping his head to some of it. He starts laughing.

"What's so funny?" I ask.

"Do you remember the movie *Taken*?" He sits on the bed.

I stuff another shirt into a new bag. "Yeah? What about it?"

"The whole reason they were in Europe was because of U2. Two fucking young girls were traveling to Europe to see U2 the band." Will starts howling in laughter.

I start laughing at him. "And you remember this because?"

He holds up a U2 band shirt. "It was Jay's favorite fucking band."

I cannot help but join in. "Who in that writing room was like, you know young girls fuckin' love? Bono."

Samantha starts to laugh.

Will can barely breathe. "Right? You literally had any choice of bands, and you picked U2? How out of touch do you have to be with the younger audience to think we like this shit?"

We all start laughing uncontrollably. After a few minutes, the laughter dies down, and the room falls silent.

I continue to shove T-shirts and whatever I can find into the black bags. "Seriously, that band really does suck though."

"I don't know. They have a couple of good songs. I like 'Losing My Religion,'" Samantha says as she closes her bag.

"That's REM," I remind her.

"Oh, then yeah, they totally suck," she agrees.

We finally finish with twenty bags. We toss them off the side of the rail and watch them fall on the main floor. The three of us hustle down the stairs and bring them to the curb. A couple of trips later, we have completely eradicated Jay's belongings from the home. The only thing that remains, are, well, his remains.

"So about the ashes, Ma, I have an idea." Will looks at Ellen. "Let's flush him."

Ellen laughs. "Are you serious?"

"He was a piece of shit in life, and what more of a fitting way to go out is to be flushed down like a shit he was?"

Ellen thinks about it for a second. "Okay. Which bathroom?"

"Up to you. He was your husband," Will offers.

Ellen stands up. "Meh, the one over there is closer. Let's do that one."

We all take a few steps and stand outside the bathroom.

"He's going to be a few flushes," Ellen jokes. "It's a lot to flush at once."

"Do you want to say anything?" Ellen asks Will.

"Nope, give me the bag." Will grabs the bag from Ellen and starts to pour the ashes in the toilet.

No words were said, no prayer was given, just a couple of pours, and down he went. We jam into the bathroom and watched Jay swirl around the toilet bowl until he was no longer here. Every piece of Ash flushed. I looked over and saw a smile that rested on Ellen's face. All the hate and torture simply gone with only a few flushes.

CHAPTER 12

I called it. Samantha and Will break up the moment we touch down in DC. There is no theatrics; there is no crying. It is a clean cut. They both agree the relationship went on longer than it should, and they are two very different people. He did thank her for being there for him and hopes that someday she will make it in Hollywood. Needless to say, the drive back to our apartment was awkward. *Jesus, Will, you couldn't wait until we got to our apartment to break up with her? Nope. We land, he turns to her and says it's over.*

Will calls her a Lyft and pays for it while he helps her take all her things down that she has slowly tried to move in. He shows no emotion as she leaves. I don't know if I should be frightened or proud at this moment. With a hug and a kiss, Samantha is no more. Will goes into his bedroom and locks himself in. *Okay, bud, I guess I will check on you later.*

I get Will's keys and drive to our shop. It's not that late in the evening, and I figured I could just check some emails and clean if it is needed. It was a quick drive; the traffic was light. *I guess the skins were having an away game this week.*

I walk in the store and head back to the office. I notice I start to feel the same way I did at Will's, but this time with a headache. My vision becomes blurry, and my legs become weak. *Ah, shit, I should have told Will where I was going. This was a bad idea.* I use the wall to help me get to the office. I take three more steps to make it to the swivel chair and sit down. Drenched in my own seat, I steady my breathing. *Is this alcohol withdrawal? This cannot be alcohol withdrawal. No freaking way.* I go in the second cabinet to our emergency stash of greenery. By the grace of God, we have one joint left. I grab it and light it up. I inhale slowly. As I slouch down in the chair, I try to relax every bone in my body.

Goddamn it, I'm trying to do work, and I get sick? Can this be from flying in a short amount of time? Or not wearing the right clothes? I feel my phone vibrate; I look down to see Jon is calling me.

"Hey, babe, how are you?"

"Jeez, you don't sound great," he says, worried. "You okay?"

"Yeah, I just haven't been feeling the best," I admit. "I decided to come to work to check on some emails so I can get a head start for tomorrow."

He laughs. "Or you could have just gone home to rest? Because I'm guessing that's where Will is right now."

"Yeah, he broke up with Samantha." I turn on the computer and take another puff.

"Are you serious? When?" Jon asks. It's kind of loud where he is.

"The minute the wheels hit the tarmac, he turned to her and said it's over. It was an awkward ride home."

Jon laughs. "I bet." Jon moves away from the noise. "So I got good news and bad news."

"Hit me with the bad news first." I take a really long drag and hold it in.

"I can't come down for Thanksgiving. This production is taking a lot longer than I expected, and we will be shooting that day."

I exhale. "And the good news is?"

"I am all yours the entire weekend, and Christmas. Well, Festivus," Jon says cheerfully.

My mood perks up. "Okay, I can live with that. I guess Will and I can do our Thanksgiving tradition."

Jon laughs. "You guys still do that?"

"It is a tradition. Of course, we do!" I dig in the draw to find the ashtray. "But I get you the whole weekend?"

"Yes, ma'am," he agrees.

"And we can go skating on the mall?" I ask, even though I know that's exactly what we are going to do.

"I hope you know, I'm an awesome skater," he brags.

I laugh. "Calm down, Brian Boitano."

"I gotta go, but I love you. Get some rest, okay? Don't make me call Will to tell you to get in bed."

"Scouts honor! Sorry, I'm doing the scout's honor thing, but I realize I'm on the phone with you, and you can't see that."

"Love you." Jon laughs and hangs up.

I laugh and toss my phone on the desk. I scroll through some emails and respond to some authors who would like to come to the shop to showcase their books. Self-published, and I tell them I'm completely down with that. I order more cups and plates. I scroll through Amazon looking at shit I don't need and then log off for the day.

I feel my stomach start to tighten, and then, it dawns on me: when was my last period? I grab my phone and check my calendar. I click on it to see the last log in for my period and calculate I'm six weeks late. Maybe more, I'm not that great with Math. A wave of nausea overcomes me, and I fall to the floor. I start to sweat and lie there and panic. *Okay, so what causes missed periods? Stress. I lost one my best friends. Drinking. I have been drinking so much lately it's crazy. Did Jon and I use a condom?* I close my eyes, trying to remember all the times we've had sex, and not once we used one. Oh, goddamn it. Maybe he got a vasectomy and forgot to tell me? That's a thing, right?

I got to get off this floor. I got to get off this floor. Just go to the drugstore and buy a test and save it for later. I mean, you aren't getting any younger? And you also hate children, Neveahly.

I slowly get up from the ground, and immediately go into autopilot. The next thing I know I am lying in my bed, praying for the wave of nausea to pass. *Whatever you do, don't tell Will. Just play it cool. I will deal with this later. I'm just going to go to bed. That's what the fuck I should have done when I got home.*

Waking up the next morning, I find Will sitting in the kitchen already with a cup of coffee in his hand, reading his iPad. I didn't even bother trying to look decent today. I feel like the ass end of a cow. I grab a cup myself and join him. I slide down on into the chair, trying not to make eye contact as I look at my phone.

"What's wrong with you?" he asks.

"Nothing,"

"Really? Because you look like shit." He probes some more.

"I guess I caught a bug or some shit. I'll be fine," I keep my eyes down on my screen. Pretending to scroll through social media.

He puts down the iPad. "Nev, you never get sick. The last time you got sick was in Florida, and you were in the hospital for a week."

I put my phone down. "I am aware of this, William. I just don't feel good. That's all. I'll go to CVS and pick some medicine up."

He stares at me some more as I pick up my phone and continue to sip and scroll. We finish our drinks and exit the apartment. As we load into the car, the car ride was silent to the store. *I haven't really been eating that well either. Maybe if I put more veggies in my diet and less fast foods, that would help.*

As we pull up, Will walks in, and I walk the few stores down to CVS. As I walk in, I put my hood and shades on as I book it to the family planning aisle. *I mean, really, Neveahly, you're a whole-ass woman. Women get pregnant all the time.* I look at all the options as I stand in there, nervous to even check my fate. I start biting my nail as a worker comes up to me.

"Can I help you find something?" she asks politely.

I jump. "What? No. I'm just looking," I quickly say. "I mean, I'm not just looking. I'm going to buy one of these. I just don't know which one yet."

"Okay," she says slowly. "Let me know if you need any help." She walks away.

Okay, Nev. They are all pretty much the same, so just pick a fucking box. I grab three, just to be safe, and all digital so I am clear with the results. I need a straight answer: pregnant or *not* pregnant. I take them up to the front, and the same woman rings me up. I constantly look around to make sure no one I know sees me. I grab the plastic bag and shove it into my purse and I pull my hood further down on my face as quickly leave.

Just make it through the day and take them tomorrow morning. I walk in to find Will standing behind the counter ringing up a customer. I am able to escape to the back office without being seen. I slowly shut the door behind me. *Fuck me, I completely forgot to get any form of medication.* I cannot help but laugh.

I've been on edge all day. Will can sense it, and it's getting harder and harder to keep this from him. As we close up, I rush through the process of closing as if it will bring tomorrow morning faster. As if somehow, I can time bend and *poof!* It's morning. Will finally steps in front of me as I frantically clean.

"Okay, enough is enough. Either you tell me what is going on with you, or I play bird is the word on a loop when we get home," he threatens.

C'mon, think of a good lie.

"Dude, if I knew, I would tell you, but I don't." *Not exactly a lie because I don't know what is wrong with me.*

"Well, go to the doctor. We have health insurance," Will demands.

As soon as I step inside the apartment, I give a half wave and a goodnight as I make my way to the bedroom. I shut my bedroom door and start pacing back and forth. *Okay, keep calm. Just take the test in the morning. I read somewhere that it's best to do it first thing in the morning. You should probably call Jon and let him know what's going on. Or just wait until you actually take the test. No, a phone call is not how someone should find out they are a dad. Text message. No, that's a shitty thing to do. FaceTime?* I jump when my phone rings. It's Jon.

"I was just thinking about you." I try to sound not so nervous.

"Really? That's probably why I called. That, and Will said you are acting weirder than normal," Jon confesses.

"Oh, did he?" I raise an eyebrow. "I wouldn't say weird. I think it's a mix of being tired and still not feeling super good and missing you, that's all. He's such a worrier."

Jon laughs. "I figured, but I was going to call you anyway to tell you I love you and that I can't wait to see you in a couple of weeks."

"Me either." I hear a booming voice calling everyone to places.

"Okay, I love you. I'll talk to you tomorrow." He hangs up fast.

I throw the phone on the bed and fall next to it. I stare up at the ceiling with my hand behind my head.

I wake up the next morning, barely able to move my arm. I grab my phone and realize I overslept. I don't even care at this point as I slowly slide off the side of my bed. I walk out into the living room to grab two red solo cups off the beer pong table and rush back into my bedroom. I take the pregnancy tests out of my purse and into the bathroom with me.

I look at the red solo cup and plan to fill it up as much as I can. *It's like the piss tests your parents gave you in high school, Nev. You got this.* I place the cup between my thighs as I sit on the toilet. I struggle to pee. *Seriously? Now you have a shy bladder?* I think of oceans, rivers; anything with running water, and soon I'm filling up the cup. I put it gently in front of me, and flush the toilet. I bring it to the sink and dip every stick that comes in the kit in the cup and cap them up. *Now I wait.* I watch them all have the loading sign. As I wait, I wash my hands and pour the rest of the urine back into the toilet and flush again.

Okay, just be cool. Just relax. Everything will be fine no matter what the outcome is, Nev. Whether you're pregnant or not, whether Jon is with you or not, you got this. Also, adoption is an option. You will get through this. The anticipation is killing me. I feel the palms of my hands start to get sweaty, my heart starts to race, and nausea starts to set in.

After sweating through my t-shirt, I decide to take a shower. I just stand there, letting the water hit me as I stare at the blue-and-white tiles before me. I think about my future with Jon. If there is going to be one, once I flip the tests over. I turn off the water and get out.

I come back to the tests and flip them all over. *Oh well, isn't this good news!*

Will and I go from aisle to aisle as we get our things for our Thanksgiving Day tradition. He's talking a mile a minute about his script he submitted to this competition and how he thinks he has a chance of winning, and I am not remotely listening to him. We come up to the beer, and he loads up the cart with our favorite beer.

"So do you think I'll win?" he asks.

"I don't see why not." I shrug. "You're a talented writer, bro."

"Right?" He grabs a couple of bottles of wine. "They announce the winner in, like, two weeks."

I stop the cart. "Wait, so you did a late entry? You never do that shit."

He shrugs. "And I had to do a video submission."

I turn down the candy aisle and load a ton of chocolate in. "What? You hate doing those."

"I know, but sometimes they are worth it. I mean, not all the times, but sometimes."

Will watches me as I load up on sweets. "Jesus, did your period just start?"

"What? No. I just want chocolate." I start pushing the cart.

Will steps at the end of it. "You and Jon didn't break up, did you?"

I laugh. "No, we didn't break up. He's talking about moving down here."

Will lets out a sigh of relief. "Okay. Because he really likes you."

"Good, because I really like him."

We make it to the checkout line and end up spending over seventy-five dollars on alcohol alone. As I push the cart to Will's SUV, I realize how gloomy and gross the November day is. November is always gloomy in DC. We start to load the groceries in the back and in the trunk.

"Would you move in with him?" Will asks.

"I don't know. I like living with you," I say. "We've only been dating for a couple of months anyway."

"But you've known him for eight years," Will points out.

"Okay, but that's not the same as dating," I retort.

Will sighs. "Actually, it's kind of better." He slams the trunk down. "Not only have you seen him at his worst, you know all his bad habits, and you still like him."

I laugh. "I mean, yeah, you could look at it that way."

Will starts to drive back to the apartment.

"You've heard him snore," Will continues. "And technically, you have lived with him before. Just with two other roommates. It wouldn't be that much different if you two just moved in together."

"Wait, are you saying you don't want to be roommates anymore?" I start to tear up.

Jesus, stop being so emotional, Nevie.

"What? No. I'm just saying, your points are invalid." Will steers the gas guzzling machine into the garage.

I roll my eyes and wipe the tears away. "Okay, what if he gets sick of me?"

"Jesus, are you that damaged like I am? He's not going to get sick of you." Will finds a parking space close to the elevator.

"I'm just saying, all good things must come to an end, am I right?" I hop out and start to load my arms with bags of groceries.

"No, they don't. Especially when a good man is involved." Will grabs the groceries out of the trunk.

We wait for the elevator in silence. As we get in front of our door, I make a mad dash to the kitchen island and drop the groceries on it before the plastic bags rip open and spill the contents on the floor. My arms feel heavier than a twenty-pound bag of rocks.

I start to put the food away as Will begins to pound down some beers. He turns on some tunes.

"Hey, do you mind if I go out tonight?" he asks, looking down at his phone.

I laugh. "I'm not your mom. You are more than capable of making somewhat decent decisions."

"Cool, cool, cool, cool. I've got another Tinder date," Will says slowly.

I groan. "Oh, come on, dude. What did we learn from last time?"

"To be fair, she really was supposed to be a hit it and quit it," Will admits, "but it just lasted way longer than expected."

I roll my eyes. "New rule: no more bringing them home until like three dates in."

"Deal." He starts heading toward the door.

"So I have to put everything away?" I ask.

"You got this," Will says as scurries out the apartment. I sigh and finish putting away the groceries.

As I clean up the apartment, I decide to make some sloppy joes for the night. I sprawl out on the couch watching TV and a glass of wine resting carefully between my fingers. I look down at my phone to see it's getting rather late. Will left around seven, and it's almost midnight. I decide to watch one more episode of *Pretty Little Liars*.

I pull the blanket off the top of the couch and snuggle up for another episode. The screen pops up with: "Are you still watching?" Of course, Netflix, I am still watching. Honestly, it's kind of rude to ask and bold of you to assume that I have a life. As I continue to watch, a teacher take advantage of his authoritative power over a young student because that's exactly what the relationship is; I hear banging at the door. I kick the covers off me and look through the peephole. Will. *Jesus.* I open the door.

"Nev," he draws out, "What's up?"

"Why didn't you use your keys?"

Will busts through the door and walks over to the couch. "Because I knew you were going to be up."

"What? How did you know?"

"Are you not watching *Pretty Little Liars* right now?" He stammers. Will starts to pull off his shoes and throws them at the door.

"Oh my god, what did you drink tonight?" I walk back over to my side of the couch.

"Honestly, I don't even remember, but it was good." He grabs a fry off my plate.

I slap his hand. "Stop eating my food. If you're gonna sit here and watch the show with me, then shut up."

"Wait, ask me about my date." He turns and looks at me.

I roll my eyes and let out an exaggerated sigh as I pause my show, "How was the date, William?"

"Awful. Now we can watch *PLL*." Will slurs his speech. He grabs the remote from me and presses play.

I reach over him and try to grab it back. He holds it over his head and strong-arms me. I try to karate-chop his arm, but it's too strong. Will begins to laugh and tosses the remote to the other hand. *Goddamn it! His arm span is so fucking wide! It's got an entire foot on me!* I pounce on his arm and grab the remote.

"Now was that so hard?" He laughs.

"I hate you." I laugh with him.

He starts to annoy me by poking me. I swat his hand away as I try to focus on the show. Will stops for a second and goes back to being annoying. He keeps poking me at my side, tickling me.

"Bro, I'm trying to watch the show!" I yell at him.

"Okay, okay," he says as he tries not to laugh. "I'll stop."

He holds his finger next to my eye. "Is this annoying? I'm not touching you!"

I swat his hand away again. "Oh my god! What are you, like five? It's like having Asher here with me! Jesus!"

Will wraps his arms around me. "You know you love me!"

"Ugh, get off me." I playfully push him off. "Did you have tequila tonight?"

"Yeah, like five shots of it," he admits.

"That explains a lot, you get so annoying when you drink tequila." I play the TV show once again.

Will grabs the remote again and holds it over his head. I try to reach for it. He starts to lean onto his side as I climb on top of him. I realize how much I am in his personal space, as the laughter slowly stops. I gaze into his blue eyes. I never really noticed how blue they were. I feel my heart begin to race. I get off him and move back to my spot on the couch.

"I probably should go to bed," I say softly.

"Yeah, me too." He throws the remote to me.

I turn off the TV. "So same time like we normally do every year?"

"Yup," he says, looking at the dark screen.

I walk back to my room. I hear Will get up from the couch, but his footsteps aren't going toward his bedroom. I turn around, and he spins me around and kisses me. I don't push him away. I feel him pull me close as I put my arms around his neck. I feel his hand grab the back of my head as he kisses me deeply. *What in the fuck are you doing, Neveahly Skye Walker?* I start to take his jacket off as his lips move down my neck, and our steps move closer to my bedroom. Will picks me up as he gently pushes me up against the wall. *Stop, you gotta put a stop to this.* I feel his hands start to lift my shirt up as

I reach down toward his belt. *Dude, Neveahly, you gotta stop.* I come back to my senses and push him off me.

"Wait, dude," I say softly, letting my feet hit the floor.

He keeps kissing me. "Yeah?"

I pull back and push him away. "I'm pregnant."

He stops at the halfway mark, trying to take off his shirt. Will slowly put it back down, covering his chest. "Look, I know kissing leads to making babies, but the actual kiss itself, Nev—"

"What?" I shake my head. "Okay, we need to go over later how babies are made, but yeah. I'm pregnant."

He stares at me. "Kissing doesn't cause pregnancies, right?"

"You cannot be that fucking drunk. No, it doesn't. Jon and I had unprotected sex, which led to pregnancy."

"Oh." He draws out.

A light bulb goes off in his head. "Holy shit! Does Jon know?"

"No, I am going to tell him when I see him next. Also, we are friends, dude. We can't do this," I remind him.

Will leans against the wall and bangs his head. "Dude, I'm sorry. I don't know what I was thinking."

"It's okay. It was hot though," I admit.

"Right? So hot!"

"But it's not happening again," I warn.

"No, never again," Will agrees.

"Also, you're super wasted, and we can have this conversation again in the morning." I tap him on top of the head.

"Okay, but congratulations!" Will says as he starts to walk back to his room.

I give him a thumbs up as I close my bedroom door behind me.

Thanksgiving. The day where it's completely okay to overeat and start family fights over politics and throw shade at family members you do not like, or is it just my family? That's why I don't go over there. I haven't been to a family Thanksgiving in over eight years. I think the last one I went to was when I was in college. The guys came up with me, and my mom's husband (my stepdad) was there and acting like a complete asshole. Me, being the complete "hair dyeing, no one should die because they can't pay for medical insurance"-type person I am, versus his "well, when I was your age, I had to walk [insert a fake number of miles to school] and work hard for what I wanted." Movies are for hippies, and writing is a fantasy. Get a real job. Yeah, dinner didn't go over too well. I never looked back, and all I do is send a text message, if that.

I wake up this year feeling the morning sickness. I lie in bed, praying for the wave of nausea to go away so I can start my day in my pajamas on the couch, watching the Macy's Day Parade, beer pong, and smoking. Well, now today will definitely be altered due to my current situation of dumbassery. I mean, no, all God's children are no accidents or whatever. As my hearing gets fuzzy, I bolt to the bathroom, cupping my hand over my mouth as the vomit spills out, barely making it.

I heave into the toilet bowl. *Is this going to be my life for the next nine months?* I stay there for a bit to make sure I don't have any residual vomit making its way out of my throat. Feeling confident that I'm absolutely done vomiting, I slowly rise from the floor. I hold on to the sink as I brush my teeth and wash my face. I zombie-walk my way to the living room. *Well, I guess no drinking or smoking or anything of fun today.* Grabbing the entire bottle of ginger ale and a sleeve of crackers, I shuffle my way to the couch and sprawl out. I reach for the remote on the coffee table and turn on the TV just in time for the parade's first round of musical numbers. I turn up the volume in hopes it will wake up Will so I don't have to watch it alone.

First number is amazing. I forgot how much I love Broadway and how much I love *The Book of Mormon. Beetlejuice* comes on, and I sit up. *I didn't know they made this a musical.* Beads of sweat form on my upper lip. My phone rings, and I look down to see it's Jon. No one else actually calls me but him. My arms feel like they are in cement, and I can barely answer it in time. I take a couple of deep breaths before answering it.

"Hey, Happy Turkey Day," I say, out of breath.

"Hey, did you race for the phone?"

"Yup," I lie. "I heard it from the kitchen, and I dove onto the bed. How are you?"

He laughs. "I would've called you back. I'm good. I miss you a lot, but I'm good. I can't wait to see you tomorrow!"

I hear a knock at the door. I groan. "I think Will went back out again and forgot his keys. He did it again last night. Like, dude, how hard is it to remember your keys?"

I open the door, irritated, and there he is. Jon. I start to cry.

"Surprise," he says into the phone.

I pull him into the door and kiss him. I take his bag off his shoulder. We stumble back onto the couch as I struggle to take off his jacket. *Oh no, please, vomit. Not now. Not at this second.* I keep going as Jon starts to kiss my neck. I sit up a bit, hoping I could stop the cold sweat from forming, but it happens anyway. *Ah, shit. Here it comes.* I stop kissing Jon and run into my bathroom. I'm not a quiet vomiter either. I'm very loud; even when I try to close my bedroom door and the bathroom door, I still feel like people can hear me. I turn on the faucet to muffle the sounds. I have nothing left in my stomach and flush. I hear Jon open my bedroom door and knock on the bathroom.

"I know I haven't showered in two days, but I don't smell that bad," he jokes.

I laugh. "No, you don't smell bad at all. I'm just fighting this stomach bug."

I splash some cold water on my face and start brushing my teeth again.

I open the door and pretend like nothing happened. "So did the production wrap up early? Or what?"

I make my way toward the bed, slowly sliding on, making sure the motion of the ocean doesn't start the tidal wave of nausea all over again.

"Uh, yeah, we finished ahead of schedule. So we're not going to talk about it?"

"About what?" I play dumb.

"How we were getting hot and heavy, and you decided to throw up," he reminds me.

"Oh, I feel better now," I say cheerfully.

"That maybe so, but still the fact that it happened is probably not normal?"

I shrug. "I don't know. I used to throw up all the time as a kid. I had the weirdest stomach."

Not a total lie. I did throw up in the monkey house at the National Zoo because the smell of shit had gotten to me.

"Okay," he says slowly. "I thought you would be at least a bottle of wine deep by now. It's ten in the morning. You and Will are somewhat hammered this time of day on Thanksgiving," Jon presses.

I lay back, putting my head on my pillow. "Will was super drunk last night. I highly doubt he will be going any type of hard today."

"Okay, so do you want to play beer pong?" Jon asks as he slides on the other side of the bed.

"Not really." I close my eyes, trying to get the room to stop spinning again.

He leans on his side and looks at me. "Is there something wrong? Look, whatever it is, you can tell me. I feel like you've been sick for a while now. Have you been to the doctors?"

"Nope," I admit.

"Are you going to go?" Jon presses.

"Probably not."

"Neveahly Skye Walker."

"Jonathan Allan Flay," I match his tone.

"So you're just going to be sick until you feel better?" Jon asks with a hint of sarcasm in his voice.

"Yeah, I mean, isn't that the adult thing to do?" I lean over to face him, slowly.

Jon laughs. "No, go to the doctor."

"But why?" I groan.

"Because why be miserable?"

I sigh and stare at him. We have an intense staredown. *I can win this. I am the queen of staredowns.* With his soft hazel eyes, Jon moves his hand onto mine. *Ah, shit, I gotta tell him.*

I sit up. "Okay, I gotta tell you something, and you have to be cool about it, okay?"

Jon sits up. "What's up?"

I sigh. "I'm dying. I've got six months to live and—"

Jon laughs and playfully pushes me. "Stop." He kisses my hand. "C'mon, whatever it is, it can't be that bad. It's not like you're pregnant."

The room falls silent. My gaze breaks away from his, and I feel my face become red and my mouth run dry. Jon leans over and tries to look me in the eyes, but I refuse to meet his gaze.

"Nev, look at me," he says in a singsong tone.

I take a deep breath. I exhale with a laugh. "But what if I was pregnant?"

Jon laughs and realizes I'm not joking. "Holy shit, you're serious."

"Yeah," I say slowly.

His face goes completely white, as if he's going to pass out. I move the pillow on my lap so he can lay down. Jon puts his head in my lap and curls into a ball.

"You okay?" I ask.

"I feel like I'm going to vomit."

"Welcome to the club," I mutter.

He springs back up. "How long have you known? When did you find out?"

"Well, a couple of weeks now, and I took not one, not two, but three tests." I get up and go into the bathroom. I come back with all three tests so he can see them.

Jon grabs them from me and looks at all of them. "Wait did you pee on these?"

"Yeah, I mean, that's kind of the general idea of taking a home pregnancy test."

"Well, I don't know how this works, Nevie!" he exclaims. "I'm sorry. I didn't mean to raise my voice."

"It's okay. I've had weeks to process this. You just got this news."

He looks at me and smiles. "Holy shit, you're pregnant."

"Yeah, looks to be that way." I sigh. "I mean, we have options though. We just started dating—"

"Nev, we have been friends for almost a decade," Jon interrupts.

"Yeah, Will said the exact same thing."

Jon's mouth drops. "Will knows?"

Ah, shit. Backtrack, Nev.

"By accident, it slipped out. He kept forcing alcohol on me, and I had to tell him," I lie.

"Fair," Jon agrees. "It's not like I'm some stranger."

"Also, true," I acknowledge.

"So"—Jon grabs my hands—"this isn't exactly how I wanted the order to go, but we can make it work if you are willing to try?"

I give a half smile. "I don't want me to be the reason you give up your career."

"I'm not giving up my career, Nevie. I'm just adding a family with it," Jon says.

I lean in to kiss him deeply. "That is the corniest shit I have ever heard, but also super sweet. We can make this work. Career and family. I will never make you choose."

"Well, it would be you guys if it came down to it," Jon says without missing a beat.

"Again, I would never make you choose," I reiterate.

Jon gives me a kiss on my forehead, and my entire body begins to relax for the first time in weeks. I feel as though a huge weight has been lifted off my shoulders, and I'm no longer keeping this big secret from him. We lay back on the bed and sit in silence. I feel myself start to doze off in Jon's arms.

As I come back to the realm of the living, I hear Jon snoring loudly next to me. I smile as I slowly slide from his gentle grip. I get up quietly, trying to let him sleep; he immediately wakes up.

"Where are you going?" he says, half-asleep.

I laugh. "To the bathroom."

Jon puts his head back on the pillow. I decide to take a quick shower since I'm in there. After throwing up all morning, I feel so gross. I hop in and out within five minutes and wrap the towel around my body. I take my hand and wipe the steam off the mirror and just stare at myself. Unable to recognize the person in front of me. *Holy shit. Me. Neveahly Skye Walker, a mom. Literally one of the last things I ever wanted to be on this planet. Although there could be worst things. I can't think of any, but there could be worse.*

I open the door and see Jon is still knocked out. I go into my dresser drawers and grab a pair of sweats and an oversize T-shirt and slip the clothing onto my body. I wrap the towel on my head and tiptoe out into the living room where I find Will sitting on the couch in his boxers.

"Where are your clothes, bro?" I ask as I continue to walk to the fridge.

"In the bedroom where the rest of my wardrobe is."

I grab a bottle of Gatorade out of the fridge and drink it slowly. "Jon is in my bedroom, sleeping right now."

Will turns his head and faces me. "Oh yeah? Does he know?"

I nod. "Indeed he does. He took it rather well, actually."

Will laughs. "I knew he would. He is the dad type. Did he say he would choose you over his career?"

I stop drinking and put the bottle down on the island. "Yeah, how did you know that?"

Will turns back to the TV. "Nev, I don't think you understand how much that man loves you."

I narrow my eyes and book it over to Will. I step in front of the TV. "Do you know something?"

Will tries to lean over to look around me. "Know what? Could you move?"

"I don't know, anything?" I pry.

Will pauses the TV. "I don't know shit."

I glare at him. "But you would tell me if you knew something, right?"

Will laughs. "Like what, Neveahly? If he was going to propose? I guess. He knows you hate marriage."

I move from the TV and sit next to him. "It's a barbaric and archaic—"

"And ancient practice, yeah, I know," Will finishes. "You've been saying this since college, bro. Did you ever think with the right person it could be maybe okay?"

I laugh. "Says the guy who never wants to get married."

"Yeah, marriage isn't for me. I want to die with a hot chick fucking me while she's on top, but for you, I want that."

I sit there, a little grossed out by Will's words but taken aback by his sincerity. We sit and watch A Charlie Brown Thanksgiving, waiting for Jon to wake up. *Should I bring up last night? Does he even remember, or should I just let it go?*

A couple of hours go by, and Jon emerges from my bedroom. I'm not sure when he took off all his clothes, but he comes out in nothing but his boxers.

I laugh. "I honestly love how comfortable you guys are around me."

Jon slides in the middle of Will and me. "What's up, dude?"

"Not much. Congrats for pumping a baby into Nev." Will gives Jon a high five.

"Thanks, man," Jon says as he puts one arm around me. "What are you guys doing?"

"We were watching *A Charlie Brown Thanksgiving*, but now we are watching *Malibu's Most Wanted*," I say.

Jon laughs. "Are you guys hungry?"

"Yeah," Will says, "I guess we should eat something Thanksgiving-y?"

I nod. "I honestly would love a Thanksgiving Day sandwich. Remember that place down in Florida? They served it all year round! God, that place used to be the shit when we would get high, or drunk."

"Oh yeah!" Will exclaims. "I think it was Pom Poms. It was so good!"

"Do you have anything like that up here?" Jon inquires.

I laugh. "What? No. We could probably make something like that, though."

I grab Will's phone off the coffee table.

"Yeah, sure, go ahead and use my phone," Will says sarcastically.

I scroll through Grubhub and look for a place that would possibly serve all Thanksgiving food. Boston Market was on the list for once, so I place the order, a large one at that, and wait for them to bring the food. I throw Will's phone back on the table. Jon and Will look at me.

"What?" I ask.

"Are you not going to ask us what we want?" Will asks.

I laugh. "I'm sorry, was I supposed to? It's Thanksgiving. What else could you possibly want?"

"She does have a point," Jon says. "There's only so much we could ask for."

"Don't side with her just because you pumped a baby into her," Will says defensively.

"Please stop saying that," I say with disgust.

"What? He did!" Will reiterates. "His sperm met your egg, and therefore you have a baby inside your vagina."

"I have questions on where you think this baby actually is placed inside my body," I say as I try not to laugh.

Will looks at me. "Is it not inside your vagina?"

I laugh and realize he's serious. "Jesus, dude, what the fuck did they teach you in Catholic school about the reproductive system?"

"Apparently not the right shit," Will says.

Forty-five minutes go by before there is a knock on the door. I leap up from the couch to answer it. I rip the bag from the delivery guy's hands and unintentionally slam the door in his face. Racing over to the island, I grab the somewhat fresh bread from the bread box and begin to create the masterpiece I remember from all those years ago. Will and Jon slowly peel themselves from the couch.

I toast the bread as I lay out all the food out that was in the bag. Turkey, mashed potatoes, candied yams, cranberry sauce, stuffing, and the gravy: all in a perfect row. The bread pops up from the toaster; I glide as if on air to pluck them out of the black box. Placing them down on the brown island top, I slowly spread the mashed potatoes first and then the turkey. Carefully, I place the yams on the warm bread and then the cranberry sauce. The stuffing sits beautifully on top while I take the second piece of toast and place it on. Gently, I push down on it, having a little bit of ooze coming from the side. A little smile creeps across my face.

"Is it me, or do I find it kind of creepy how Nev is so happy right now?" Will asks Jon.

Jon laughs. "It is both creepy and cute?"

"Silence!" I half whisper.

I grab a knife from the side drawer and slice the beautifully built sandwich. I take one of the pieces and dip it on the gravy and bring it to my mouth.

"Holy fuck, this is amazing," I say with food in my mouth.

"So are you going to make us one?" Jon asks.

I snap back to reality. "Oh shit, you guys wanted one?"

Will sighs. "Jon, I'll make us one. Preggo over here is in her own little world."

I continue to eat my sandwich and sway back and forth in glee.

"Can I have a bite?" Jon asks.

I stare at him and think about it. "Sure." I move my hands over to his mouth, holding only where he is allowed to take a bite.

Jon looks at me. "Nev, seriously? That's such a small piece."

"Take it or leave it, babe."

Jon sighs and takes a bite. He lets out a little moan and grabs the sandwich from me and takes a huge bite. My mouth flies open. I pick up the second half of the sandwich.

"Holy shit, that is pretty good," Jon admits.

"I told you!"

"So am I making two or just one?" Will asks.

"Three. Jon took half of mine, and I'm going to need another one."

Will lets out an annoyed sigh. "Fine."

All three of us sit at the island and eat our Thanksgiving Day sandwich. We sit and chat for a bit to catch up on how we all have been doing. Well, mostly Jon and Will as I sit in euphoria with my sandwich. I hardly contribute to the conversation.

For once, I am able to keep everything down. A mixture of ginger ale, Gatorade, and an amazing Thanksgiving Day sandwich. Jon and I retire back into my bedroom.

Jon and I lay in my bed with the TV on as I scroll through Google on my laptop, looking for OBGYNs. The list is overwhelming, and I don't even know what to look for in a doctor. I mean, I don't want an asshole for a doctor, but that goes without saying. I start to chew on my thumbnail, Jon turns and sees a worried look on my face.

"What's wrong?" he asks.

"There's, so many fucking doctors, and I don't know what to do," I admit.

Jon leans in to look at my laptop screen. "Well, look for someone who is local?"

I laugh. "Gee, that's so helpful."

He shrugs. "Well, I'm just as green as you are!"

I look at him. "Point taken."

"Do you want a female doctor or a male?" he asks as he takes the laptop from me.

I laugh. "I definitely don't want Dr. McDreamy staring at my lady parts, so female."

"Good point." Jon scrolls some more. "Well, how about this one?" He clicks on a practice.

"That's a doula," I point out.

"What's the difference?" he genuinely asks.

"Honestly, I'm not sure, but no, keep looking." I put my head on his shoulder.

He stops scrolling. I look at him. "Or you could stop?"

"How about we just find out how far along you are for right now?" he suggests.

I nod my head. "I like that idea, but why not find a doctor though?"

He closes my laptop. "Now hear me out—"

"Jesus Christ"—I sit up—"every time you or Will say, 'Hear me out,' it either leads to a drunken night or us running from the cops."

"Fair, but not this time. What is keeping us in DC?" he asks.

"My store, I guess."

"Okay, what about your family?" Jon inquires.

I laugh and see he's serious. "Oh my god, you're serious. Jon, I haven't talked to them in over a year. I could care less."

"So our kid's not going to know that side of the family?"

"I mean"—I think of how I can carefully navigate this—"I guess our child can know Asher, but that's about it. Where are you exactly going with this?"

"I'm just saying, you could sell the bookstore, and we could take that and move to California." Jon looks at me, trying to gauge my reaction.

I ponder this idea. Will and I can actually write movies, and Jon can help shoot them. This is literally the dream life we all have been wanting. On the flip side of the coin, we are taking this on a gamble. We can completely fail, with a baby in the mix and a mortgage and bills, with no safety net.

"This is a huge gamble, dude," I finally say.

"I know," Jon says softly. "I also know this is your grandfather's store, and it means the world to you."

"I mean, we would have to talk to Will about this, regardless," I warn him. "I am sure he would be down no matter what, but this is a huge step for him."

Jon laughs. "Will would leave this place in a heartbeat. Are you kidding? A new change of pace and California titties? Yeah, he would be down."

I laugh. "Fair."

"So"—Jon scoots closer to me, cupping both of my hands—"how about we have this conversation with him tomorrow, and we just look for a doctor for to see how far along you are and to make sure the baby is okay for now?"

I nod my head in agreement. "All right."

Jon kisses me on the forehead. "This is going to be amazing!"

I sure hope it is.

CHAPTER 13

I could barely sleep last night. Between Jon's paint-peeling snores and the possibilities of moving across the country, it was damn near impossible. I even busted out my laptop and moved to the living room to look up houses in different areas, and to my dismay, California isn't as bad as people make it. It's like the rest of the country; depending on where you want to live, it can be affordable.

As I hear the fridge open in the kitchen, I leap out of bed, with my laptop, and race into the hallway. The sudden movement makes me extremely light-headed. I grasp the wall and feel my way to the kitchen. As the wave of nausea passes, I make it to the stool and sit down quietly, placing the laptop on the island. Will turns around and jumps.

"Jesus, put a bell on you," Will says, putting his coffee down beside me. "Why are you up so early?"

I smile. "Can we talk?"

Will sighs. "I already know you're pregnant, and it's not mine, so what else could we possibly talk about?"

I basically am trying not to jump out of my skin.

"How could you like to move across country?"

Will slides onto a stool and takes a sip of his coffee. "I mean, that would be ideal, but what about the store?"

"We could sell it!" I exclaim.

"Calm down, Spunky Brewster," Will says as he takes another sip of his coffee. "You would be okay with that?"

I look at him.

"Fair point. What would we do? And I'm assuming you mean California?"

"Follow our dream of starting a production company, duh," I say so matter-of-fact-like.

Will nods. "With what money?"

I sigh. "With the money from the store. How are you not following this?"

"I'm just trying to figure out how this is all going to work since you're with child," he says, pointing to my stomach.

I look down. "We have enough money saved in our savings for a cushion. We can start looking now."

"I'm assuming you have already."

"I have," I agree with him, "in Sacramento, West Covina, Baldwin Park, and East Los Angeles."

Will looks at me with disbelief.

"You should know already once I have an idea in my head, I map it out, and also now that we have three men, well, two men and a woman and a future baby in the mix, we have an extra mouth to feed. So yeah, I had to map everything out."

"Why not everything in LA?" Will asks.

"I mean, we could, but we would have to struggle a bit, and not everything has to be in LA. There are production companies all around the world," I offer.

I open the laptop and let it boot up. As I type in my password to log on, I click open the screens where I have all the tabs available for him to look at the houses.

"Oh, dear God, Neveahly, how in the hell are you able to focus with all these tabs open?" he asks, baffled.

I shrug. "I mean, it's just like my brain. Fifty million tabs open, and I have no idea where that music is coming from."

He gives a little chuckle and continues to look at the computer screen. I hover over him and look over the options again. I love the thought of living in Sacramento. It's so beautiful, but I also like the idea of living by the water. Will types in something in the browser and begins to search. He comes up with another city and starts looking.

"What the hell is that?" I ask.

"Crescent City. It's a beach town,"

"It looks pretty nice," I say, looking over his shoulder. "I guess we could ask Jon how he feels too."

Will laughs. "I'm sure he will love this. This would be a great place to start a production company. It's family friendly apparently," Will points to pictures where there are happy families frolicking about.

"Hurray," I say sarcastically.

Will looks at me. "I detect a hint of sarcasm."

I shrug. "I mean, it's cool and all, but I'm not going to be a soccer mom if that's where you were going with this."

Will looks at me and puts his hand on my shoulder. "Neveahly Skye Walker, at no point in time will I ever let you become a soccer mom or own a minivan. Do you understand the words that are coming out of my mouth?"

I laugh and nod. "Yes, sir."

At that very moment, Jon comes out with a tank top and boxers on, half-awake. Will and I both look at him and smile.

"So I take it this talk went well?" Jon asks in a groggy voice.

"Indeed, it did," excitement flows with every word that escapes from my lips.

"Yeah, man. I'm always down for a new set of titties in new cities," Will says.

"Told you," Jon says.

I roll my eyes. "Okay, whatever. So, Jon, you are on realtor duty in California, and I will be on realtor duty here in DC. And doctor duty as well."

Will laughs.

"What's so funny?" Jon asks, confused.

I let out an annoyed sigh. "I said duty."

I manage to find a clinic that's about fifteen minutes away from the apartment. I make an appointment for today, just to get it out of the way. I don't know why I'm so nervous. I don't think I've been to the doctor, yet alone a lady doctor in years.

I run over the possible things to expect online from your first doctor appointment: my medical history, Jon's medical history, both of our family backgrounds, which brought me to the conclusion that

I know really nothing about Jon's family life except that he has one older brother and his mom was a single mom. I've met his older brother once when he came to visit him down in college and his mom when he moved all his stuff in, in the apartment, but other than that, I have no idea. Fear and dread set in immediately. *Holy shit, what if she thinks I'm a whore? What if she's a God-fearing woman?*

I realize I've been sitting on the bed draped in my towel for longer than I intended to, when I feel Jon's touch around my shoulder, snapping me out of my fear-induced train of thought.

"What's up, space case?" he asks.

Jon sits next to me on the bed as I just stare out into space again.

"So I was looking online on what to expect from the first visit, and I know nothing about you," I confess.

Jon laughs. "Yeah, you do. You just don't know my medical history. That's completely different."

I turn my body toward him. "I mean, should I know this stuff about you? I don't even know your blood type. Shit, I don't even know my own blood type."

Jon gently touches my face. "My blood type is A, and I think the only bad thing we have in my family is high blood pressure."

"Weirdo, who knows their blood type?"

"Literally everyone who donates blood," Jon says as he starts to get dressed.

"Oh my god, who donates blood?" I fall back onto the bed dramatically.

"Everyone who is trying to save a life? Or be a good person." Jon starts to slide on a pair of sweats. "Look, I know this is scary, but we will get through this, I promise."

I sigh. "I know. Also, I have really small veins, which is why I don't donate blood."

"Hey, no judgment being passed on my end."

I get up from the bed and walk toward the dresser drawers. I find a pair of sweats and a not-so-worn-down sweatshirt and throw it over my body. I start to look around the room for my slide-on Vans when I see Jon has them in his hand. I feel the tears form in my eyes. Jon smiles as he walks over to me and wipes them away.

"Why the tears?" he asks.

I cry even harder. "I don't know, honestly. I think it was incredibly sweet that you found my shoes and had them ready for me."

"Oh, I mean these are your favorite shoes."

I start to sob. "Oh my god, is this going to be for the entire pregnancy?"

Jon laughs and gives me a hug. "Probably, and you know what? It's going to be fine."

I cry it out for a few more moments before taking the shoes and placing them on my feet. As we walk out to the living room, Will is sitting there, waiting for us.

"What are you doing?" I ask, confused.

"I'm going too," he says.

I shake my head. "What? No! Only one of you is fucking me, so only one of you is going to see my lady parts."

"True, but who is going to be babysitting all the time? Also, who has the car, and where is the car seat going to go?" Will asks.

"I have a car," Jon chimes in.

"Touché, I was not expecting that at all." Will gets up from the couch. "Truth is, I don't want kids or will have them, so this is as close as I'm going to get. I don't want to see your gross lady parts—"

"Hurtful," I interrupt.

"But since I am your best friend, I do want to be there for you," Will continues, "so can I come? I'll buy you pancakes afterward."

"Deal," I agree.

Jon, Will, and I walk out of the apartment and down to the car. The ride to the clinic was a bit awkward. Jon and I are nervous, and Will is telling jokes. Jokes that are falling short and that are just not funny right now. We hit every single red light known to mankind and almost end up being late to the appointment. Once we get there, parking isn't so bad.

I don't know what my expectations are walking into this clinic, but once I opened the heavy door, all of a sudden my worries slip away for a brief moment, and my mind calms itself down.

The nurse behind the sliding glass gives me a thick stack of papers for me to fill out. *Awesome, a test. Just what I wanted.* I don't even really know my dad's side of the family. How the fuck am I supposed to answer these things? I feel terrible. Not physically but kind of like human garbage; I have no idea what my family history is. My mother and I were super close when I was younger but never had that talk about the history of her family. I know depression and bipolarity are in the family gene pool. As well as schizophrenia. I try my best to fill it out, but I struggle.

I get to the father section and hand it over to Jon. He laughs and fills it out with such ease. *Ugh god, must be nice to have such a decent childhood, dude.* Jon hands it back to me within five minutes, and I go back up to the sliding glass and hand it to the nurse. She offers a kind smile, and I return to the seat between Will and Jon.

Jon and I wait patiently as Will taps on the chair and plays on his phone like a child. *It's going to be like having two kids, honestly.* Finally, after what seems to have been an eternity, my name is called.

"Neveahly Walker?" The nurse butchers my first name.

"Yeah, that's me," I say as I spring up from the chair.

Jon follows suit, and so does Will. Jon and I look at him, trying to figure out where he is going.

"So I'll wait out here then?" Will says as he points back to the chair.

"Yeah, dude," I say.

Jon and I follow the woman down a long hallway where a scale is. *My mortal enemy.* I stare at it for a few moments and then back at Jon.

"I will stand back,"

I take a deep breath in and step on the scale. I don't even look at the number. I don't want to at this point. All I know is, I didn't hear an "Oh, geez" from the nurse, so it can't be that bad. We move from the scale to a small room where there is an examining table and an ultrasound machine. My heart skips a beat. The thought that we are going to be able to see our baby is kind of exciting and scary all at the same time.

The nurse goes in the overhead cabinets and pulls out a salmon-colored paper gown. She places it on the examining table.

"I'm going to take your blood pressure, and after that, I'm going to need you to change into that gown for me," she says.

I slide my arm out of my sweatshirt for her, and she slides the cuff up my arm. The cuff tightens around my arm, and just when I thought the pressure was getting to be a bit much, air slowly escapes the device.

"All right, everything looks normal," she says, taking it off me. "Now if you can change into the gown, the doctor will be in to see you."

She leaves Jon and me in the room. I stare at Jon. He looks at me, baffled.

"Could you possibly turn around?" I ask politely.

"Uh, sure," he says, slowly turning around. "I mean, I've literally seen all of you."

I take off my clothes quickly, fold them neatly as possible and place them in the empty spot on the examining table. I slide the gown on my body, the opening part facing forward, and wrap it around myself. I hop onto the table, just as Jon turns around.

"I'm assuming I can look now?" he jokes.

"I mean, yeah, if you want to," I say.

He laughs and shakes his head. We wait in silence for the doctor. I scroll aimlessly through my phone, not really having the attention span, or willpower to even focus on anything. The knock on the door startles me, almost causing me to drop the device on the dingy looking floor. The young male doctor walks in. Dr. McDreamy. A huge grin creeps across Jon's face. It is literally the one thing I didn't want, and it's the one thing I got.

"Hello, I'm Dr. Johnson, and you must be Ms. Walker?" he says, looking down at my chart.

"Yes, that's me," I say, looking at him, extending my hand.

He meets his hand with mine. "Nice to meet you"—he looks at Jon—"and you must be the father?"

Jon extends his hand. "Yes, I'm Jon Flay. Nice to meet you."

"Nice to meet you too," Dr. Johnson says. The doctor sits down and looks at me. "Now I know you took a test, but I need you to go pee in a cup once more."

I laugh. "Yeah, I can do that." I grab the cup from him before he can even extend his arm to give it to me.

I look down the hallway to see that the bathroom door is completely open. I book it down the narrow pathway and shut the door behind me. I do as the instructions tell me on the wall and fill the cup up way past the mark. As instructed, I leave the cup on top of the toilet and walk back to the room.

I see that Dr. Johnson and Jon have been talking as I step into the room quietly.

"That was fast," Jon says.

"Yeah, I really had to pee." I shimmy back onto the examining table. Kicking my short legs back and forth.

"Great," Dr. Johnson continues. "Now, here comes the not so fun part. Jon, would you like to stay?"

"What is this part?" Jon inquires.

I look at Jon. "He has to swab my lady parts and give me a breast examination."

Jon's eyes widen for a moment, and some of the color drains from his face.

Jon looks at me. "I mean, do you want me to stay?"

"No, it's fine. You can go," I encourage.

Jon grabs his stuff and leaves the room, gently shutting the door behind him.

Dr. Johnson starts with a general breast examination and finds nothing out of the ordinary. He listens to my heart and lungs to make sure everything sounds normal, and everything does. Dr. Johnson then starts to lay me on my back.

"When is the last time you had a Pap smear?" he asks.

"I'm not going to lie to you, Doc, I can't remember," I confess. "Maybe when I was in college? No, I was out of college, and I thought I had the clap."

He laughs. "Thanks for your honesty. I'm going to need you to scoot your butt down as far as it goes. I want you to feel as though you are going to fall off the table and then place your legs in the stirrups."

"Geez, normally guys would have to buy me a drink first," I mutter.

"What was that?"

"I said is that far enough?"

"Yeah, that's fine," he replies as he sits on a rolling stool. He grabs a piece of equipment out of wrapping and unwraps it. "Okay, now this isn't going to feel exactly the best, but if you just relax, I promise you it won't take long."

Literally what every man has said to me, but continue.

I try to relax every muscle in my body as I feel the instrument inserted into my vagina. It doesn't feel good, but it also doesn't exactly hurt. It's uncomfortable. I close my eyes, but all I can think about is how uncomfortable this is. *Jesus. Is this going to be every month?*

What seems to be like an eternity, he is finally done. He hands me a piece of cloth for me to wipe off with. *Wow, just like a true college experience.*

"Okay, I will go get your husband," Dr. Johnson says.

"Boyfriend. He's my boyfriend," I quickly correct him.

Dr. Johnson laughs. "Okay, I will go get your boyfriend."

The doctor leaves, and I sit up a bit on the table. I feel a tad bit uneasy over the fact that I was so quick to correct him like that. I probably shouldn't have done that. I mean, he is just my boyfriend, but it wasn't that serious. I see the door open, and I flash Jon a smile. He kisses the top of my head and sits next to me. The doctor sits back on the rolling stool and brings the ultrasound machine closer to us both.

"All right, the fun part," he says.

As he boots up the machine, I feel Jon's hand grab mine. I look at him and smile. This is a magical moment. A moment that I never thought I would have or share with anyone. Honestly, I never thought I would want to even have this, but with him, it makes it worth it. As the screen comes on, the doctor grabs the wand and puts some lubricant on it.

"All right, let's see where this little one is, shall we?"

I smile. "Let's do this."

Dr. Johnson places the warm wand on my stomach and starts to move it around. We immediately are able to see it. My jaw drops when I see this tiny creature roaming inside of me and that's been making me sick for weeks. I feel the tears start to roll down my cheeks when I look over at Jon and see he is crying too. I smile and squeeze his hand.

"This is pretty cool," I say, looking over at him.

Jon kisses my hand. "Cool? This is amazing. We created a life, Nev."

The doctor moves in closer and starts taking measurements.

"I'm assuming y'all want pictures?" he asks.

"Yes," Jon and I agree.

After a few snaps and a couple more measurements, he looks at us.

"I'm going to be honest with you, Neveahly," he begins, "you look a lot further along than what you think you are. From the measurements, you are about eleven to twelve weeks. When was your last period?"

I sit up. "I honestly don't know. Ms. Flow comes and goes as she pleases."

"Well, I will print out these pictures, but to get a better estimate of arrival, you will need to set up another appointment—"

"Oh, we aren't staying in the area," I quickly interrupt.

"Well, you should get set up with an OBGYN as soon as possible. Pregnancy is a big deal, and if you have been as sick as you say you have, you might want to keep an eye on it," Dr. Johnson warns.

"Will do," I agree.

"Congratulations. From what I can tell, you will be due sometime in early June." Dr. Johnson begins to clean the wand and turn off the machine.

He hands me another towel to wipe off my stomach as I begin to sit up and wipe off.

"The nurse will be in to take some blood, and since you won't be in the area much longer, I can put a rush on it if you would like," he offers.

"Yes, that would be nice," I reply as I clean off every part of my stomach thoroughly.

Dr. Johnson gets up and leaves the room, leaving Jon and me alone. Jon leaps up from his chair and kisses me without any warning. I barely have time to breathe before I feel his lips on mine. His hands touch my face gently before he pulls away.

"We are going to have a baby," he says gently.

"Yeah, I know. I kind of saw the pictures too, my dude," I joke.

I start to get dressed but leave my top off so the nurse can find a vein. Jon continues to stare at me.

"What?" I say, looking at him.

"I just notice your stomach is kind of out now," he says with a smile.

I immediately look down at it and see that it has started to come out a bit, and my breasts have gotten fuller. My eyes widen.

"Look, it's not a bad thing. I just think you are going to look beautiful pregnant," he says.

A nurse comes bumbling with a tray. She looks a bit in disarray but also like a seasoned nurse. I sit in the chair Jon was once sitting in and plop the good vein arm down immediately. Without saying a hi or exchanging pleasantries, she goes to work. To my dismay, she finds a vein on the first try. That never happens. It's normally a three to five stick before they have to get the vein whisperer in, and that's even a problem. She finds a good one and fills the vials up and then leaves.

I place my sweatshirt over my body and fix my messy bun. We leave the room and walk into the waiting room where Will is still sitting but now talking to some woman who is sitting by her lonesome. Jon and I exchange uneasy looks, unsure if he's actually trying to hit on an unmarried or possibly married woman or is just having a conversation. I walk into his line of view and catch his attention.

"Nevie," he says pleasantly, "how are you?"

"I'm good," I say slowly. "Are you ready to go?"

"Sure am. Nice meeting you," Will says.

Will opens the clinic door, and we head off to the International House of Pancakes.

CHAPTER 14

Will, Jon, and I formulate a plan for the upcoming months. Jon's lease is up next month, so he will move down here to DC and stay with us. There is no sense in staying in an expensive studio apartment when you can live with your pregnant girlfriend and best friend. Will and I will look for a realtor in DC for our bookstore. The bookstore should be an easy sell. It would even be a nice coffee shop. Jon is in charge of the movers for California and getting all our stuff there. Easy, right? Should be, but I am a complete control freak, and I have to have everything under my belt, and it's so hard to let everything go and delegate tasks to people. Especially two men I've known for over eight years, and I've seen how they do their laundry.

I lay next to Jon as I scroll through the realtors in our area. Nothing really stands out. I don't even know the first thing about it; I just need it sold. I click on a name, and I see their background and years they have been in the industry, and I get so overwhelmed. Luckily, the one thing I can put off is having a doctor. The next visit isn't for another month, and I can go back to the clinic if need be if we have to stay a bit longer here in DC.

Finally, I find someone who looks like they won't be a complete pain in my ass, and I give him a call. He sounds a bit eccentric but nonetheless interested in helping us out with the store. We stop on the way to get them coffee and for myself tea because I can't have any damn caffeine anymore. I'm still bitter about it. I'm so exhausted all the time. I can fall asleep anywhere at any time, and it's actually kind of impressive.

We park the SUV behind the store and open up for a couple of hours. A tall slender man comes in in a black Armani suit with black-rimmed glasses with a large briefcase. At first glance, I would not think he is a relator but more of a businessman. Will, Jon, and I look at him.

"Hi, can we help—"

"Shh!" the man says while holding up his hand.

We all look at one another. I cannot tell if this man is serious.

"The vibe is so bohemian. I love it," the man says as he walks around the store.

I come from behind the counter and begin to follow him. "I'm sorry, are you Phillip?"

"Shh! I'm taking in the vibe," he says to me again. "Yes, I am Phillip."

I turn and look back at Jon and Will, completely baffled that I just got shhed again by a grown man. The man touches every book in the aisle. He walks down in and then grabs my hand and leads me back to the registers.

"Tell me, are you Neveahly?" he asks.

I take a moment. "I'm sorry, am I allowed to speak now?"

"Yes! Speak, darling! Speak!" He touches my face.

I move his hands away from me. "Please don't ever do that again, but yes, I am Neveahly."

"I'm Jon, and this is Will," Jon says, trying to take the attention off me.

"I will give you six hundred thousand dollars cash for this place with the books included," he says without taking his eyes off me.

My mouth drops. "I'm sorry what?"

The man takes a long, exasperated sigh. "I'm bored, Neveahly! You see, I have nothing but time and opportunity, and I see this as an opportunity. Take it or leave it."

"Take it," I said without thinking.

"Wait, now hold on," Jon says, "How in the hell do we know you are—"

The man drops a huge briefcase down on the counter and opens it up with money in it. I get out the pen and start marking them to see if they are real, and they are. I start pinching the man to see if he's real.

"Ouch, stop that!" he says.

"Sorry," I say. "It's just been a really shitty year, and the fact that this happened so quickly is kind of baffling to me."

"I buy and sell buildings," Phillip begins, "and this is something that I absolutely want!"

"Okay, but just like that?" Jon asks.

"Just like that, sir!" Phillip snaps his fingers.

"This seems a bit weird. I contact you, you give us money, and then that's it?" I ask.

Phillip sighs. "When you go into the store, does the proprietor sit there; think and want to talk about whether or not they want to take your money? Or do they take it?"

"He's got you there, Nev," Will chimes in.

"Look, darling, I don't have all day. If you don't want the money, then I can go somewhere else with it." Phillip starts to grab the case.

I slam my hand on it. "Nope, definitely didn't say that."

"So you do want this money?" Phillip asks.

"Yes," all three of us say without hesitation.

"I promise you, this is no joke. I may come off a tad bit strong, but that's just who I am. I know what I want. You made a great decision here." Philip kisses my cheek. "I will contact my lawyer so he draw up a new deed, and we can do that awful lawyer dance, and I can get the old one and all that rubbish! Thanks for making this less painful for me."

Phillip leaves, leaving the briefcase on the table. Will, Jon, and I stare at it in disbelief and say nothing. We just stare at the large lump sum of money. We all have never seen that much money before in our lives, and I can hear all our hearts racing.

"What the fuck just happened?" I finally ask. "And what do we do with all this money?"

"Well, clearly this is going in the bank, Nev," Jon replies.

"Yeah, no shit, but like, do we open a new bank account for all three of us for the house? Holy fuck, we can buy a fucking house with this money!" I scream.

"Did I just have a stroke? Do you guys smell toast?" Will asks as he grabs his chest.

"First of all, why are you grabbing your chest if you think you had a stroke, and second of all, no you didn't," I reply.

"Okay, here's what we are going to do," I say slowly. "We are going to go to the bank right now, start a house account, and put it in there, okay?"

"Yes, that's a really good idea," Jon agrees.

"So no Vegas?" Will asks.

"Absolutely not, bro," I say without hesitation.

"Well," Jon says slowly, "maybe a little of that money can go to Vegas."

"Okay," I turn to Jon, "we have a kid coming on the way. Let's not forget that."

"I literally forgot all about that," he admits. "God, money does crazy things to you."

"Let's close for the day and handle this." I suggest.

"Deal," Will and Jon say in unison.

Jon carefully takes the briefcase and walks to the back of the store with it slowly.

I look at him. "Jon, honey, it's money, not a fucking baby."

"But there is just so much of it!" he exclaims.

We pile into Will's SUV and take off to the bank.

Banks sure do ask a lot of questions when you have that much money, but they also are very nice to you when you do. We were able to get an account and secure our money, and all the bills were in fact real. For some reason, that was still lingering in the back of my mind that they were fake. Will drove us home, and we are all in a daze to what had just happened. Okay, cool, one thing good has happened, but you know we have three more issues to worry about and two more months to get this shit done, so I'm just saying, anything can happen.

The weekend goes by so fast, and I hate saying bye to Jon. Every time I cry, and I know it makes it harder for him, but hey, I will be able to see him in two weeks for good. Jesus, for good? That sounds so final and formal, and for some reason, that really scares me. Commitment. I've never had a successful relationship ever, and things are going so well with Jon, and then I got pregnant. I don't want him to be with me because I'm pregnant. Maybe I'm overthinking this.

I lay here in my bed for the rest of Sunday until I hear a knock on my bedroom door. Will does that one-two tap and then flings my door open. There really isn't a point in knocking if you're just going to barge right in.

"Hey, come on in, bro," I say as I sit up in bed.

He comes busting and then turns around. "Shit, are you wearing any clothes?"

I look down. "I'm in a tank top and some shorts."

Will turns back around. "Okay, good! I found a house for us."

Will pushes his way through the junk food pile on the bed and sits next to me. He realizes what he did and looks at me.

"Should I ask if you're okay?"

I laugh. "I'm fine."

"Okay, whatever." Will shoves the iPad in my face. "It's a four-bedroom, three-bath house, and guess how much money it is?"

"Six hundred thousand dollars?" I ask sarcastically.

He makes a buzzing sound. "Wrong! It's four hundred thousand dollars!"

I laugh. "Okay, so?"

Will lets out an annoyed sigh. "And it's right by the water, and it's closer to LA!"

"Did you show—"

"He's already into it!" Will interrupts. "We are just waiting for your go-ahead."

I look at him. "You're serious?"

"Like a heart attack," Will says, looking me dead in the eye.

"Okay, don't you think this is moving hella fast? Like, do you want to slow down and pump the brakes a little?" I ask.

"What? No. I want to be set so I can fucking relax, bro. So what? Are we pulling this trigger or nah?" he asks. Will looks at me as if I'm a mom waiting to give an answer if I will allow her child to get the candy bar.

"Okay, the house is beautiful, but what if there are other houses out there we like? What if we could get a bigger house for less money?" I offer.

Will sighs. "I guess you're right. I just got so excited because we wouldn't have a mortgage."

"Oh, no doubt, but how about we find three houses, and all in the same price range, and we pick the best out of the three. Deal?" I ask.

Will sits there and thinks about it. "Fine, deal. I hate when you make sense." Will gets off my bed and walks back to the door. He stops in the frame and turns around. "Seriously, should I be worried? There's like a week's worth of food on the bed."

"No, I just hate it when he leaves," I say, trying to fight back the tears.

"I knew I should have kept walking," Will mutters loudly. He walks back and sits on the other side of the bed. "I know it sucks, but look at it this way, you will be stuck with him for life."

"That is the worst way to put it, but I appreciate the effort."

"I did try," Will says, taking an Oreo cookie. "What are we watching?"

"*Bridezillas*," I say, taking the TV off pause.

"Want company?" Will offers.

"Yeah, I used to love being alone, and now I hate it," I confess.

"Hah, wait till that crotch goblin comes out of your lady regions. You will enjoy it again." Will takes a sip of my Gatorade.

"Okay, one rule, if you're going to eat my food, eat the off-brand shit. That's why I bought it," I warn.

"Wait, for me?" Will asks.

"Yeah, and Jon. I get the good stuff, and you guys get the off-brand shit."

We sit in the bed and continue to watch *Bridezillas* and laugh at the ridiculousness of the show.

Monday rolls around, and I meet back with Phillip's attorneys in the store. I look over the deed and sign it under one condition: they have to change the name. Phillip agrees to it, and we shake hands. Will and I start to clear out our personal things while Michael and Mickey continue to keep their employment. They are sad to see us go but are very lucky to keep their jobs.

Bringing the stuff back to the apartment was a pain in the ass. I never realized how much shit we accumulated over the years and just left there. It is a solemn day yet a joyous one. I should feel more sadness, but I don't. I feel more hunger than anything. Will treats me to IHOP again.

We sit in our favorite booth, scroll through endless listings on the iPad. I feel a tap on my shoulder and look up and see Michael.

"Neveahly, long time no see," Mike says with a huge grin on his face.

"Yeah, and it's been so fucking pleasant," Will says.

I shoot Will the death stare and look up at Mike. "Yeah, dude, it's been a minute."

"What? No hug?" he says, trying to show off to his new girlfriend.

I roll my eyes.

"What have you been up to?" Mike, embarrassed, tries to keep the conversation going.

I let out an annoyed sigh. "Nothing. Sold the store, I got pregnant, what about you? Who's this? That's not Maggie," I say, pointing to an unfamiliar blonde.

The girl turns to Michael. "Who's Maggie?"

Mike laughs an uncomfortable laugh. "What do you mean you're pregnant?"

I slide out of the booth and show him my little stomach. "Pregnant."

His eyes grow wide as he looks at my bump.

The young woman taps Mike on the shoulder. "Excuse me, who the fuck is Maggie?"

People in the restaurant start to look over our way. I don't even care anymore; with Michael, it's always a spectacle.

"Maggie is his baby mama," I tell her.

"When? How?" Mike stammers.

I laugh. "It's not yours, Michael. Calm your tits."

A sense of relief washes over his body. The statuesque woman on his arm starts to walk away. Mike chases after her, without saying goodbye.

I sit back down in the booth with Will. I scroll through the endless houses while Will stares at me in disbelief.

"What?" I ask.

"Did you see the color drain out of his face when you stood up and showed your stomach?" He laughs.

"Oh, I know. Priceless. It was even more priceless trying to see him do the math in his head. We always used a condom." I continue to look down at the screen.

My stack of pancakes, bacon, and eggs come out as well as Will's French toast. I inhale mine and start to pick at Will's. I didn't realize I was so hungry. We pay our bill and make our way back to the apartment.

I pass out for a couple of hours and wake up to a missed call from the clinic. I call them back immediately.

"Hey, this is Neveahly Walker. I got a call from Nurse Wilson, I think that was her name, about my test results?" I say, trying to stay calm.

"Oh! That's right!" I can hear the nurse rustle through papers. "All your levels are normal, baby is healthy, all your tests came back everything looks normal, and do you want to know what you are having?"

I smile. "Wait, you can tell me that through a blood test?"

"I sure can!" the nurse says.

My heart is pounding. *Wait, should I wait for Jon? No. I love him to death, but I need to know!*

"Yeah, I guess," I say nonchalantly.

"You're having a girl," she squeals.

Dread consumes me.

"Hurray!" I try to sound excited. "That's great news!"

"Call back if you have any questions, concerns, or need to make any appointments," she says and hangs up the phone.

Well fuck. Another little me? That's just fucking fantastic.

CHAPTER 15

I stand awkwardly in the kitchen by the island with the pink cake waiting for Jon to come in. *Wait, is this how you're supposed to do a gender reveal? Fuck the balloons and shit. That's a lot of cleanup afterward.* Jon is on the last leg of the drive coming from NYC. I'm so nervous. What if he wanted a boy? I'm not trying again. This is a one-and-done-type situation. This wasn't even supposed to be a situation.

I start to pace the kitchen floor. I hear Will's bedroom door open as he comes out for the first time all day. He sees the cake and smiles.

"Oh, another you. You guys are fucked," he jokes.

I shoot daggers into his soul. "I know this, man! What the fuck have you been doing all day?"

Will grabs a beer from the fridge. "Writing."

I shrug. "Cool. Do I look okay?"

"For someone who's pregnant? Yeah, I guess," Will says, going back into his room.

Wow, that was absolutely no fucking help. I start pacing again. I see my phone light up, and Jon's name appears. I immediately answer it.

"Are you downstairs?" I ask.

"I sure am,"

"Okay, I will open the front door." I rush over to the door and open it.

I stand in the front entrance with the cake in my hand. I'm so nervous I almost drop it. I stand there and stand there for what seems to be an eternity.

Jon comes in carrying two suitcases and sees me. He smiles as he walks into the apartment, and his eyes shift focus to the cake. Jon drops the suitcases and covers his mouth in disbelief.

"How long have you known?" he inquires.

"A couple of weeks. I didn't want to tell you over the phone. I wanted to tell you in person."

Jon comes over toward me and takes the cake, placing it on the countertop. He kisses my lips gently while putting one hand on my stomach.

"A girl," he whispers.

"Yeah, a girl."

"That's so amazing." He beams with joy.

"Is it?" I say in a high-pitch tone.

Jon laughs. "Why wouldn't it be? I would have two of you. Well, one and a half."

I roll my eyes. "Is there anything I can help you with?"

"No, where's Will?" he asks, scanning the room.

"Writing, apparently."

I knock on his door before barging in. I see he's sitting at his desk with his headphones on. I sneak up behind them and rip them off, sending him flying out of his seat.

"I am going to die one day because you do that," he says, grabbing his chest.

I laugh. "No, you won't. Jon's here. Go help him."

Will lets out an annoyed sigh and pushes himself dramatically from his desk. Like a child, he drags his body toward the door and out to the living room. The two exchange pleasantries and they make their way down to the garage, to grab a couple more bulky items.

About two hours of back-and-forth, Jon is moved in. All three of us fall on the couch and stare at the blank TV screen. Jon and Will drink a beer as I sip on some water. I rest my head on Jon's shoulder as I kick my feet up on the coffee table.

"Well, guys, one move down, one more to go," I say.

"Yeah, just one more." Will takes a sip of his beer and lets out a satisfying sigh. "Speaking of that, I found three houses, and I think you will like at least one of them."

Will leaps up from the couch and goes into his room. Moments later, he reappears with his iPad loaded up with the three options.

"See," he says, shoving the device in my lap, "like you said, I gave you three options, and here they are."

"You did," I agree.

I scroll through the endless pictures of all three houses. I must admit, Will has immaculate taste when it comes to housing. From structure all the way down to decor. I hand over the iPad to Jon so he can see, and we can finally make a decision.

"I like the second house," Jon finally says. "The ranch style is kind of cool."

"Good, I was hoping you would pick that one. There was a thirty-thousand-dollar price cut, so now it's only four hundred thousand dollars," Will says as he pushes my head back to look at Jon.

I remove his hand from my face. "You know, if you guys would like to talk, I can move."

Will gets up and scoots between Jon and me, forcing me to the other end of the couch.

"Also," Will continues, "it has a guesthouse in the back so we can have an office out there."

"Can I see?" I say as I try to reach for the iPad.

Will throws the iPad to me. "Here."

Jon looks at me. "So, Nev, what do you think?"

I look at the two eager beavers and then back down at the iPad. "I mean, I do like it. So let's pull this trigger. I guess you can—"

"I will call her tomorrow! I've already talked to her about it. Since we won't have to apply for a mortgage and can pay in cash, it only takes a week, which is fucking awesome," Will explains. "Technically, we could leave tomorrow and never look back!"

I laugh. "Hakuna your tatas, my dude. We still have to organize the moving vans from here to California, and the holidays are about to come up. So call her tomorrow, we celebrate the holidays for the last time here in DC, and we move at the beginning of the year or whenever the movers can move us. Sound like a plan?"

Will makes a disappointed face. "Fine, that does sound reasonable."

I tussle his hair. "Attaboy, slugger."

"So pizza and a movie?" I suggest.

"Sounds great!" Jon says.

I order the pizza. All three of us end up falling asleep on the couch. I wake Jon up around two in the morning to come to bed and try to shake Will awake, but he is out cold. Jon and I cuddle close in bed, and I instantly go back to sleep.

The next week is hectic. Moving is always a stressful time, but moving and being pregnant is even more stressful. Also, trying to remember to take my prenatal is the absolute worst. I have to set an alarm on my phone every day, which I feel like I shouldn't have to do. Half the day, I'm either in bed because I'm too tired to move or I'm in the bathroom because I can't stop throwing up. Jon suggested that maybe we should postpone the move, but I will be damned if we stop this train from leaving the station because of me. *I thought after the first trimester you were supposed to stop being sick? Oh god!*

I wake up on Saturday around two thirty in the afternoon. I had no idea how late it was, and I rush to get ready for the day. I find Will and Jon sitting around the kitchen island looking at the iPad.

Jon smiles. "Are you late for something? Was I supposed to wake you up?"

I stop short of the kitchen, completely out of breath. "Why did you let me sleep so late?"

Jon puts down the iPad. "Because you couldn't sleep last night."

I lean over. "Jesus Christ, I'm out of breath."

"Yeah, we can see that," Will chimes in. "Take a seat."

I hobble my way over and sit down. "What are you guys doing?"

"We found a moving company, and the cheapest we got was ten thousand dollars to move across country," Jon slides the iPad over to me.

"Jesus, who do they think they are moving? The Jonas brothers?" I look at the cost.

"Out of all the references you could have made, you pick the Jonas brothers?" Will says.

"I'm still waking up," I snap.

"Still, though," Will says as he glares at me.

"I mean, we can afford it, Nevie," Jon intervenes.

I look at him. "I know, but still." I sigh. "I mean, we might as well book it at this point."

"For when?" Will asks.

"I don't know. You guys pick a date," I suggest.

"Cool, January second," Will responds.

Beads of sweat form at the top of my forehead. I feel my face get hot and my hearing become fuzzy. I see that Will and Jon are talking, but I have no idea what they are saying. I start to zone out again, and I feel Jon touch my leg gently. I come back to reality.

"Hey," Jon says, "you good?"

I smile. "Yeah. I think I'm going to lie back down." I excuse myself and head back to the bedroom.

I slide back under the covers and close my eyes. Moments later, I feel the weight of someone on the other side. I roll over and see Jon, with his hazel eyes staring into mine. His soft yet strong hand gently touches my soft brown skin. I lean over and kiss his lips. I hear the wrestling of the sheets as Jon moves his body closer to mine as I feel his arm wrap around my waist, forcing me on top of him.

Leaning down, I place my lips on his. Jon runs his hand through my curls. He gently rolls me onto my back and slides my shorts off as he removes his shorts. Suddenly, he stops.

I look at him. "What's wrong?"

He seems a bit uneasy. "This isn't going to hurt the baby?"

I try to hold in my laughter. "No."

"I mean, I'm not going to poke her or anything?" he asks.

"Jon," I say again, trying not to giggle, "you are big, there is no question about that, but there is not a chance you could do that."

Jon leans down to kiss me. "Okay, but are you okay?"

"You are killing the vibe here, babe."

He laughs. "I'm sorry, I'm just trying to make sure you are all right."

"I appreciate it."

He slowly enters between my thighs. It's been a while, and for some reason, it feels better than before. Hearing him moan my name, feeling his lips on my neck, I feel myself get wet. I feel myself about orgasm as I grab my headboard. Jon grabs my breasts, and I can't hold it in any longer.

I lay next to him as we both try to catch our breath. Jon wraps his arm around me and pulls me close, kissing the top of my forehead. I place my head on his chest and run my finger through the hairs on it.

"You know," he clears his throat, "I've never really taken you out on a date."

I laugh and look at him. "What do you mean?"

"We go out with Will all the time, and when it's the two of us, we get pizza, but we never actually go on a date, date."

Holy shit, he's right. We never have been on an official date before. I guess I figured he never really had to take me out.

"I mean, I'm not a really fancy type of person," I confess. "I haven't been on a date in so long."

"Can I take you on a date tonight?" he asks.

"Be serious," I joke.

He sits up and looks at me. "I am serious. I will find a fancy restaurant. No Will, just the two of us."

I grab the blanket and wrap it around my chest. "Really? Just us?"

"Yes."

I sit there for a moment. "Okay, we can do that."

Jon leans toward me and kisses me. "Great. I will let you shower first, I will look for a nice restaurant to go to tonight."

I throw the blanket off me and start heading to the bathroom. "All right, it's a date."

The showering part was the easiest. I can still shave my legs, I can still see my lady friend down there, but finding an outfit was a tad bit harder. I went from dress to dress, trying to find what I could wear.

I finally settle on a flowing black dress that isn't so tight around the stomach. I decide to straighten my hair and take my time doing my makeup. Not too much yet enough to look like I'm wearing makeup. Since it is winter, I opt for a closed-toe shoe with a wider heel, and hopefully, we won't have to walk too far because I haven't worn heels in like three months. I haven't worn any shoes in two weeks, to be honest.

Jon looks amazing in his suit.

I want to rip it right off him and say, "Fuck the dinner. You can take me out once we get to California. Let's go for another round." Alas, I just admire how sexy he looks.

As I step in view of Jon and Will, the two immediately stop talking. Jon's face lights up, and Will's eyes widen.

"What? Is this too dressy?" I say, looking down at my outfit. "Honestly, this is one of the few dresses that's not clinging to my stomach."

"No," Jon says as he walks over to me, "you look amazing."

"Yeah, you really do, Nev. I literally just remembered you are a woman," Will says.

I roll my eyes.

"Okay, are you ready to go?" I ask Jon.

"Almost," he says.

Jon goes behind the counter and gets out a bouquet of long-stem red roses. "These are for you."

I smile. "When did you get these?"

"When you were asleep earlier today."

I bring the beautiful flowers to my nose and smell them. "These are beautiful. Thank you so much."

"You're welcome. Will is letting us borrow his car tonight, so the question is, Are *you* ready?"

I smile. "I am."

Jon holds his arm out for me to grab, and I oblige.

On the way to the restaurant, Jon made an amazing mix of old R&B songs. As we listen to the soothing vocals of Luther Vandross, Jon takes his time getting to the restaurant. I don't mind. The town is beautifully lit with Christmas lights. Each twinkling in the dark night; dancing in the cold wintery breeze. Twenty minutes of driving, we finally arrive at a cute, quaint little restaurant. White Christmas lights strung along the building, illuminating the brick siding. So beautiful. Snow starts to come down from the sky. If I didn't know any better, I would have thought Jon would have planned the forecast.

Jon goes around to my side of the door and opens it. Like a true gentleman, with his hand extended, waiting for mine. Years of mistrust completely gone as I allow him to grab it. We walk toward the small building. Jon reaches for the door and opens it for me. I look inside and see no one is there. Are they closed? Did he make a mistake? I turn back to him and look confused. I redirect my attention back to the front of the restaurant and see a young woman standing there.

"Ah, Mr. Flay," the young woman says, "your table is ready for you."

I look at Jon. "What is going on? Where is everyone?"

Jon says nothing as the woman leads us to the middle of the restaurant. A table with a candle lit and a bottle of champagne opened, chilling on ice, wait. A young man takes my jacket and Jon's. Jon rushes over and pulls my chair out for me. I scoot in, and Jon saunters back over and sits down. I smile. Moments later, a man comes over playing the violin.

"Okay, what is going on?" I ask.

"Nothing," Jon says casually. "I told you I was going to take you out on a date, and I'm taking you out on a date."

I look around the restaurant. "This restaurant is completely empty, and I'm assuming you did this?"

Jon grins. "Maybe I did, maybe I didn't."

"So now you're going to be mysterious?" I ask.

"Perhaps." He chuckles.

I roll my eyes and laugh. "Okay, keep your secrets, but this is very lovely."

The violinist starts to play a song I remember from the car. A song that always reminds me of Jon and that would forever be our song. All of a sudden, I realize what could possibly be happening.

"I'm glad you like it. You deserve all this and more. I mean, we are getting ready to uproot our entire lives and start a new one. Well, and start a family."

I take long sip of water.

"It's kind of crazy, Neveahly, starting a family with you," he looks at me and smiles. "Who would have thought two kids from film school would fall in love?"

A nervous laugh escapes from my lips. "Right?"

"It's just kind of crazy that life brought us down this road, and I know what you think about relationships and especially marriage."

"That it is barbaric and archaic ideas? Okay, but you know if the right person comes along, I might think differently," I say.

"Right," he says slowly, "which is good to know that if the right person were to come along, things would change."

The violinist plays, Jon and I become quiet as the salad is brought to us by the waiter.

"So what would that right person look like?" he inquires.

I accidentally drop the fork, making a loud clanging sound. "Shit, sorry. I don't know. Someone who understands me. Someone who isn't a stage four clinger. Someone who can turn the world on with his smile, someone who can't take a nothing day and make it all seem worthwhile."

Jon looks at me. "So you want Mary Tyler Moore?"

I laugh. "You put me on spot. I got nervous! In all honesty, I just want someone who loves me for me and accepts me for all I am."

Jon shakes his head and laughs.

"What would your right partner look like?" I ask.

"You," he says without hesitation.

I look at him. "Really?"

"Yup." He goes back to eating his salad.

"Good to know,"

A huge grin creeps across my face. *Okay, I can't eat. Just tell him the truth, Nev. You wouldn't mind being his lifetime partner. You wouldn't mind waking up next to him for the rest of your life. You don't even mind the fact he snores like a freight train sometimes. Just fucking tell him.*

"So do you think I chose a good place?" Jon inquires.

"I do. I think it's so beautiful." I polish off the rest of my water. "If you'll excuse me, I have to use the restroom."

I get up and excuse myself from the table. I briskly walk to where I see the bathroom sign. I open the door and head toward the sink and stare at myself in the mirror. I see someone who needs to tell Jon the truth. I brace myself for the inevitable and walk back to the table. I see our main course is there as I slide back in the seat.

"Everything okay?" he asks.

I smile. "Yeah."

Jon begins to eat. I start to poke and prod at the chicken and pasta before I put my fork down and look at him.

"I lied," I blurt out.

Jon looks at me, confused. "About what?"

"About the right partner is for me. You. I would want you. I mean, dude, bro, shit, I suck at this." I take a deep breath. "Babe, ah, that's better. I know I'm not really good with emotions and all, but if there's anyone I would want to spend the rest of my life with, it would be you. For the first time ever, I let down my defenses when we got together. I wake up every day and smile, knowing you are next to me, and I cannot imagine what my life would be like without you."

Jon smiles and reaches into his coat pocket. "So would you want to wear this?" He puts a box onto the table.

My entire body starts to tremble. "I mean, I'm not really a jewelry person." I grab the box and open it. It's gorgeous. Square-cut diamond. "But I can be."

"We don't have to get married right away, but I want to spend the rest of my life with you and only you." Jon gets up from his chair with confidence, walks over to me and gets down on one knee. "Neveahly Skye Walker, will you marry me?"

"Yeah, sure, I guess. I mean, you already put a baby in me," I say. I lean down and kiss him.

The entire restaurant starts to clap and cheer. He gets off his knee and wraps his arms around me. I'm not even hungry at this point. I just want him all to myself and for the rest of my life with our daughter.

Excitement and joy overwhelms me, but my mind goes back to the night with Will. *Do I even tell Jon? Or do I take this to the grave?*

Jon is beaming with joy, and I'm all over this place with my emotions. *Will Will take this to the grave? Do I need to have a talk with him?* I shake my head to rid my mind of such thoughts and stay in the moment with Jon. No matter what happened then, it's over and done with. There is no point in trying to play the "what if" game.

I rush into the apartment. Will, sitting on the couch, watching TV, I jump on the couch and shove the ring in his face.

"Ah, he finally asked you," he says slowly, moving my hand away from his face.

My mouth flies open. "Finally?" I turn to Jon. "How long have you been planning this?"

"For a month or so?" he confesses.

"Wait, how did you know my ring size?" I inquire.

"You are such a heavy sleeper," he says.

"So you just measured my finger while I was sleeping?"

"How else was I supposed to get the measurement?" Jon asks.

"Touché."

"Well," Will says, pausing his show, "you're pregnant and engaged. Two things you said you would never do, Nev."

"Thank you for reminding me, William."

Will pats me on top of my head. "That's what I'm here for."

CHAPTER 16

Moving day is finally here. Our house is paid in full, and everything is packed and ready to go. We all decide to drive across the country to see America in all its glory. I don't know how much fun it's going to be with a pregnant woman, but hey, it's an adventure. I am the first to wake up. I walk to the café down the street and get the guys come coffee and bagels.

I set everything up on the kitchen island one last time. Sitting there, I patiently wait for them as I scroll through the iPad, looking at the daily news. I start to scroll through our checklist to make sure we have everything for the road when I hear Will's door open. I turn my head around to see him dressed and ready.

Will grabs a bagel and a cup of coffee. I hear my bedroom door open, Jon comes out bright-eyed and ready. He kisses the top of my head as he reaches for a bagel and the last cup of coffee.

"This is it," I say, looking at him. "This is the last time we will ever be on the East Coast."

"I mean, we can come back," Jon says.

I look at him. "This is the last time we will be on the East Coast unless we are coming back for a funeral."

Jon laughs. "Okay."

"We are actually doing this," I look at both of them.

"Yeah, man." Will takes a sip of his coffee. "What time are the movers coming?"

Jon looks down at his watch. "Any minute."

"Are you guys nervous?" I ask.

Will shakes his head. "I'm ready to get laid again."

I roll my eyes. "What about you, Jon?"

"The only thing I'm nervous about is screwing up our kid."

My eyes widen. "Shit, I didn't even think about that."

"Your kid, our screwing it up?" Will asks.

"Why must I choose, bro?" I put my head in my hands.

Jon rubs my back. "Everything will be fine, Nev. Just one day at a time. Let's just get through this pregnancy."

We sit and wait for the movers. Thirty minutes past by and Jon's phone rings. They alert us they are downstairs. We stay out of the way as the men begin to load our entire lives into this huge van parked out front of the building. Box after box and piece by piece, our lives slowly start to disappear from the apartment. Once filled with parts of us, it is now becoming a void. A hallow of what once was. I feel tears fall from my face. Before I could wipe them, Jon does it for me.

I can't decide if these are tears of sadness or joy. Every poor decision and every good one led up to this moment for us to come together to take this journey to where we are about to go, even in this unknown territory. Two and a half hours go by, and the entire apartment is bare. I double-check to make sure everything is empty before we leave. I pick up a few things of mine, and of course, Will left a couple of charges behind.

I stand at the apartment door for the last time and take one last look. Scanning the room one last time, I smile and close the door behind me gently. As I ride the elevator one last time, I realize I will miss the off-putting smell it always gave. The smell of shitty alcohol, cheap cologne, and bad body odor. I get off at the first floor and slide the apartment keys under the landlord's door and walk down the flight of stairs to the lobby.

I see Will's car idling in the front of the building, waiting for me. The front seat is open. Jon is driving, with Will in the back, lying down already. *Okay, so I guess we are up for the first half of the drive then.*

"All right, what shall be the first song we listen to?" Jon asks us.

I take his phone and type in the song title. Within a few seconds, I find the band and hit play. I wait for it to load and anticipate the reaction of Will and Jon. Not even five chords in, Will sits up and reaches across the console and turns off the music.

"We are not listening to *The OC* theme song, Neveahly," he says, glaring at me.

I laugh. "I mean, California, here we come, right back where we started from."

"That doesn't even fucking make sense!" Will screams.

Will takes control of the tunes. We all wait for the song to load, and "Bad, Bad Leroy Brown" comes on.

"To Nicki," Will says.

"To Nicki," Jon and I say.

Jon puts the SUV in drive. The sun slowly spills into the car, briefly blinding me. The music continues to play as we begin to drive, and I feel Jon's hand grab mine. I look at him, and he gives my hand a brief squeeze. As we leave the city and merge onto the highway. Looking in the rearview, I see the city get smaller and smaller, before it disappears all together. I feel my body relax and close my eyes, letting Jim Croce, lull my to sleep.

ABOUT THE AUTHOR

Courtney Dinkins is a novelist, poet, and screenwriter. Her debut novel, *Perfectly Imperfect*, was published in 2021. When she's not writing, she can be found in independent local cafés or road-tripping around the Northeast. She lives in Virginia.

CPSIA information can be obtained
at www.ICGtesting.com
Printed in the USA
LVHW031549050821
694493LV00003B/311

9 781637 102770